W9-AEB-452

ETERNAL
SONATA

Also by Jamie Metzl

Fiction:
The Depths of the Sea
Genesis Code

Nonfiction:
Western Responses to Human Rights Abuses in Cambodia, 1975–80

ETERNAL SONATA

JAMIE METZL

Arcade Publishing • New York

First Edition

This is a work of fiction. Names, places, characters, and incidents are either the products of the author's imagination or are used fictitiously.

Arcade Publishing books may be purchased in bulk at special discounts for sales promotion, corporate gifts, fund-raising, or educational purposes. Special editions can also be created to specifications. For details, contact the Special Sales Department, Arcade Publishing, 307 West 36th Street, 11th Floor, New York, NY 10018 or arcade@skyhorsepublishing.com.

Arcade Publishing® is a registered trademark of Skyhorse Publishing, Inc.®, a Delaware corporation.

Visit our website at www.arcadepub.com.

10 9 8 7 6 5 4 3 2 1

Library of Congress Cataloging-in-Publication Data is available on file.

Cover design by Laura Klynstra

Print ISBN: 978-1-62872-679-4
Ebook ISBN: 978-1-62872-682-4

Printed in the United States of America

ETERNAL
SONATA

1

Hope springs eternal, but life, which it carries on its wings, slowly deflates like a leaky basketball.

Or maybe hospices are just depressing.

The hacienda-style Wornall Center for Palliative Care may look cozy from a high altitude drone or through Augmented Retinal Display lenses, but here at regular ground level every surface is designed to be quickly hosed down, scrubbed of the wreckage of human demise, of the evidence of each body's last desperate struggle to expel the humors it no longer accepts as its own. It's not a warehouse of broken dreams; it's the last gasp before sinking into the quicksand of life's cruel hoax.

I've been in the atrium for all of ten seconds but already have the visceral sense I'm breathing in death itself.

"Mr. Azadian?" I hear from behind. I turn toward the pleasant voice.

"Suzanne Ferguson," the approaching middle-aged woman says. Her medium-length red hair frames a round, inviting face.

"Thank you for seeing me," I say, extending my hand. "Do people disappear from this place often?"

My words come out sharper than I'd intended, stopping Suzanne Ferguson in her tracks.

"No," she says coldly, not lifting her hand to meet mine.

"I didn't mean to say . . ."

"This has never happened before, Mr. Azadian. We take it *very* seriously."

At least somebody does, I think.

Two weeks ago a renowned octogenarian scientist on his death-bed vanishes from hospice care and the news only reaches me this morning? Even now, I probably wouldn't be here if Martina Hernandez, my editor, who doesn't seem to give a damn about my career advancement these days, hadn't grudgingly sent me. The tip about the disappearance was no big deal, and who else do we still have covering the science beat in our diminished newsroom?

But I'm here, and Professor Benjamin Hart did disappear, and almost-dead people don't vanish into thin air every day of the week. At least not in Kansas City.

"I presume you've notified the police?" I say gingerly.

Her look asks if I think she's an idiot.

"Did they come up with anything?" I continue.

"They asked a few questions, reached out to a few neighbors. They spent about an hour here, then said on their way out they'd get back to us if they learned anything."

"Have you heard from them since?"

She shakes her head. "I don't get the feeling this is much of a priority for them. Our guests at the hospice don't have much runway left."

The compassionate look on Suzanne Ferguson's face makes clear she values that little strip at the end of the airfield far more than does the Kansas City Police Department.

"I see," I say, imagining myself someday sputtering off the end of a remote runway into a gurgling sea. "Do you mind if I look around?"

"Please. That's why I was willing to see you, Mr. Azadian. We don't normally do much with the press, but this is very unsettling to all of us, especially the Hart family."

"How are they doing?"

"Not well, as you can imagine. Mrs. Hart has come by or called every day for the last two weeks. She's beside herself. Says she keeps calling the KC police, who assure her they're searching."

"But you don't think they are?" I reply, unsure if Suzanne Ferguson knows it was Mrs. Hart, Dr. Katherine Hart, who called our newsroom early this morning with the tip.

"If they were looking seriously I'd imagine we'd know something by now."

I pause to let her words settle. "Can you show me his room?"

She leads me down the sterile, pastel-green corridor. An eerie silence, punctuated by intermittent whispers and the quiet whir of Robotic Delivery Carts rolling through their rounds, blankets the hall. "Of course," she says, "we now have a new guest occupying the room."

The ancient man plugged into the respirator perches somewhere between sleep and death as we tiptoe in. The room is standard hospital design, with a bookshelf and a large painting of a sunset on the wall across from the bed. The sunrise has obviously long since passed.

I approach the window, softly unfasten the clasp, and lift. It opens about six inches before locking. "Any chance he could have opened the window more than this?" I whisper.

"Mr. Azadian, Benjamin Hart was at a very late stage of terminal cancer. He would have had a hard time just turning the clasp. Even if he did, he couldn't have opened the window any more than you just have."

"Can we talk outside?"

She follows me out.

"Could he still be here somewhere? Is there anywhere you might not have looked?" I ask.

"We've scoured every inch of the facility."

But if Benjamin Hart, University of Kansas professor emeritus of microbiology, is not inside the hospice, where else might he possibly be and how might he have gotten there? "Exactly when did you notice he was missing?"

"We know he went to bed after dinner on October 19. When the nurse went in to check on him the next morning he was gone. We searched the premises and couldn't find him."

"I presume you had a look at the surveillance feeds."

I can't quite read the pained look on Suzanne Ferguson's face. "We did, but . . ."

I perk up. "But?"

"There was a glitch in the program. Apparently there was a break in service for two hours that night between 2 and 4 a.m."

My mind pings a faint alert. "And I take it there was no sign of Dr. Hart leaving his room before or after then?"

"Yes."

I pause a moment to think. "Do these service breaks happen often?"

"We had the same question. Our VP of operations called Everguard, the surveillance camera monitoring company. They told her there wasn't a scheduled upgrade that night but sometimes strange things can happen to the feeds. They said they'd look into it." It's clear from the look on her face they haven't heard back.

"These delivery carts going up and down the halls, don't they have sensors helping them get around? Wouldn't they be capturing images?" I ask.

"They do, but they're docked for recharging that early in the morning."

"And wouldn't Professor Hart have been wearing a biosensor on his wrist?"

"We found it in his bed."

Another ping. "Is that normal?"

"We usually take them off when our guests are washing up, but . . . no, it's not really that normal."

My mind begins wrestling with the coincidences as I whisper the notes into the u.D—universal.Device—on my wrist. "How many exits does this facility have?"

Her eyes glance up as she counts in her head. "Eight."

"Can you show me?"

I note the position of nurses' stations as Suzanne Ferguson leads me around the building. It's at least conceivable someone could reach an exit without being seen. "Are the exit doors locked?"

"At night, from the outside. We never lock them on the inside because of fire regulations."

"Okay," I say, then whisper more observations into my u.D. "What more can you tell me about Professor Hart?"

"People come here at their twilight, Mr. Azadian. We rarely get a glimpse of what they were like in their prime. He seemed quiet and contemplative. Dignified. But there wasn't very much left."

"Did anything about him appear different before he disappeared?"

"Not that we were aware of, but we only knew him during the five weeks he was here."

Maybe the guy did just disappear, I think to myself, but I'm here, digging is my job, and—probably to a fault—I've never been able to leave questions unanswered. "Was he on any medications that might have changed? Did you keep any ongoing records of his condition?"

"This is a hospice. Most people go off most of their medications when they come here; some don't even wear biosensors. By the time people get here it's generally too late for technology. Our nurses file short notes on our guests at the end of each day, but they're by no means comprehensive."

"Can I see the notes about Professor Hart from before he disappeared?"

"I'm not supposed to and I'm not sure it will tell us anything." Suzanne Ferguson takes in a slow breath. "But this seems like a special circumstance." She pauses again before speaking. "I can't let you see any files themselves. . . . Let's go to my office."

As we enter, she places her palm on her desk for biometric identification before dictating her commands. "Open file. Nurses' Log. Patient. Benjamin Hart. October and November 2025."

Her ashen face darts upward as the text flashes across her tabletop screen:

No items match your search.

2

In Jorge Luis Borges's magical short story "The Circular Ruins," a father dreams his son into being, then spends his life worrying the son will discover he's not real. Only later, when the father does not burn in a fire, does the father realize that he himself is the product of someone else's dream.

Wandering into the *Kansas City Star* newsroom, a Borgesian look of dreamy contemplation of life's ephemerality must be smeared across my face.

Martina Hernandez, as always, homes in on it like a laser. "Earth to Jorge, come in Jorge," she says, marching by and not looking in my direction.

Her formerly jet-black hair shifting toward gray, the lines and indentations etching across her face like Maori moko tattoos, Martina is as dressed for battle today as she was the first day she arrived at the *Star* thirty-three years ago as a junior assistant in circulation.

"Martina, I need to talk with you," I say, filing in behind her, caught somewhere between assertive and submissive.

Even after I broke the story of the US government's secret genetic enhancement program two years ago and was promoted to reporter at large, not to mention the success of my book *Genesis Code: Genetic Engineering and the Future of Humanity*, there's no question in anyone's mind about how the hierarchy is structured here. That is why Martina still ridicules me and my seemingly useless PhD in philosophy by calling me by Borges's first name instead of Rich, and why

I'm still following her around the newsroom knowing full well she's not going to stop.

"Not now, Jorge," she says dismissively. "Halley, come in here," she orders over my shoulder.

I turn to see Sierra Halley in the middle of the newsroom. Sierra glances at Martina, then fleetingly toward me.

Tall and thin, with the all-American athleticism of a lacrosse player, her deliberate glide toward Martina's office brings to mind the lope of a gazelle. Just twenty-six, her no-apologies, post-post-feminist expectation of absolute equality on her own terms, along with her focused drive and determination, have forged an impressive wake through the newsroom in the eighteen months she's been at the *Star*.

Her spring-like Mayflower freshness stands in contrast to my Armenian American hint of dark-haired foreignness. My wiry, five-foot-eleven, forty-one-year-old body, the perpetual hint of afternoon scruff and pensive air of wonder on my face, and my slightly long black hair make me seem more like the philosophy professor I once aspired to be, or a barista, than an on-the-ball reporter.

Six weeks ago, Martina transferred Sierra from the business desk to the health-care beat—confirmation of an ascent that's beginning to feel preordained. Given the role that health care is playing in the US economy and in keeping the lights on at the *Star*, I'm not entirely surprised it's Sierra, not me, being summoned to Martina's office.

But it's more than personal. The revolution in the news business keeps happening, every turn a bit worse for the old-style media companies like us.

Since the News Protection Act—the law that provided federal subsidies to news organizations that accepted national security restrictions on what they published—has been rescinded, media companies have become freer of government influence but far more vulnerable financially. We can publish what we want, but we still need to figure out how to pay for it.

In the past couple of years, two ideas have guided our transformation to address this challenge. The first is to focus on the local market. Where the *Star* once had national aspirations and bureaus in Washington and New York, and even wrote about global issues like the developing world's fresh water crisis or the constantly unfolding chaos in the Middle East, our editors now eschew most anything beyond the greater Kansas City area. We once competed with the great national news organizations but now pit ourselves against community media, fighting for relevance in the sandbox of our little Paris of the Plains.

If that's not bad enough, the second idea is even worse.

With so many advertising revenue streams drying up over the years, all we have left to sell are our stories themselves. Of course, we don't call it that. It's not prostitution, just dinner and some flowers followed by sex. But how else can anyone explain why we are writing so many stories about the miraculous innovations of the health companies who just happen to be our largest advertisers? And is it really a surprise that all the positive stories about big health in news outlets across the country are pushing up those companies' stock valuations as they fight each other for market share, as their collective power grows, and as the Congress, awash with political contributions from those same companies, becomes ever less willing to regulate them?

But no one ever got to heaven (in which I don't believe) by ignoring the devil (in whom, for that matter, I also don't believe). Maybe compromising our integrity in this dying business is the price we need to pay for staying in the game. I'm not sure I agree, but that probably explains why most everyone seems agitated as I wade through this collective emotional fog toward Joseph Abraham's cubicle. He's waving his hands, moving words and images across his cubicle e-walls, and doesn't see me approach.

"Abraham," I say sharply, trying to startle him. Sometimes I can't help myself.

He doesn't flinch.

I wonder for a moment if he actually saw me approaching and is just getting tired of my shtick.

Joseph has begun to come out of his shell in the three years he's been my researcher at the *Star*, but he's still the quiet, serious young-old man he always was. Short and sturdy, with the dark skin and curly hair of Southern India, he exudes the calm mustiness of an ancient forest spirit. He looks at me with a mix of warmth and what I've started to interpret these past few months as caution. Joseph and I have been through a lot together, but I'm starting to get the impression that on some level he feels that continuing to be my researcher is holding him back from coming into his own as a reporter.

"I need you to look into something for me."

He nods hesitantly, awaiting additional information, but I read into the small gesture a sense that the power in our relationship is somehow changing now that he's been assigned some preliminary stories of his own. I rely on Joseph completely but don't think I'm being self-serving in my assessment that he's not quite ready for that next step. He has all the brains, resourcefulness, and then some, but he'd be well served by a generous helping of Sierra Halley-like assertiveness, by building the confidence to make his own case. The tortoise beats the hare in the children's story, but in the real world he'd be well-advised to get a move on it.

"See what you can learn about retired University of Kansas professor Benjamin Hart. He's the one who disappeared from the hospice. The surveillance cameras in the facility are monitored by a company called Everguard. The feeds stopped for two hours between 2 and 4 a.m. on the morning of October 20, just when he seems to have vanished. See if there's any way to figure out what happened. Okay?"

"Sure," he says quietly, looking down.

I pause a moment, unsure how to respond to Joseph's expression of even less enthusiasm than his limited range of natural expression would normally allow. "Are you sure?"

He looks at me wide-eyed without responding.

"Thank you, Joseph."

He offers a slightly conflicted nod, leading to a somewhat awkward pause.

"Okay then," I say hesitantly, pivoting back toward Martina's office.

Sierra is just coming out as I approach. I detect a hint of irony in her stare as she glides past.

I pause a moment, wondering if she's warning me about Martina or mocking me in some way, before turning toward Martina's office.

The door is still open. "Knock, knock."

Martina looks up, sighs, then shifts her gaze down toward the massive screen of her desk.

I wait for her to speak.

"What is it?" she finally says without looking up, as if speaking to an exasperating child.

It's funny with Martina. I'd have thought the success of the Genesis Code story would have sealed a bond between us. In a way it has. We both got pats on the back and promotions, she to deputy editor. But I sense deep down that Martina is still thoroughly annoyed that I was first offered an assistant editor role, which would have put me in a category of her perceived competitors in the company, that I turned it down because I still wanted to be a reporter and didn't want to deal with all the politics, and that, worst of all, I may be in my current subservient position in Martina's internal hierarchy by choice rather than necessity.

"The hospice story," I say tentatively.

She shakes her head, pretending not to remember what I'm talking about and still not looking up. It was at the bottom of the priority list when she assigned it to me this morning and she's not about to indulge me now by acting like she affords it the slightest importance. Her gaze shifts back down toward the screen. "Just do the little story I sent you to do, Jorge."

"The guy disappeared two weeks ago," I blurt out, knowing I have at most one more sentence to make my case. "The police aren't doing anything, the security cameras went dead at just the time he vanished, and any record of him in the hospice database has been erased." It's a compound sentence.

"An old guy near death goes missing from hospice. I'm sure there are lots of good reasons why a geezer missing a few screws can wander off into the darkness. Why don't you just do what you were assigned in the morning? All I wanted was a little copy for Metro. A thirty-minute story. Old guy disappears, police looking," she drones, unimpressed.

"I could," I say, avoiding Martina's bait, "but isn't it at least worth asking a few questions, sitting down with his wife? I thought that's what we did these days—cats in trees, house fires, potholes."

"Don't be a smartass," she says impassively. No one knows more than she what we've traded to stay alive.

I stand obsequiously, starting to get annoyed that Martina has yet to look up from her table screen.

"Shouldn't you be covering Senator King?"

"I'm covering King's health-care forum in Lee's Summit tomorrow morning, Martina." With the centrist Republican President Lewis reelected and the next presidential election three years away, King is starting to position himself as the inevitable Republican candidate, and then President of the United States, by taking every opportunity to criticize Jack Alvarez, the Democratic vice president in America's Republican-Democrat centrist national unity government. "And I can chew gum and pat my ass at the same time."

Martina lifts her head and chuckles. A hint of exasperated warmth crosses her face. "A few questions, Jorge. A few," she says, clearly in spite of herself.

3

Imposed on vast farmlands one massive subdivision at a time, Overland Park, Kansas, is a testament to the cumulative power of prefabricated parts.

If you saw a photo of almost any home in Overland Park, any strip mall, any restaurant, and were asked where in America these might be located, the only logical answer would be "anywhere."

But every locality has its unique stories, I think to myself as I knock gently on the front door of the large ranch-style house at 9518 West 146th Street. The whispering November wind brushes my face with the first hints of winter across the vast Great Plains.

Through the crack in the opening door, her intelligent hazel eyes stare at me plaintively. The woman's erect posture, slender frame, and elegant dress seem almost an act of defiance against advancing age. But even from first glance, it's obvious a fog of sadness has descended upon Katherine Hart. I can only imagine what she's been going through.

"May I come in?"

She takes a step back. "Thank you for coming," she says softly as I enter. "Can I offer you coffee?"

"Thank you, Dr. Hart," I say, feeling somewhat uncomfortable that she, the one in this terrible situation, is offering me coffee. "I'm okay."

Katherine Hart may not have had the stature of her husband, but Joseph's small file on her was impressive enough on its own: private practice neurologist, clinical professor of neurobiology at Kansas

University Medical Center, pioneer in the mental resuscitation of stroke victims.

We sit quietly in her living room. The room has high ceilings, a Marc Chagall print, and a few abstract paintings on the walls. A large photo of the Hart family over the mantle. I notice Professor and Dr. Hart surrounded by two younger couples with a gaggle of kids of various ages. "Your family?" I ask, trying to break the ice.

Katherine Hart stands and walks toward the photo.

I follow.

Her voice lifts slightly as she points to the different people. "It's Ben and me, our two daughters Dalia and Ofira, their husbands Michael and Sanjay, and our five grandchildren, Ava, Daniel, Chloe, Zoe, and little Gabriel." Reciting the list of names adds a fractional smile to her otherwise deadened face. "I asked Ofira and Sanjay to take their kids to the park when you said you were coming."

"And this," I say, pointing. The framed miniature album cover catches my eye. Four tough guys in black leather jackets stare out defiantly from in front of a set of drums. It looks strangely out of place.

She smiles again briefly. "Ben got me that for our fifth anniversary. It's the album cover for the song 'Crazy Little Thing Called Love,' from Queen, the old rock band. It came out that year." Her face holds on to the memory for a brief moment, then collapses under its weight.

"I'm so sorry," I say. "I'm so sorry for your . . ."

Katherine Hart closes her eyes. "At this point, I think we need to accept that Ben is gone. I only wish I knew to where. We lived in this house together for thirty-five years. It was always alive with his presence. Now it feels so empty in his absence."

I want to hand her something to wipe her tearing eyes, but she takes a handkerchief from her pocket before I can.

"The police don't seem to be doing anything," she says softly, shaking her head. "I talk to the wonderful people at the hospice every day. They don't know anything. I just don't understand how some-one in his condition could just disappear into thin air. That's why I called the *Star* this morning. No one seems to be doing enough. It doesn't make any sense. My biggest fear is that he wandered off into the night somewhere and died all alone." Her body begins to cave forward. "We've been together for fifty-one years. He couldn't tie his shoes without me. I worry his body is all alone, that it's being eaten by animals." She holds her hand over her eyes, then seems to straighten her body by sheer force of will. "The rabbi wants to start *shiva*, but I keep telling him to wait another day. Somehow I need to know where he is, where his body is, before I can . . ."

"I'm so sorry, Dr. Hart," I say.

"Please, call me Katherine."

I nod slightly.

"It's funny," she adds wistfully. "I'm a scientist, but I can't help being a sucker for hope at a time like this." She pauses a moment, then her shoulders begin to curl inward.

I feel I should do something to break the oppressive silence, but I feel helpless.

Katherine Hart stares at me plaintively. "I'll give you any infor-mation you need, just please, I beg of you, find Ben . . . even if it's just what's left of him. I need to be with him one last time."

"I promise I will do my best."

Her intense stare makes clear that's not good enough.

I feel the overwhelming urge to say something, anything. My mind cautions me about making blind promises but the words are already escaping my mouth. "I will find him. You will be together." I regret them immediately. If the police and the hospice can't locate Benjamin Hart, who am I to promise more?

Katherine Hart's eyes lift with an infusion of hope as she takes in my words. "Thank you, Mr. Azadian."

"Rich."

"Thank you, Rich. I can't tell you how much this means to me and my family."

My calm face betrays my inner turmoil. I'm already dreading the likelihood I will let her down. I plod on. "Can I ask you a few questions?"

Her eyes remain locked on mine.

"Was Professor Hart in any condition to get out of bed by himself in the middle of the night?"

"He is . . . was," she says, clearly struggling to keep her composure as she weighs the possibilities, "a very strong-willed person. He had so little strength left, but I have to believe that if a tiny neuron fired somewhere in the depths of his cerebral cortex, he could have pulled himself out of bed through will alone."

"But it would have been hard?"

"Of course. I know a lot about what mental decline looks like. We can track it on fMRI and MEG machines. He was terribly close to the end when he arrived at the hospice."

"Was his mind together? Could he have become disoriented and just wandered off?"

"It certainly is one of the possibilities. At times I would see the spark of recognition, of his brilliance in his eyes, and then just as quickly the fog would settle back in. What cancer didn't steal from him seemed to go after the experimental treatment regimen failed. But science doesn't always explain everything. Somewhere in there I knew he was, on some level, the same compassionate genius I fell in love with."

"Could the cancer treatment have disoriented him in some way?"

"Maybe, but he'd already been off the trial for three months at the time he—he . . . disappeared. We'd had a lot of hope for a miracle, but maybe miracles never . . ."

"How old was Professor Hart when this photo was taken?" I say, pointing at the family portrait and trying clumsily to steer the conversation to safer ground.

"That was five years ago. He was seventy-eight then. A lot has happened these past five years. He hasn't looked much like that for some time now."

"Do you have any more recent photographs I can see? I'd like to get a sense of how he might look today. So I can know what . . . whom . . . I'm looking for."

"Yes," she says softly, placing her hand on her coffee table. The tabletop screen lights up. "Photos. Ben. 2020 to 2025," she dictates.

The now all-too-familiar words flash across the screen. NO ITEMS MATCH YOUR SEARCH.

"That's impossible," she whispers. "How could they have disappeared? 2020 to 2025," she repeats desperately, as if a few lines for compassionate override might have been embedded somewhere in the billion lines of code.

She looks up at me with wide, unbelieving eyes. Then her face collapses into her hands.

4

"Jerry, it's Rich," I say into my dashboard screen as my silver Tesla XY streaks toward Toni's. "Can I get your quick advice on something?" I say.

Jerry Weisberg's gaunt, pale, and perpetually sweaty face peers out from my screen, his brown hair seeming slathered on as an afterthought. From the strained look on his face, I get the feeling he is fighting the urge to lock himself away in his cave-like basement office in the University of Missouri–Kansas City Computer Science Department, where he is a professor, so his wall-to-wall screens can immunize him from human interactions through the intimacy of distance.

Jerry may be a bit awkward, I think to myself, but he really came through for me when I needed him a couple of years ago, and I'll be forever grateful for that. So grateful I can't help pestering him for more assistance.

"Um, sure," he mumbles, making intermittent eye contact.

I tell him of the missing surveillance feeds and data files at the Wornall hospice and the missing photos on Katherine Hart's home computer. "How can we know if this is just a chance blip or if something more is going on?"

"It all sounds suspicious but it's hard to know," Jerry replies, warming as the conversation bends toward his home turf. "It would be an odd coincidence that two files about the same person disappear from two different systems in two different places. I'd need to get inside the two networks."

"Can you?"

A look of nervous consternation crosses Jerry's face.

"With their permission," I add.

Jerry has proven he's a master of breaking into electronic networks designed to keep him out, but he still probably believes at his core that good guys don't violate network privacy unless they really have to. "Um, well, I guess—"

"Great, Jerry. I really appreciate it. What do I need to do?"

"Umm," Jerry murmurs. We both know I am railroading him but I hope he trusts I wouldn't push him like this for no reason. "I'd need their universal network identifier codes and they'd have to request access while connecting through their biometrics."

"Can I have Joseph work with you to help make that happen?"

Jerry nods tentatively.

"Great. Thanks," I say quickly, locking in my gains before caution can convince him to retract. "I'll have Joseph call you." I tap my u.D and his face vanishes from the dashboard.

One more quickie call as my Tesla glides itself effortlessly around Meyer Circle.

"Yo, Mo," I say as he answers.

Maurice Henderson eyes me cautiously, not responding to my provocation. Nobody else would ever address Kansas City Police Department Deputy Chief Henderson with "yo," and the idea that any abbreviation of his full name could ever legitimately be used to address him is virtually unthinkable.

"May I help you?" Maurice says formally after a long pause.

Maurice doesn't really do humor, or informality, or small talk, or man hugs, or any of the expressions of human connection the rest of us struggle to carry out. He is, however, one of the most upright people I know, even if I often have the impression he's holding a silver dollar between his butt cheeks.

"May I have the pleasure of inviting you for coffee tomorrow morning?" I say, matching his formality with a small dose of irony.

I've learned to see through Maurice's tough exterior over the past two years. Maurice would have probably lost his job instead of being promoted had it not been for my part, with his help, in exposing the Genesis Code genetic enhancement program and stopping the fanatical murderer who had snuffed out so many pregnant women. But then our connection cooled for a while until Maurice's son, Maurice Jr.—MJ—started taking a shine to Hellenic philosophy at the Kansas City Classics Academy charter school. Maurice is the type of person who hates asking for things, but how many other people did he know with a PhD in philosophy who could walk MJ through Aristotle's reflections on the essence of happiness from the *Nicomachean Ethics* or push him to take a side in the great debate between Plato and Aristotle on the universality of forms? To Maurice, it was just Greek.

"What do you want, Dikran?" he says in the same warmly exasperated tone more and more of the key people in my life seem to use with me these days.

Only a few people know how much I dislike being called by my given name, which is perfectly normal in Armenian but sounds alarmingly like "dickwad" in English. As a child, I'd switched immediately to the English version of Dikran, Rich, in the face of puerile harassment on my first day after switching from Armenian day school to public school. "I need to talk with you about something in person. Something important."

Maurice waits almost ten seconds before the words leak reluctantly from his mouth. "Eight a.m., twenty minutes, Broadway Café. I'm drinking water." He's probably as close to smirking as his physiognomy will allow.

"See you then, deputy sir," I say cheekily as I tap out, wondering why I always feel like I'm herding iguanas, straddling the line between inviting people to do the right thing and outright harassing them, albeit lovingly.

But deep down I know, as I pull into Toni's driveway, that the most elusive iguana is still probably me.

5

"Honey, I'm home," I announce, reveling in the cliché as I push open the door to her kitchen from inside the garage.

She looks up from her bowl of mint chocolate chip ice cream, and I know it's not going to be good. "Are you sure? Aren't you the guy who lives in Hyde Park?"

The words carry with them the distance that has slowly crept between us these past months. "Are you feeling any better?" I ask.

Toni's eyes don't afford me an opening, but then her mocking half smile softens the blow. "If wanting to eat grass until I throw up is a sign, then definitely yes."

Even when she's upset, there's always been something irresistible about Toni. Her graceful, slender frame, sharp green eyes and olive skin, the quirky bob of her charcoal hair, and her ever-so-slight dimple are all alluring to me, but it's the kindness exuding from her every pore that's what ultimately draws me to her. I have to admit it's all just a tad more resistible when she's as annoyed with me as she's been these past months. "Can I get you anything?"

Her eyes widen, inviting me to answer my own question.

Two years ago, she and I probably each realized the other carried a little piece of ourselves we hated to admit we were missing. Now, we've somehow settled into a pattern of being together but not fully connecting. It doesn't take much to not notice a new dress or fail to decipher a hidden brood. Each transgression is hardly a crime. But little by little it adds up until you find yourself in a new place, not quite sure how you got there. Our magic feels a bit more distant. There, but just beyond our reach. "Was your day okay?"

The simple question almost feels like papering over the real issues hanging in the air. We've now been together for nearly three years, with one seven-month break toward the beginning, but we're not engaged, we still have two separate houses, and I've even been resisting getting a dog together. And Toni, shot up with hormones as she prepares to have her eggs and a small skin graft extracted and frozen, is not happy.

"Fine," she says, taking a spoonful of ice cream into her mouth, "notwithstanding."

It doesn't seem to matter that we, like everyone else, would use IVF even if we were having kids, which we're not. It also doesn't change things that most women across the country, regardless of their marital status, are having their eggs extracted, frozen, and stored at twenty years old based on the new National Cryopreparedness Protocol. Notwithstanding, of course, the induced funk we've somehow entered.

The momentary silence is beginning to grow heavy so I resort to shameless cheating. "How were the waifs?"

Toni lifts her eyebrows. "You can't trick me that easily, Dikran."

I stand my ground with a pitiful half smile. Toni volunteers once a week after work at Wayside Waifs, the Grandview animal shelter that rescues, heals, and puts up for adoption dogs, cats, and other furries rejected by their past lives.

"But," she adds, throwing me a verbal bone, "I'm a pushover for those puppies."

Toni not only loves dogs, she also loves underdogs, and the Wayside puppies are both. She knows I'm not a big fan of pets, which she, like most everyone else in America, recognizes as a vile personal failing. Seeing how her eyes soften at even the mention of the dogs, I feel once again a bit like a jerk that Toni and I don't have a dog of our own. But a dog is connected to a commitment, which is connected to a life, which is connected to a fear still pinging out irregular signals of caution from somewhere deep inside of me.

Her eyes betray a hint of the debate I sense is going on in her head. Instead of making me feel worse that we don't have a dog or a life fully conducive to such a dog, her expression softens. "Well if that's the game we're playing . . ."

I'm not sure where Toni is going until she lifts her right wrist and whispers into her u.D. Looking over my shoulder, her face blossoms. I stare at her for a brief moment, taking in all that could be if I'd just get over myself, before turning to see a video box opening on the freezerator door.

"Auntie Toni!" Nayiri's happy voice coos. The eighteen-month-old daughter of Maya Armstrong, the young woman from Oklahoma Toni and I saved two years ago from the rogue US government agent systematically murdering women who, like her, were carrying genetically enhanced embryos as part of the Genesis Code conspiracy, Nayiri's wild mane of puffy blond hair, radiant blue eyes, and buoyant smile dominate the screen. "Uncle Dikran," the ecstatic baby adds as I join Toni in front of the camera.

"Aww," I say, overwhelmed. I'd scrubbed references to Maya in my stories two years ago, and we've been hiding her ever since at my mother's home in Glendale, California, where she's assumed the name Magda Aramian to try to avoid notice in our Armenian American community. "How is my little *hokees?*"

"*Shad lav,*" Nayiri responds.

I turn toward Toni for a brief moment. Our eyes connect.

"What are you doing today, Nayiri, honey?" Toni asks in her most sugary voice.

Maya's angular face pops into the screen. Still only twenty-seven, she has clearly blossomed and matured in the two years we've known her.

"Hey guys," she says nonchalantly, "what's up?"

"We just wanted to say hello," Toni says.

I love Maya and the baby and my mother a lot, but I'd be in much less regular touch with all of them were it not for Toni.

"Want to see our new trick?" Maya asks.

Toni and I glance at each other and we are back on the same team. Every video call seems to elicit another manifestation of what little Nayiri is capable of.

Maya taps her u.D and a familiar colored fish begins dancing above the words on our screen. She rubs Nayiri's head softly. "What does that say, *yars*?"

Nayiri points to letters as the words form in her mouth. "O-o-one f-ish, two-o-o f-ish," she says, starting to gain confidence, "red fish, blue fish."

"That's so wonderful, honey," Toni sings.

"Amazing," I add.

Two barks reverberate through Toni's room.

"Is that who I think it is?" Toni calls, a crooked smile budding. "Is that who I think it is?" she repeats in an even more playful voice.

"The one and only," Maya responds, lifting my mother's Shih Tzu, Shoonig, to the screen.

The dog wags his head and barks excitedly.

Toni's face again lights up. "There's a good dog," she declares in her silliest dog voice. "There's a good Shoonig."

"What have you guys been up to?" I ask.

The connection endures for another ten minutes with more feats from the baby and updates from Maya and my mother about life together, cooking, and various bits of modern technology Maya is exposing my mother to.

I turn to Toni as we tap off the call. "I'm sorry, sweetheart."

My words are vague but she doesn't need to ask what I mean. "I appreciate your saying that," she says after a pause. "This is tough. They keep saying they'll eventually be able to make eggs from induced stem cells and skip the whole extraction process altogether, but my ovaries will probably be dried-up craisins before that happens."

I hate it when she references her age. Thirty-three is still young, especially in these days of scientifically managed reproduction. But we both know that the clock still ticks, even if it's a bit slower than it once was. "Two more days and you'll be off the hormones," I say, trying pathetically to add a positive spin.

She humors my humble offering for a few quiet moments. "Two more days and they'll stick an electronic arm up my hoo-ha."

I reach my hand slightly in her direction, then stop myself.

Toni sees that I'm not sure how to respond and throws me another bone. "Your mother and Maya were so proud of their little *janig*. She's becoming a real little Armenian."

Of course, Armenians also excel at nasty words just as much as endearing ones, and Toni has learned enough about my culture these past years to pull back from my pivot with one of them.

"*Eshoo kak*," she says with a mischievous grin.

It's not the most appropriate use of the words "donkey shit," but she somehow both makes her point and diffuses the remaining tension at the same time. I sit in the chair next to hers and take a spoonful of her ice cream.

"It was an interesting day," I say.

Her eyes focus warmly on mine for the first time since I walked in the door. "Tell me, honey."

6

I'm waiting calmly with two bottles of Badoit water, two café Americanos, and two cinnamon rolls on the table in front of me when Maurice walks in at 8:02 a.m. As always, he looks sturdy and well-kempt, his afro cropped close to his head like the US Marine he once was. I get the feeling he's forced himself to be two minutes late just to make a point.

"What do you have?" he asks sharply. He doesn't mean the food.

"It's nice to see you, Maurice."

Maurice unscrews the top of his water bottle and pours a glass. "Good morning, Rich," he says in a slightly sardonic tone as he sits.

"Is your family okay? MJ, the dog?" I ask.

"They are fine," he says with a faint smile, not asking me about Toni even though the four of us—Maurice, his wife Janae, Toni, and I—have been out to dinner three times in the last two years. He takes a perfunctory sip of his water, no doubt waiting for me to tell him why he's here. Maurice Henderson doesn't do social coffees.

"The department?"

The words bring a hint of life to Maurice's face. "Health-care costs are bankrupting us. We have to cut back on hiring new recruits to take care of the old codgers living out their golden years. With everything happening in the Middle East, we're having to put round-the-clock protection at the synagogues around town, not to mention the people we already have keeping an eye on the fertility clinics and biotech labs. If anybody has a beef in Kansas City, eventually we need to send a team out to patrol something, but the beefs keep adding up as the country metastasizes and our budget keeps getting cut." Maurice shakes his head. "The department is great."

I smile.

I may be one of the few people who see this side of Maurice, though his expression suggests he's not quite sure that's a good thing. "What am I doing here, Rich?"

"Does the name Benjamin Hart mean anything to you?"

"Not really. Why?"

"He is—was—a retired KU biology professor. He was dying of cancer before he disappeared from the hospice at a hundred and twentieth and Wornall a couple of weeks ago."

"I didn't recognize the name but I saw that in one of my briefing notes a while ago. What about him?"

"He just vanished. The guy was practically a vegetable. There's no trace of him."

"Strange things happen. There aren't always answers. You know that."

"A few people told me KCPD hasn't been doing much to look into the disappearance."

"I'm sure a few people are saying that about lots of things. I don't know the details about Hart, but we have young kids disappearing all the time and don't have the resources to follow up. Those kids have their lives ahead of them."

"I started looking into this yesterday and there seem to be some strange coincidences."

"Look, Rich, I don't need to get pulled into another one of your wild goose chases right now. We're a police department. We prioritize. That's what we have to do."

I don't need to say that one of my "wild goose chases" turned out to be the biggest case of Maurice's career. "Can I just tell you the circumstances?"

His face maintains its mild annoyance as I lay out what I've learned.

"That's it?" he asks when I'm done.

The image of Katherine Hart's desperate stare into her coffee table screen flashes through my mind. "I need to ask you a favor, Maurice, a personal favor."

Maurice eyes me impassively.

"All I ask is that you look into this a bit more. I'm sure there are more important things on your plate right now, but just do me this little favor and have an extra little look. At worst it will waste a bit of your time, and at best there might be a stone somewhere that's gone unturned."

Maurice taps the table a couple of times. Then he shakes his head with a wry smirk, stands, and walks out the door.

Z

"Now I'm sure that when you're not living your lives and going to church and cheering for your kids in soccer and baseball games, when you just take a step back in a quiet moment and think about it, most of you good people are wondering once in a while, 'what the heck are those crazy people in Washington doing?'"

Slipping into the back of the Chapel Hill Clubhouse in Lee's Summit, Missouri, I watch Senator Carleton King—tall, lean, and chiseled, his brown hair parted over the side of his triangular face—pause for humorous effect. If rumors are to be believed, King's series of health-care forums around the state are just a prelude to his expected run for the presidency three years from now, in 2028.

"But when you have to be in Washington week after week as I do, it forces you to ask that question every day."

I look around the room. The almost two hundred people in the audience seem the epitome of country club privilege.

"Well, I'm just a country boy from the boot heel, but I've been looking around for eleven years, and to tell you the god's honest truth, ladies and gentlemen"—he pauses and leans forward as if about to reveal a deep secret—"I'm not exactly sure what they're up to. They're certainly having a lot of meetings. They're certainly spending a lot of your tax money."

The crowd releases a collective guffaw, King's humor seeming to confirm what they know deep in their hearts to be true: that they are victims of a secret government plot to give their hard-earned money to slackers living lazily off the fruits of other people's labor.

But then a face catches my eye. I have no idea why she's here.

Sierra sees me and gestures for me to come over to her side of the room, near the opposite door. I pause a moment, my mind flipping through the possibilities. Did Martina send us both? Is Sierra now taking on the politics beat as well?

"You know, ladies and gentleman, Robin Hood may have been good at racing around the forest in little green tights," King continues as I walk toward Sierra, "but he wasn't trying to keep a country competitive. He didn't have to make sure small business owners like you had the incentives you need to grow your companies without worrying that the more you made, the more would be taken from you. That's why Robin Hood isn't the symbol of America. We don't have his picture on our dollar bills. Our symbol is the American eagle, who doesn't sit in his nest waiting for it to rain frogs but heads out every morning to find them himself."

I reach Sierra, trying my best to appear unperturbed. "What brings you here?"

"Should I not be?" she whispers, probably reading my tone better than I had intended.

"I'm just a little surprised," I say quietly. "Did Martina—"

"Yes. You, too?"

I nod.

"I guess health and politics are becoming inextricably linked," she says.

"Senator, are you going to let them take away our health care?" a tight-faced elderly woman in a red, white, and blue sweater shouts to King.

"Now that," King says emphatically, "is an important question."

The United States has been debating health care for decades, but in spite of the major progress we made through the National Competitiveness Act, we still spend more per person than any country in the world, have far worse health outcomes on average, and remain shackled to politicians promising everything to everyone even as high prices and miraculous innovations make health care so expensive it threatens to sink the US economy once and for all.

"You all know that Jack Alvarez and the liberals don't want you to be able to go to your doctor's office or to the hospital and get the treatments you need and have worked your whole life to afford. You know what they call this kind of discrimination?" King pauses, a mischievous look on his face. "What do they call it?"

"Health democracy," disparate voices from the crowd yell out.

"You said it, my friends," King replies, boomeranging into a rhythm. "They call it health democracy, but it doesn't make us healthier and it undermines our democracy. How can it make us healthier when it's denying good people like you the opportunity to get the health care you need? How can it strengthen democracy by limiting your rights?"

"How about by making access to health care a little more equitable in our increasingly dividing society?" I whisper to Sierra. Advances in medical science—from applied genomics to neural conditioning to even the preliminary progress in the brain-machine interface—have been astounding these past years, but some of the most cutting-edge treatments are still out of reach for people less privileged than everyone in this room.

She looks at me and shrugs. "It's complicated."

"Alvarez and the liberals say they're trying to control costs," King says, "but how are they going to do that? The only way to control costs is through a free market. They say they want to regulate, but the government bureaucrats I see in Washington couldn't regulate their way out of a paper bag."

"How much money are King and the other Republicans getting from the big health companies and hospitals betting on them to hold back any type of regulation that might cut away at their bottom lines?" I whisper to Sierra.

"Yeah," she replies, unimpressed, "but the health companies are also counting on the Democratic candidates they support to push for higher levels of government investment in new drugs and health-care technologies."

Sierra clearly knows her stuff.

"Alvarez and the liberals shouldn't be playing politics with your lives," King continues. "If you want to spend your money making yourselves healthier or taking care of your parents, then it's your fundamental, God-given right as Americans to do so."

The heads continue to nod as I imagine the big health stocks ticking up. "With no regulation of costs, we'll go from the 24 percent of GDP we currently spend on health care to whatever number will finally push us over the edge," I whisper to Sierra, probably trying to impress her with my statistic.

Sierra nods, finally agreeing with something I say. "But the acquisition of smaller companies with promising technologies and drugs in their pipelines will have already been made based on the inflated share prices, and the big health stock options will have already been exercised by then."

As King thunders on, I start to worry again about why both Sierra and I are here, but then pride gets the best of me. "I'm going to head out," I whisper to Sierra. "Why don't you take it from here?"

"Suit yourself," she says, no doubt recognizing why I'm leaving.

I'm annoyed at Sierra, Martina, the *Star*, and most of all myself as I stand there, still not moving. But then I feel the slight vibration on my wrist and tap my u.D.

"It's Maurice," he says.

I can hear his seriousness in my earbud even through the din of the room. I rush out the door and into the clubhouse hallway with purpose.

"Sir," I mumble softly.

"I came across something I thought might interest you. William Wolfson is a retired scientist living in St. Louis. Old guy. Used to work for Monsanto."

"Okay," I say, not sure where Maurice is going.

"I just came across a short reference in one of the statewide police reports. He's been dying of cancer these past five months." Maurice pauses. "And he disappeared nine days ago from the St. Louis hospice."

8

The mezuzah strikes me as an odd coincidence.

I've been on screen with Joseph for much of the three and a half hours it took for my Tesla to glide itself from Lee's Summit to St. Anthony's Hospice House in south St. Louis County. We've gone over William Wolfson's impressive bio in detail—PhD from the University of Illinois, former professor of complex adaptive systems at Washington University and director of the university's Biodesign Institute, former chief scientist at the global agriculture conglomerate Monsanto. Joseph and I have discussed the mathematical probability of two leading scientists vanishing from hospice care within a week of each other in the same state.

I've also gone through the paces with the nonplussed staff at the St. Louis hospice. Like their Kansas City counterparts, they looked everywhere and had no idea what might have happened. As in Kansas City, the overworked and underfunded St. Louis Police Department hadn't done much of anything to search for the missing old man dying from cancer. Although the St. Louis hospice didn't have surveillance cameras installed, as in Kansas City, their digital files had also been compromised.

But as I approach the cozy red brick colonial in University City, it's the mezuzah that somehow calls to me from the growing pile of coincidences. Two *Jewish* professors with cancer vanish from hospices in the same state at roughly the same time along with their records?

I pause a moment and pick up the reverberation of activity from inside the house before ringing the bell. The hospice had been unwilling to provide the home address, and Jerry Weisberg had to do some digging to get it, but we hadn't been able to track down a working number to let me call in advance.

A pale teenager with thick eyebrows and frizzy, shoulder-length red hair opens the door wearing blue jeans and a hooded sweatshirt.

"Is this the Wolfson home?" I say.

"Yes," he says guardedly.

"Is Mrs. Wolfson here?"

"My mother?"

The math doesn't add up. "Is there a Mrs. Wolfson who's your grandmother?"

A middle-aged man I sense is the boy's father approaches the door. "Can I help you with something?"

"My name is Rich Azadian. I'm a reporter with the *Kansas City Star* looking into the disappearance of Dr. Wolfson."

The man's demeanor shifts defensively, his suspicious look making me feel momentarily self-conscious.

"May I come in?"

He doesn't budge.

"I'm interested in trying to find out where Dr. Wolfson might be," I continue awkwardly.

"Why?"

The question is a fair one. What is a Kansas City reporter doing in St. Louis investigating a story that even the *St. Louis Post-Dispatch* hasn't covered?

"Because there seem to be some strange circumstances surrounding his disappearance," I say tentatively.

"Stranger than just him vanishing?"

I sense my opening. "Another scientist disappeared from hospice care in Kansas City a week or so before Dr. Wolfson. May I come in?"

The man takes in my words, still not convinced. "I appreciate your interest, but my father-in-law is gone. We really hope his body can be found, but he was in the final stages of terminal cancer and

Alzheimer's was kicking in. I hope we find him, but there may not be that much left of him to find."

"I understand completely, but there could be more to this," I say, feeling like I'm tripping over my words.

"Perhaps there could be, Mr. Azadian, but my mother-in-law is in a very weak state. My father-in-law's cancer treatment gave her a bit of hope. When that didn't work the floor started to drop out for both of them. Now she has her family around her. That's her life now. It's probably best to leave it there."

A slight ping rings in my head. Two Jewish scientists dying of cancer on drug programs . . . "Can you tell me a little more about the cancer treatments?"

The man pauses reluctantly. It's not clear I have the latitude for an additional question. Then he relents. "He was on an experimental cancer regimen. It didn't work and actually made him worse. That's when we moved him to the hospice."

"I'm really sorry to ask, but might you be able to tell me what type of treatment it was?"

The man shakes his head slightly, making again clear I'm beginning to overstep. "An experimental treatment protocol from the company Santique. They said it had a lot of promise. Now please . . ."

"Just one more question?" I say quickly, pushing my luck.

The man moves his son out of the way and begins to close the door. "I'm very sorry, Mr. Azadian, but I need to ask you to—"

"Have any of your data files with recent photos of Dr. Wolfson been replaced?" I blurt into the closing door.

A look of surprise flashes across his face. The door stops moving. "How could you have known that?"

"Let's just say there's starting to be a pattern."

He looks at me then behind him into the house. "I can't let you in. Everything is fragile here. But take down my number and call me later if you need more information. My name is Joel Glass."

I downlink his number, then stand reflexively before the closed door for a moment before walking back to my car.

"Take me home," I instruct.

"Routing to 3624 Charlotte, Kansas City, Missouri," the sexy robot voice responds.

I realize my mistake. "Take me to Toni Hewitt's house."

As the Tesla resets its route, I instruct my u.D to connect with Katherine Hart. She appears on my screen, leaning in over her coffee table, staring blankly and waiting for me to speak.

"Are you okay, Dr. Hart?"

"I'm here," she says morosely. "And it's Katherine. Have you learned anything?"

Her eyes brighten when I tell her about William Wolfson.

"It's certainly strange there are so many parallels," I tell her.

She nods.

"There was one thing his family mentioned about the experimental cancer drug I wanted to ask you about."

"Yes?"

"They said it was supposed to be some kind of miracle treatment and that Dr. Wolfson got worse after it didn't work."

Dr. Hart's head lifts slightly. "That's what they told us, too."

"Who?"

"The doctors and the health agent."

"What health agent?"

"The representative from the company, Santique."

2

"It's not just two scientists disappearing, Maurice," I say into my screen as my Tesla glides west on I-70. "Both of them were part of the same experimental drug treatment from the same company."

Joseph and I have spent the past thirty minutes onscreen gathering information about Santique, the Geneva-based health company currently using its stratospheric stock valuation—spiking even higher right now on vague rumors of a miraculous cancer treatment in the offing—to go on a global buying spree, snapping up hundreds of the most promising smaller companies. Santique made a small splash in Kansas City three years ago when it opened a new biomedical research institute next to the massive Sowers biotech park on 87th Street and I-435.

"Definitely an unlikely coincidence but still not impossible," Maurice replies from his desk. "This still just isn't a priority for us."

I'd thought Maurice would be more easily convinced, especially after telling me about William Wolfson's disappearance in the first place. "There's really nothing you can do to raise the profile of these cases?"

"There's a lot I can do," he responds. "I can divert the entire department to work on them. It's just not the right use of our limited resources."

"There's *no* action you can take?" I repeat, my mind whirling to generate suggestions. "What do you do for runaways and missing kids?"

"Not as much as we should."

"Nothing?"

"We search. And we enter their names into the NamUS database."

"What's that?"

"The National Missing and Unidentified Persons System."

"Did you enter Benjamin Hart's name into the system?"

"It's not used for that sort of thing. We have protocols—"

"Maurice," I say, "just please do me a favor and enter his and William Wolfson's names. What's the downside?"

"It's not the way—"

"Maurice, please. I've met with their families. They are at a loss. No one is doing anything. What's the cost of adding their names compared to what their families are going through? Just this once."

"Yeah, right," Maurice says, shaking his head as he taps off.

It's almost 10 p.m. when my Tesla turns down Toni's Brookside street. I take control of the steering to navigate her driveway.

I know from our quick conversations over the course of the day she's not been feeling great, so I'm not surprised to see her wrapped in blankets on the media room couch as I walk in. Her disheveled hair and tired face peek out from the top of the wrapped quilt.

"Hi, baby," I say, my tone perched somewhere between tentative and enthusiastic.

"Hey," she moans, dragging out the vowel. Even her little groans I still find adorable.

"You doing okay?" I sit on the couch in front of her and place my hand on the side of her face, then tap her u.D, which flashes the icon for normal biometrics.

"With all the miracles of medicine, you'd think they'd have come up with something a bit less primitive," she says.

She's being generous. The science of reproduction keeps charging forward, but even if egg freezing at twenty years old is the norm, that doesn't make the extraction process any less personal, especially for Toni, whose naturalist streak led to delaying the procedure a good thirteen years. Sure, she should have done this years ago; sure, she'd need to freeze even if we weren't even dating or were having kids tomorrow; sure, we keep hearing of the miracles of induced pluripotent stem cells to someday generate unlimited eggs, but none of that seems to quite matter right now.

"Only one more day, baby." I take off my shoes and lie beside her on the couch. "Could you survive work?"

Toni gives her all to her patients in the Neonatal Intensive Care Unit at Truman Medical Center, babies struggling to survive, but she's been the one struggling these past weeks to maintain her high standards as a nurse while battling the overdose of hormones surging through her body.

"Survive is the right word," she grumbles, wrinkles creasing her forehead. "Find your old guys?"

She focuses intently as I update her on what I've learned.

"What do you think?" I ask when I've finished.

"I don't know. Could be a random coincidence, could be something more. If I thought the worst I'd wonder if someone wasn't trying to hide evidence of something."

"Like?"

"I don't know. Maybe the treatment was so disorienting they lost their minds and wandered off and it just happened that these two guys haven't yet been found. So what's next?"

"I'm going to the Santique research center in the morning. I'm not sure if they'll tell me anything, but at least I can ask."

Her raised eyebrows ask a question she doesn't need to verbalize.

"You know I'll be there," I respond.

Toni is actually working a full day and only taking the time to have her eggs extracted during her lunch break. Still, I wouldn't imagine not being around to support her. "Can I get you anything? Are you hungry?" I continue, feeling yet again that we're cramming too much that's unsaid into daily formalities not capable of bearing such a heavy load.

She shakes her head slightly.

"Can I massage your bum?" I add mischievously, sliding my hand through the seam of the wrapped quilt.

Toni's hand reaches down and gently catches my arm. Her long fingers tap it twice. "Maybe some other time, Dikran."

10

Every blade of grass surrounding the Santique Biomedical Research Institute is perfect. The Scandinavian-style modernist glass building is shaped like a giant sail gliding forever forward into the future.

As I enter, large walls of frosted glass along the cavernous front entrance flash images of research facilities around the world and patients whose wide smiles make abundantly clear they've been given the gift of life by the Santique Health Corporation. The sharp sun radiating through the eternally blue early November sky illuminates the room into a crystal cathedral.

The lobby is an enclosed cube with no people visible. As I enter, a pulsating blue pastel arrow flashes before me on the floor, advancing with each step I take. The arrow leads me toward the far wall, where a video image of the receptionist materializes as I approach.

"Good morning, Mr. Azadian. Welcome to Santique," the clean-shaven young man says, every piece of him as put together as this building and his hair as neatly cropped as the lawn. "May I help you?"

I immediately power down the u.D on my right wrist that has so willingly betrayed my identity.

"I'm a reporter with the *Kansas City Star*," I say into the wall. "I'd like to speak with someone about an experimental treatment for cancer your company has put into trials."

"I'll be happy to connect you with someone in media relations. Please stand by a moment. Can I offer you a seat and some water while you wait?"

Before I can answer, the screen fogs and is replaced by the Santique logo, a flexed bow forming the bottom half of the "S" pointing its arrow to the stars, with the remaining letters printed in classical Roman script as if etched into the Pantheon. No Limits, the tag line below adds, as if spray-painted on by a graffiti artist.

A curved chair rotates out of the wall toward me on a track, a bottle of Badoit water resting atop one of its arms. A pair of VR glasses sits on a small illuminated stand. The flashing light beneath the glasses makes it clear I am supposed to pick them up. I put them on, and the impressive, detailed story of Santique's spectacular rise from Swiss family company to European champion to global darling unfolds in virtual reality. I'm inside the clinic in the African camps where a series of rhinoviruses is being sequenced and overcome. I am walking down the aisle with a young survivor to meet her groom. The experience is designed to be overwhelming and it is.

The images mist out as a sinewy thirty-something woman materializes. Her perfectly erect posture and blond hair pulled back in a bun suggest a childhood immersed in ballet. I assume she is a real person, but it's ever harder to know in virtual reality.

"Hello, sir," she says with only the slightest of accents, balanced, I'm guessing, somewhere between Paris and Oxford. "My colleague tells me you are doing a story on one of our cancer drugs? I see in our records that Ms. Halley covers this type of story for your paper. Has that changed?"

"No, it hasn't," I say, annoyed that Sierra is again crowding my space and alarmed but not surprised Santique has kept such close tabs on the *Star*. Is there any information on the rest of us these companies *don't* have, I wonder. "I'm looking at these issues in a different context than Ms. Halley."

"I see. And that is?"

"I'm collecting information on two people who were part of an experimental cancer regimen run by your company."

"I understand," she says. "As I'm sure you can appreciate, we are unable to provide information on any individuals who may have been engaged with our protocols."

Her words somehow grate on me, as if each of them has been parsed by an army of lawyers. "I know that. I'm actually more interested in the protocols themselves."

"A briefing can certainly be arranged for specific treatment protocols once the findings have been released and published."

"And for those currently in trials?"

"I'm afraid we are not able to discuss those in any way."

I feel a bit stupid for even trying to get information from Santique in such a rookie fashion. With populations aging fast in the developed world and China, cancer is the coin of the realm for the big health companies. They are not about to share information with a reporter wandering in off the street. A company like this didn't get where it is by responding to the media; they got here by shaping it.

"Might it be possible to speak with one of your scientists?"

"I'm very sorry, Mr. Azadian, but our internal regulations are quite strict. I'm sure you can understand our need to protect our intellectual property. Our firm exists to foster health and well-being around the world. We are very careful about only releasing information and data once it has been fully vetted."

She is so precise and logical, it's hard for me to counter. It seems fruitless to tell her I'm not asking for data to be released, just to talk with someone who knows more about a specific cancer treatment. She is refusing to help me, albeit in the most polite manner possible.

"Thank you," I say with a slight nod, then pull off the glasses. I stand and turn toward the entrance door. The arrows lead me where I already know I am going. Out with no information.

Joseph is waiting for me onscreen as I boot up my car.

"Any luck?" he asks.

"Nothing. It was at least worth trying."

"I'm not surprised," he responds, his tone suggesting that just showing up at Santique was a questionable idea in the first place.

I'm sure that's right, but I've also found in my nine years at the *Star* that just poking around turns out to be a decent strategy from time to time. "There's got to be more information out there. Can you look?"

Joseph pauses. He has his own stories to worry about.

But half of his time still belongs to me.

"Let me see what I can find," he says warily.

11

"Here goes nothing," Toni says dryly as she approaches me in the NICU waiting room.

Her noon appointment is in ten minutes, so I'm not surprised she's not her most enthusiastic self.

I stand and face her.

She takes my hand and stops for a moment. "I'm glad you're here."

"Of course I'm here. I know I don't say it enough, but you're the most important person to me in the world."

"More important than your mother?" she asks mischievously, catching me off guard.

"Yes," I say, feeling guilty as the words escape my mouth. Baby Nayiri notwithstanding, I still don't visit or speak with my mother as much as I probably should.

"I'm just teasing you."

I relax.

"More important than yourself?" she fires once my defenses are down.

A part of me wants to protect myself. It's overruled by the fact that I'm here escorting her to a surgical procedure that may be commonplace but is still traumatic for her—and by the possibility she has a point.

Maybe I'm being defensive, I think, but I've made sacrifices, too. I had a pretty exciting offer from the investigative news organization ProCivica to move to New York last year. We thought about it seriously. But at the end of the day, Toni didn't want to leave her parents and her friends and probably knew in her heart she was not a big-city woman. Her parents live in Independence, Missouri, and Kansas City was also half a country closer to California and Maya and Nayiri, she had argued. I guess I could have gone on my own or tried to convince her to change her mind, but I knew then as I know now that I value Toni more than my work. So I turned down the offer but bought myself the Tesla as a guilty consolation. If I was going to slow down my life, at least I could do it in an obscenely fast car.

Toni notices my mind drifting. "You really are a pain in the ass sometimes."

We both stop walking and face each other, then she wraps her arms around my neck. Our bodies pull together.

"I'm scared," she says.

"I know, baby," I say softly, focusing only on her and holding her tightly.

The walk through the hospital takes under ten minutes. The deliverybots and Robotic Nurse Assistants on their rounds courteously steer themselves out of our way as we pass. We arrive at the OB/GYN ward and get in line behind a small army of women all here for the same ORC—oocyte retraction and cryopreservation—procedure. The well-oiled machine of the clinic makes it seem like a McDonald's drive through. The fact that the entire procedure is carried out by surgical robots only heightens the perception of mechanical efficiency.

I'm not allowed in, so after she enters the ward I pace the surprisingly empty waiting room. Maybe this procedure has become so routine, like a teeth cleaning, that people come on their own. To my surprise, she emerges twenty-five minutes later with a small bandage on her arm and a relaxed smile on her face.

"Well?" I say expectantly.

"Piece of cake," she says nonchalantly, as if our earlier conversations had never happened.

"Are you sure? Are you okay?" I'm unsure how much I should ask. I'm not the one who's had a robotic arm inside of me.

"Yeah, of course," she says, making clear she doesn't want to go into the details.

I've learned over the past few years to stop pressing immediately in the face of that look. "Okay," I say hesitantly.

"Walk me back to work?"

"Um, sure," I say, taking her hand.

Her step somehow feels more carefree than it's been for weeks, maybe months.

"All right, honey," she says outside the NICU doors. "I'll see you later?"

"What time are you done?"

"My shift ends at seven thirty."

"Meet at your place at eight? I can bring dinner."

The mention of her place seems to cause a momentary flicker in her eye. "Sure."

12

"What do you have for me?" I fire, approaching Joseph's cubicle.

He doesn't look up. "Scientific papers, patent applications, pharmaceutical and gene therapy trial guidelines."

"Anything jump out?" I say, chewing my sesame flagel.

"Relative to what?"

"Any reference to Benjamin Hart or William Wolfson?"

"Not connecting them to Santique."

I take a slug of matcha. "Anything about recent cancer protocols?"

"Lots of references to sequencing the cancers, stem cell treatments, pharmagenics—"

"Does it list the names of specific Santique employees connected with the most recent trials?"

"Lots of them."

"Can you narrow it down?"

"With the right search terms." He turns his head toward me as if to say, *well?*

I pause. "How about getting a list of their researchers associated with Santique's cancer work over the past few years to see which names are cited most, at least to get us started?"

"I can probably do that," he says, mumbling into his u.D and waving his arms to move files across his wall. "I'm guessing there will be a lot of names."

In ten minutes, the list in order of citation frequency appears. There are around eighty in total, mostly French-sounding. None of them mean anything to me. Michel Noland, Mathieu Gignac, Celine Henri, Olivier Meilleroux . . .

Joseph transfers the list to my u.D.

"Let me see if I can track down any of these people individually," I say. "Keep looking."

He stares at me blankly.

"Please," I add, turning back toward my cubicle.

It takes me almost an hour to cover the first eleven names on the list, and I'm beginning to get frustrated by my complete lack of progress when Joseph steps gingerly to my desk.

"I think I may have found something interesting," he says, tapping his u.D to splash a document on my cubicle wall.

It's hard to know what he's referring to from the tiny print. "What is it?"

"A footnote in an article in the *American Journal of Cancer Research* on stem cell treatments for specific cancers from March 2022, three and a half years ago, that references both Michel Noland, chief scientific officer at Santique Health, and a Santique scientist named Dr. Noam Heller."

"And?" I ask, not clear why this is significant.

"They'd publish something like this as the foundation of a patent application. It's like a preemptive claim."

"Okay," I say cautiously.

He takes a breath then a small step back. "I downloaded all the cancer papers filed by Santique over the past decade and put them in a database. Then I ran an association algorithm targeting the names of the scientists and the compounds mentioned in each of their studies."

I'm not entirely sure where Joseph is going but have, like most everyone else, developed a profound appreciation these past years for how big-data analysis can uncover narratives far beyond our limited brains.

"Heller and Noland only published one article together, which appears to be Heller's only publication as a Santique scientist. All the other Santique research seems to stem from that single article,"

Joseph says, tapping his u.D to splash a heat map on my wall. "This shows all the associations over time between Santique scientists and the compounds they reference in their papers. Heller and Noland's paper is represented by the bright blue dot in the middle. See how it gets so much larger just after the *American Journal* article is published in March 2022? Their work is the foundation of the other studies. It's like they're showing the way and the other research is following the lead. Forty-two papers are filed in the next six months, all referencing the original article. Noland is a co-author on all of them, but Heller is only co-author on that single paper. Then, just as fast, the blue dot shrinks very quickly, as if Heller and Noland's work is taken out of the equation. It's not just that they stop releasing papers referencing the Heller and Nolan article; they completely stop publishing cancer papers."

"And this is a company betting its future on finding a stem cell–based cure for cancer?"

"I had the same question," Joseph says. "That's why I ran a search of the full database for references to all of the compounds referenced in Heller and Noland's 2022 article. Look what I found."

I'm not exactly sure what the red blotch on my wall is telling me, but Joseph opens his hand to bring the blotch into sharper relief. The text of an article emerges.

"This is a paper Heller published in *Cell* on revolutionary stem cell approaches to cancer therapy, the year before, in 2021, when he was at Sowers," Joseph says. "All of the compounds referenced in the paper he did the next year with Noland are there."

"Which makes you think Santique acquired Heller and his research after then?"

"It could definitely suggest that. Heller and Noland's March 2022 paper was just the codification of Heller's previous work. It's like Heller's discovery is being handed off to Santique. Then Santique starts focusing like a laser beam on this work with Noland but not Heller, then the publications stop."

"So maybe they've got Heller working quietly in the basement."

"They hire him from Sowers, focus all their energies on patenting his work, then suddenly go dark?" Joseph asks, not waiting for an answer. "This got me at least interested in seeing if I could learn more about Noland and Heller. Noland seems to be a lifer at Santique, a rising star, but look at Heller." He waves his right hand to manipulate the files. "The guy is unbelievably impressive, a genius. Born in Cape Town in 1956; University of Cape Town PhD in biology; Stanford post-doc; most of his career at the Weizmann Institute in Israel, where he was one of the early pioneers in stem cell research; came to Sowers in 2016, where he publishes a series of path-breaking papers, but then he seems to vanish from the public record in 2022."

"Wow."

"It's not just that. He seems to have mastered and pulled together a lot of different fields in his work."

"Like?" I ask.

"Computer science, deep learning artificial intelligence, biology, psychology, advanced mathematics for a start."

"Not Mayan numerology? The guy is an idiot."

"He's also apparently a concert-level violinist and composer. He and his wife used to perform together in Israel. She was also a scientist. Looks like she died ten years ago."

"So Heller was a major figure, then three years ago he just drops off the radar," I say quietly. "What about other references to him? Is there a way to map more general references to Heller over time?"

"That's easy," Joseph says, already waving his hands to manipulate the data.

The heat map that splashes on my wall a few moments later tells the same story as the research papers. Heller, like most everybody else, lives a life exuding a traceable data stream. Then, in late 2022, the stream goes dark.

"So Heller leaves Sowers four years ago to join Santique, just before Santique builds a major facility next door to the Sowers research park. He co-publishes a paper with a Santique scientist based solely on his own research, then Santique takes over the science and he's not heard from. He's an older guy. Could he have died?" I ask.

"I don't know," Joseph says. "You'd think someone like that would have an obituary somewhere. I don't see anything."

The logic is appealing, but I battle in my head with William of Occam, the fourteenth-century English theologian I sometimes channel to keep me from veering too far off track. It's easy to come up with complex theories, but the simplest explanations are usually the most accurate. "Is all of this strange or just a product of our imaginations?"

"At very least Noland and Heller could be a key if we're interested in learning more about Santique's experimental cancer research," Joseph says, making the source of our realization clear.

"And from my experience at Santique earlier today, there's not a big chance they're going to let us talk with Noland."

"Which leaves us with Heller," Joseph says, completing my thought. "If we can find him."

"What do you suggest?"

Joseph continues to wave his hands, moving files across my wall. "I still can't see where he lives or works. I can see what hospital he was born in in South Africa, where he lived in Palo Alto, his apartment in Israel, and where he lived in Kansas City until three years ago. But for the last three years, there's essentially no record. It's like he's been erased."

I stare at Joseph but my mind is elsewhere. What is it about vanishing scientists these days?

13

Flat and rectangular, the dilapidated one-story building must be about a hundred and fifty feet long and fifty feet or so wide. The cracked asphalt surrounding the building shows faded yellow markings for parking but no other cars are in sight.

I knock on the sturdy front door of the orange brick warehouse. No answer.

I yank the steel door handle. It doesn't budge.

All casual observation suggests this building is unoccupied. The Missouri River flows quietly by.

But thank dog I'm not relying solely on casual observation.

Joseph's call to Sowers human resources had hit a predictable brick wall, both on getting access to Noland and on information about where we might find Heller. Then I'd called in a bigger gun.

Once his initial reservations were overcome, tracking down Heller was the kind of challenge Jerry Weisberg reveled in.

"Death and taxes," he had said, responding to my query about how someone could simply vanish without leaving a trace.

He targeted death first. The morgues and funeral homes had not prioritized network security, and it was relatively easy to at least show that nobody named Noam Heller had been officially recorded dead in the United States over the past few years.

Taxes were another story. Jerry drew a line there. "I wouldn't be comfortable hacking the US government on this even if I could," he had said. "Not based just on what you've told me."

"This is important, Jerry," I'd pleaded, but Jerry was not going to be railroaded.

"But," he continued with a suppressed smirk, "we don't need to hack public records. They're public. We can't get the details of personal tax filings, but we can confirm whether or not a filing has been made." He wiggled his finger to track through the database links splashed on his wall. "Here we go. Noam Heller. Jackson County, Missouri. Personal taxes filed for 2024. At least you can bet he had some connection to Kansas City in April of this year."

I'd wanted to hug Jerry but knew full well that nothing would do more to knock him off his game. "How can we narrow this down?"

"We can't from the tax database, but what else do we know about him?"

"We know he was born in South Africa, that he's a cancer researcher, that he used to live in Israel, that he plays the violin—"

"What type of cancer?"

"I don't know exactly," I said. "The research he published a few years ago was on genetic sequencing and stem cell–based approaches to diagnose and treat cancers."

"Is he still working?"

"I don't know. I'd imagine that someone with that kind of passion wouldn't just quit."

"But if he was working for a big company like Santique, he'd probably have shown up in an employment database, which he didn't." Jerry had paused to think. "Does he have his own lab?"

"Could be. How would we know?"

"The easy way would be to look up the address, but we did that already."

"Thanks for that," I said ironically.

"But maybe," Jerry continued, "he'd need to order special equipment or materials for his research."

"What are you thinking?" I asked.

Jerry was already deep into his research. The files splashed across his walls. "According to this, an advanced stem cell lab would need specific antibodies for confirming the flexibility of the cells, stem cell media, and usually specific viruses to help reprogram the cells. All of this is pretty specific, but let's see what we can do."

I'd watched in wonder as he made a list of the key materials, in awe as he hacked the medical supply companies to see where they had been delivered in the Kansas City area over the past three years. Then he eliminated all the listed hospitals and known labs from the list. Two unknowns remained. So he'd hacked into the Kansas City Power and Light system and learned that the large energy bills for one of them were being paid by Santique Health, and so here I am at 1836 Levee Road in Kansas City's West Bottoms—the historical base of the city, now mostly abandoned but for a few dilapidated warehouses and struggling bars where the down-and-out cohabitate with the artsy poor.

But there doesn't appear to be anyone here, and the main entrance is locked, and nothing happens when I keep knocking.

I walk a loop of the facility, peering into the darkly glazed, grate-covered windows and banging on the back door, but see and hear nothing. If something is happening here, there's not much evidence of it.

A part of me thinks I should leave, but it doesn't take my philosophy PhD to know that much of our transient lives happen outside our direct gaze. I've also invested too much energy in getting here to back down so easily. I have at least enough confidence in my own research to keep trying. I drive around the block, then park my car beside a neighboring abandoned building with a decent view of the facility and wait.

I fill the first thirty minutes reviewing Joseph's additional notes on Heller and then scanning the international headlines, again dominated by the forever unfolding crisis in the Middle East where the Sunni–Shia wars that already destroyed Iraq, Syria, Lebanon, and most of the old Arab states are metastasizing into roving bands of militias fighting with the weapons, including tactical nukes, of the disintegrating states in a scorpion's duel with each other and Israel.

Now that the Israel-Palestine peace deal has collapsed, the jihadi terrorists have fully infiltrated the West Bank. The international commitment to keep that territory disarmed has proven worthless. As part of the grand compromise between America's support for Israel and China's still-desperate need for Middle Eastern oil, the United Nations–led consortium of big powers had agreed to provide and man sophisticated anti-missile protective domes to shield both Israel and the scattered oil fields. The UN's done a decent job working with the Israeli military to shoot down the daily barrage of missiles, but many of the UN member countries who support fortifying the oilfields are waging a rearguard action to halt the expensive, challenging, and sometimes deadly protection of Israel. The international movement to pull back has been growing for months.

Still no action from the warehouse.

I connect with Joseph, who shows me what more he's learned about the impressive careers of Professor Hart, Dr. Wolfson, and Dr. Heller.

Still nothing from the warehouse.

It's getting dark, and I'm starting to wonder if I'm really achieving anything by lurking around. But I've already sunk five hours into this stakeout and I still have ninety minutes before I need to be at Toni's. If I leave now, I'll have to start over from scratch. I eat a SaladBar from my glove compartment and wait.

Nothing.

I'm trapezing between consciousness and a daydream inexplicably involving Martina, Sierra, and my mother at the Santa Monica pier when my partly opened eyes send an urgent alert to my brain. My head jerks forward.

The light is not perfect, but even in the hazy sunset the outline of the tall, older man is clear. As he strides toward the river, I see the silhouette of an excited puppy leaping around him.

I open my car door as quietly as possible and step out, then walk briskly over and approach him from behind.

Dr. Livingstone, I presume? I reject the impulse. "Excuse me. I'm sorry to bother you."

The man turns abruptly. He is lanky and thin with a wisp of gray hair resting over his forehead. His large eyes alight his creased face over ruddy cheeks. An unmistakable vibrancy counteracts his advanced age. "Who the hell are you?" he says in a staccato that sounds British but I know to be South African.

"Dr. Heller?"

A worried, almost panicked, look crosses the man's face. "So this is it?" he asks gravely.

"I'm sorry?" I say, confused.

He stares at me sharply for a few moments before seeming to process my obliviousness. Then he takes a step backwards, turns, and begins marching briskly toward the warehouse. "Sebastian, come," he orders over his shoulder to the small brown Labrador.

"I'm very sorry to bother you, Dr. Heller," I say, rushing behind him. "I need to ask you some questions."

"Please leave me alone," he says nervously, picking up his pace.

"But . . ."

The imposing back door to the warehouse opens. The puppy is at first uncooperative, twisting its head toward me and bouncing back and forth between the sources of duty and excitement. Heller turns, perturbed, and ushers the exuberant puppy in the door.

"Dr. Heller, I need to talk with you," I say into the swiftly closing door. I hear the lock turn. "*Dr. Heller.*"

14

Toni disliked the idea from the moment I raised it.

I'd rushed in her door at 8:20 with grilled chicken and a carton of steamed vegetables so I was already halfway in the doghouse.

But for Toni there are worse places than the doghouse. "It's dishonest and deceptive," she'd said, "and I doubt it will work. From everything you've told me about him, Dr. Heller will see right through it."

She may have been right, but I can be a dogged pain in the rear sometimes and here I am at 6 a.m. back in my same West Bottoms hiding place with a still somewhat hormonal low-boil Toni in the passenger seat of my car, two large travel mugs of espresso, and Toni's mother's biscuit-tan cocker spaniel, Dreyfus, slobbering up the bio-sympathetic hatch of my Tesla.

The car is one of my few indulgences with the nearly $200,000 I earned from *Genesis Code*. I remind myself daily that the sleek, rocket-like sports car is just a frivolous object, but I'm honest enough to recognize I've developed almost romantic feelings for it. The temperature-controlled, body-forming seats ensure perfect comfort in my little ecosystem. The full-screen dashboard fully integrates with my u.D. The constant stream of augmented reality updates describing conditions ahead and potential dangers flashes across my windshield. The internal lighting system and selections from my music playlist correspond with biometric data constantly monitored from my wrist. When I sit back and give over control to the Autonomous Driving System, I feel cared for, safe.

But after paying all of Maya's baby costs, helping Joseph build a small school in his home village in Kerala, buying a gold and sapphire necklace for Toni, and putting some money away for our long-planned but—thanks to me—not-yet-realized big trip to "someplace hot," and throwing down more than I probably should have for this irresistibly indulgent sports car, I now find myself with $46,000 in the bank and not much more long-term security than I had two years ago.

On another day it could almost be romantic, sitting in the car watching the blending orange and purple hues of the sun rising over the Missouri, reflecting on the fall leaves dangling from the few trees lining the banks of the mighty river. But today we wait quietly, and Toni stews.

I've learned the hard way over the years that there are some things I do well and some things not so well. I can dazzle people with intellect or, as is painfully obvious right now, overcome their resistance with a mix of idealism and pugnacity, but I don't have the simple ability to make people I've just met trust or sometimes even like me.

Toni, on the other hand, is a natural genius at this. Her calm manner and deep Midwestern graciousness almost magically put people at ease. She connects. It's not only what makes her so good at her job, it's also why the world, which sometimes feels charged and tense around me, seems more at ease around her. She, of course, knows all of this. It's just that she doesn't like her best qualities being used as a prop, or her love and knowledge of dogs being woven into another of my schemes.

The plan, I think as I look at jovial Dreyfus in the rearview mirror, isn't entirely contemptible. And Dreyfus, my unwitting agent, is quite simply the most likable dog I've ever met. Even I, who somehow lack the pet-obsessed gene most everyone else in America seems to possess, have a soft spot in my heart for Dreyfus. Floppy-eared, with a constant look of excited expectation on his face, his expression and demeanor, if verbalized, would probably translate into something like "oh boy, really, can I, can I?" It's hard to imagine any man or beast not taking pity on poor, needy Dreyfus, who seems to want only to be loved, and granting him at least a few moments of sympathetic attention.

After forty or so minutes of waiting, we see the two figures emerging from the back door of the warehouse. Heller is walking, erect and brisk, with Sebastian darting peripatetically around him.

"Told you," Toni says proudly. "Puppies have to make kaka and run around in the morning."

"You were right and you are on," I say.

She eyes me with a mix of annoyance and appreciation.

"And thank you," I add.

She shakes her head. "Come on, Dreyfus. Let's do this."

Dreyfus has less appreciation that he's being exploited. He lifts his head excitedly at the sound of his name. *Dreyfus? Hey. That's me. Oh boy, really, can I, can I?*

I watch them walk around the building to approach Heller from the other side. I see Dreyfus sprinting over to Sebastian and the two dogs first sniffing each other and then leaping and yelping together, their tails wagging excitedly. Then Heller moves briskly toward the dogs and Toni follows suit. I see them start talking.

At first Heller's body stands stiff and erect, but as the minutes pass his stiffness seems to melt. After about fifteen minutes, I see him nod slightly. Toni bows her head as if to say thank you before Toni and Heller begin walking toward me. I get out of the car as they approach.

"Rich, this is Dr. Noam Heller. Dr. Heller, this is Rich Azadian."

"I'm sorry about yesterday," I fumble.

Dr. Heller looks at me as if sizing me up, then scans the horizon in both directions with an expression that seems, for a moment at least, somehow nervous. "Why don't the two of you come in."

15

Stepping through the substantial door of the decaying warehouse, I am overwhelmed.

From the look of the building's exterior I would have expected some dusty boxes and a few battered remnants of better days. Instead, the glistening, fully automated, state-of-the-art laboratory blows me away.

The immaculate white walls gleam under incandescent light. Immense cabinets, looking like glass refrigerators filled with test tubes and agar plates, line the wall to my left. Near them, a massive cart is stacked with hundreds of small plastic cubbies, a white mouse twitching in each. A series of conveyor belts, reminding me of one of those endless sushi bars, runs from each of these areas toward the middle of the room, where an outsized scope rests under a translucent plastic dome.

To my right, clear plastic sheeting walls off fifteen or so compact machines arrayed in a rectangle. Inside the rectangle, quietly whirring yellow robotic arms pull plastic plates in and out of each machine in a symphony of coordinated movement. Each time an arm reaches over, a small window opens on each machine, allowing the plates to be transferred from one to the other.

At the far end of the lab, a massive silver door makes the smaller white door next to it look downright Lilliputian. The violin sonata playing in the background only heightens my sense of bizarre juxtaposition. It's hard to grasp so much happening in so concentrated a space.

"Incredible." The quiet word leaks from my mouth. I hardly notice Dreyfus and Sebastian nipping each other happily as they race toward the far corner of the lab.

"Welcome to Heller Labs," Heller says, the wrinkles around his eyes contracting warmly. He is not at all young but there is definitely a certain youthfulness about him.

"I don't know where to begin," I say awkwardly, still trying to get a handle on what I'm seeing and wondering why he has let us enter in the first place.

Toni steps in. "Thank you again for inviting us in."

"You didn't give me much a choice," Heller says with a hint of irony.

"I mentioned to you outside that I'm a nurse, but I've never seen a lab quite like this."

"Why, thank you. I don't get many visitors. It's nice to show off a bit."

"Would you mind showing off a little more?" she asks.

Heller's slight blush is momentarily overcome by what seems almost like a flash of worry. "I normally would not be so forthcoming," he says, composing himself, "but you've come at what we might call a serendipitous moment." He looks down for a few seconds as if figuring something out, then stares at each of us in turn before taking a few steps toward the glass cabinets. "It all starts over here."

Toni glances at me and raises her eyebrows as we follow Heller. *Not bad for a walking hormone machine.*

I smile back with my eyes. *Thank you.*

Heller opens one of the cabinet doors, picks up an agar plate, and holds it out to us. We train our eyes on the layer of murky white gel.

"Look closely," he says, moving it under a light.

"Everything is moving," Toni says.

"Exactly. *Caenorhabditis elegans*, but most people call these amazing creatures roundworms." He pauses theatrically. "I began studying them many years ago with the great Sydney Brenner. They are the little workhorses of biomedical research—the size of a standard comma, the simplest little creatures with a nervous system. They're hermaphroditic, cheap, freezable, and most importantly, short-lived."

"Sucks for them," I say.

Heller looks at me and smiles thoughtfully. "We all live on borrowed time, Mr. Azadian, but our lives exist on a relative scale. The *C. elegans* normally live about two weeks, but I'm quite confident their experience feels as long to them as ours does to us."

"Or as short," I add, my perennial fear of mortality triggered.

My words seem to catch Heller's attention. He pauses, as if processing a thought. "We all live on sliding scales."

Toni and I look at him expectantly.

Heller hesitates, as if unsure he should continue.

"How do you mean?" Toni coaxes.

An avuncular half smile builds slowly on his face. "The mice over here generally live an average of 2.3 years. The bats that swarm over the river at night can live up to fifty years. Why?"

We don't have an answer.

"It's not an easy question," Heller continues, "but essentially regulatory proteins tell hormones to instruct cells what to do. For the past decade, I've been studying how roundworms with specific genetic mutations and extra doses of certain molecules regulating their cells can live longer than normal. I'm trying to gain insights into how we might reprogram cancer cells to their younger, healthier state. Roundworms are simple creatures, far simpler than humans, but we have many of the same genes and can learn a lot about ourselves by studying them. Like all organisms, their cells are constantly balancing how much energy to allocate to growing versus to repairing themselves. That's the balance of nature. If they put more resources into growing, they put less into repair and live shorter lives. The inverse is also true. It's all regulated by insulin signaling between the cells. That's the great insight of the *C. elegans* research."

"So if all you eat is sugar, you live hard and die young," I say, my eyes glancing over and briefly catching Toni's.

"Something like that. If we suppress the insulin receptor, the daf-2 gene, they get less of that sugar high and live longer. The same effect happens if we boost the daf-16 gene and make them emphasize cellular repair. But worms don't have stem cells like higher-level organisms, so there's only so much they can tell us about cancer cells."

Toni and I nod slightly, encouraging Heller to continue.

Heller leads us toward the mouse cart. "So the next logical question I asked was whether the same mutation process would work on a far more sophisticated mammal, our little furry friends over here. In addition to boosting and suppressing the daf genes, I experimented with a number of approaches. I'm not sure if these words mean anything to you, but I explored rapamycin and everolimus kinase inhibition, sirtuins, telomerase therapy. Each is a different way of sending signals to the cell that emphasize repair. Everything worked a little. Nothing worked well. I tried delivering a chemical into the cells called nicotinamide adenine dinucleotide, NAD, to reverse the decay of their mitochondria, the little power packs of the cell. The process worked a bit better but with a twist. The mice with the mutated genes and NAD injections lived slightly longer, but they became far more susceptible to other diseases like diabetes. A number of them grew uncontrollable tumors. My fight to stop cancer was instead enabling it. Something was missing."

My mind wanders back to the bleak images of human wreckage from the Kansas City and St. Louis hospices. "I'm sure I didn't understand all of it," I interject, "but I read your article from six years ago in the *Journal of Regenerative Medicine*."

"That article was mostly theoretical when I wrote it. I hadn't actually proven anything. I just outlined the idea of using a combination of genetic manipulations and other approaches to reverse-age specific cancer cells. I needed to see if the mutations and other inputs that slowed the deterioration of the roundworm and mouse cells could be used to target cancer cells in higher-level mammals."

"And that's what you've been working on here?" Toni asks.

"Let me show you something else," Heller says, leading us toward the rectangle of machines inside the plastic sheeting. "This process is called quantitative high throughput screening. The different machines wash, incubate, sort, spin, and sequence the cells. We can sequence the DNA of the roundworms or the mice or anything else. We can reprogram blood cells into stem cells and then differentiate them into other types of cells. In a day, we can do what it would have taken a lab worker fifteen years a couple of decades ago."

"And with that you can cure cancer?" Toni asks.

"That has always been the goal, but it's an extremely difficult one." Heller looks solemnly at Toni, then slowly shifts his gaze to me, as if again weighing whether he should continue. He takes a deep, slow breath. "There are many types of cancer cells, but the ones we worry about all have one very basic hallmark. They've essentially forgotten how to die and are multiplying out of control, overcoming the body's natural immunological ability to fight back. We've gotten pretty good at identifying cancers these past years through liquid biopsies pinpointing the nucleic acids circulating in the bloodstream. For years we've also been making progress in fighting cancers through precision molecular medicine, checkpoint inhibitors, immunotherapy, antibody-drug conjugate therapies and the like, but we're always a day late and a dollar short because the cancers keep evolving and mutating. But cancer is ultimately a disease of cellular aging, so I wanted to stop trying to figure out how to fight each different cancer and instead focus on reverting the biological age of the cells to a point in time before they became cancerous."

"To slow their aging process like you did with the roundworms?" Toni asks.

"Even more," Heller says. "Slowing the cell's aging process wasn't enough. Once they were cancerous, the cells had their own internal accelerators." Heller pauses again before continuing. "My idea, my big idea, was to not just try to revert specific cells to a previous state but to also amplify the naturally occurring genes known to suppress the growth of the cancer, to send the cells back in time and give them a better chance of defending themselves going forward."

"Can cells really go back in time?" I ask.

"People didn't used to think so before Yamanaka cracked the code for inducing stem cells, but humans are far more plastic than we once thought."

My mind jumps back from the fascinating science lecture to the urgency of this moment. "So when did Santique find you?" I ask.

Heller's face tightens. "They didn't exactly find me. I'd known them for a while and our interests were dovetailing. They offered me a great deal of money and to build me this facility if I would join them."

"And you did?" I ask, still uncertain why Heller is being so candid with us after previously going to such lengths to stay hidden.

"Heavens, no. The last thing I'd ever want to do is get sucked into a big company like that." Heller takes a small step back. "But," he continues in a softer voice, "I needed a lot more money and this lab to test my hypothesis. Science can be magic, but magic can be expensive."

"I'm a little confused," I say. "Weren't you referenced as a Santique scientist in the *American Journal of Cancer Research* paper you co-wrote with Michel Noland three years ago?"

A pained look flashes momentarily across Heller's face. "You seem to already know the answer to that question, but yes. That single article was part of our deal. They needed to co-author my work to establish their lock on the intellectual property and avoid a Theranos situation. I had bigger goals and was willing to oblige."

Toni leans forward. "Please tell us about the magic, Dr. Heller."

His expression softens as he looks at her. "It's called Targeted Autologous Enhancement Therapy. The science is a bit complicated, but in general terms it involves storing genetic materials from an earlier stage of cellular development, isolating and culturing the stem cells, and then reintroducing the epigenetic information via those stem cells into the subject along with the targeted enhancements and genetic mutations at a later date. The basic point is that all of the cells come from the same person, so the body doesn't reject them, but from samples taken at different times."

"Does it work?" I ask.

Heller takes a deep breath. "It didn't at first. The issue was targeting. I was trying to revert specific cells but some of them just didn't want to be reverted. Or sometimes they did in the mice but not in cells from other mammals. I started piecing together the factors—think of it like the ingredients you would need to bake a cake: NAD, rapamycin, telomerase, acetylglucosamine, the list goes on—but I still couldn't figure out how all the parts went together, how to bake the actual cake. But then I started to wonder if there might be a piece, an ingredient missing, something that could catalyze everything else."

"The baking powder," Toni says.

"The equivalent." Heller smiles briefly, as if again deciding whether to continue.

"What did Santique get from you?" I feel a slight jab from Toni's elbow as the words leave my mouth.

"Can you please tell us what piece might have been missing?" she asks. "No one likes a flat cake."

"It's okay, Antonia," Heller replies. "We each have our own communication style." He turns to face me. "A fair question, Mr. Azadian. In exchange for the rights to my patents, they offered perpetual funding for my research and 40 percent of all future revenues going to the high-impact research division of the American Cancer Society."

"So why be so hidden here?" I ask.

Another nervous flash crosses Heller's face. "Revolutionary science can transform the world, but it often brings danger. I don't think of myself in their league, but Galileo was imprisoned, the Curies died of radiation poisoning, Einstein unleashed the nuclear age. I prefer to do my work in private."

"Wha—"

Toni cuts me off. "You have no help? You do this all by yourself?" Her words clearly convey admiration.

Heller looks at her appreciatively before answering. "The lab is fully automated, built for self-sufficiency. A lot of this type of work has been done by loners, Jamie Thomson in Wisconsin, Yamanaka in Japan. I have a Hmong couple come a few times a week to help with cleaning and some basic lab support. They also bring groceries and help tidy up. I hardly ever leave this place."

"Can you tell me more about the genes that reverse—"

"Can I ask you a question, Dr. Heller?" Toni interjects, again cutting me off.

"I ask that you call me Noam," he says, taking her arm and leading her back toward the center of the room.

"Why the fixation on cancer, Noam?"

Heller stops walking and lets go of Toni's arm.

"I don't mean to . . ." Toni says, clearly reading something on his face I can't quite decipher.

Heller looks into Toni's eyes for longer than feels comfortable. "You remind me of her in a strange way."

"I'm so sorry," she says softly.

"My wife was vibrant and vivacious and brilliant . . ."

"I'm so sorry," Toni repeats.

Joseph's background research had indicated that Yael Heller had been a top chemist at the Weizmann Institute in Jerusalem before she died ten years ago. Only now does it hit me that this was when Heller shifted his research focus from animal biology to cancer and moved to Kansas City to join the Sowers Institute.

"We used to play violin duets together, but when she died the music stopped. I decided to dedicate the remainder of my life to fighting the terrible disease that took her."

Toni places her hand on Heller's forearm.

"So that's what I'm doing here," he continues, "with little Sebastian to keep me company."

"And a little music," I say.

Toni's eyes chastise me. *Didn't he just say the music stopped?*

"A Bach sonata?" I ask.

"Very good, Mr. Azadian. Can you tell me which one?"

My mind flips through the Bach pieces I'd obsessed over when failing to recover from my sister Astrid's senseless death almost two decades ago. "One of the violin sonatas?"

"Bach wrote twelve. Anything more specific?"

I know Bach pretty well but can't seem to place it. "Number one?"

Heller relents. "I'm sorry to tease you. It's not guessable."

"Not guessable?"

"It's not a pure Bach sonata. It's an eternal sonata."

"Which is?"

"A variation on *all* of the *Sonatas de Chiesa*, using Bach's same fractal formulas but extending the mathematical variation *ad infinitum*. If Bach had written his sonatas to go on forever, each melody embedded within the mathematical formula guiding the whole, this is probably what they would have sounded like, all thanks to the miracle of quantum computing."

"That's beautiful," Toni says.

I'm not exactly sure what she means.

"A tribute to your wife. The music never stops," she adds.

Heller looks at Toni with wide, warm eyes. "Thank you," he says softly.

I'm starting to feel like a third wheel when Heller tracks back.

"My cellular reversion formula was extremely challenging to find," he says as if the earlier conversation had never been interrupted. "The daf-2 and daf-16 mutations needed to be edited into the cancer genome along with genetic material from an earlier stage of development like blood or other cells stored from earlier withdrawals, and other molecules had to be added in precise ratios," he says, walking us toward the large steel door in the back. "Still, it wasn't working properly. And then I realized I needed to step back and think differently, to challenge my assumptions and try to find a completely new source of DNA that might conceivably catalyze the transformation I was seeking."

He opens the door and leads us into what appears to be a dark closet. "If you would please close the door behind you."

Heller opens a second door in the back of the small room. The chilling air and neon blue hue reach us simultaneously through the darkness.

We step forward into pure beauty.

16

Bathed in the faint blue light, the electric jellyfish float majestically in space. The pulsating greens, pinks, and blues of their translucent domes radiate nature's magnificence down their long tentacles drifting below.

My hand meets Toni's in the darkness. We are beyond words, overcome by simple perfection.

"*Turritopsis nutricula melanaster*," Heller pronounces. "The immortal jellyfish of the deep Arctic sea. Only discovered six years ago after the melting icecaps made their part of the Arctic accessible. They age like the rest of us, but then shrink to a polyp as they get older and are reborn as young versions of themselves. The scientific term is 'transdifferentiation,' but it is nothing short of magic."

Neither Toni nor I can yet speak.

"The medusas have extraordinary cell plasticity," Heller continues, "and can maintain the stem qualities of their cells farther into their mature phase than any other known organism. Fragments of their genomes pointed the way toward making reversion treatments possible. It was the key that made the other pieces work."

"They're so beautiful," Toni says as if in a trance, "so peaceful."

"You'd think that from looking at them," Heller says, then gives a moment for his words to settle, "but don't be fooled by appearances. They are extremely deadly. Each of their tentacles is lined with tiny nematocysts that can violently discharge poisons into their prey. Within seconds, the poisons attack the victim's red blood cells and ignite a cellular potassium release leading to cardiac arrest. Once their victim in neutralized, they begin devouring the carcass cell by cell. It's a highly efficient process, the majesty of nature in its own sort of way. Watch."

He uses a small blue light to locate a metal box on the floor, opens it, lifts out a frozen salmon, and slides it through a large vent at the top of the massive aquarium. The fish rests in a chamber at the top of the aquarium. After the top of the vent closes, the bottom opens automatically, releasing the salmon into the tank.

Each individual move is almost imperceptible, but the swaying tentacles of the jellyfish begin to bend toward the half-floating frozen fish. As the tentacles connect, they slowly weave the salmon into an ever tighter web.

"In two hours, that fish will be gone without a trace," Heller says. "It's a tough world eight hundred feet below the Arctic ice. These jellyfish have evolved to seize whatever nutrients they can find wherever they can find them."

We stand mesmerized, watching nature take its course.

"And you've recreated that environment here?" I ask.

"Close enough," Heller replies. "This room is its own little world. I sometimes feel it's the only place where I can truly be alone. You'll notice your u.D isn't even connecting."

I tap my wrist reflexively.

"It's their world in here," he adds.

"Did the cancer treatments work?" I ask after a few minutes of still-stunned silence, the families of Professors Hart and Wolfson very much on my mind.

I feel Toni squeezing my hand, asking me why I'm once again disturbing such a perfect moment with my pestering.

"Let's step outside," Heller says. "It must be getting very cold for you."

I rub Toni's arms to warm her up as we step back into the main laboratory.

"It worked very well on the mice. Once the *Turritopsis* gene fragments were added to the cellular reversion formula, their cells reverted to their precancerous state."

"And humans?"

A pained look comes across Heller's face. "Humans are infinitely more complicated."

I nod, waiting for more.

Heller hesitates. "They are in human trials now . . . I guess we will see."

Something about his use of the word "they" seems a distant way of describing his own miraculous progress. "If I may, Dr. Heller," I say gingerly.

He tilts his head slightly in my direction.

"I'm looking into the disappearance of two men who were part of an experimental cancer treatment protocol from Santique. They both disappeared from hospices, one in Kansas City and the other in St. Louis, at roughly the same time."

The wrinkles around Heller's eyes deepen. "I see."

"I'd imagine they could have been part of the human trials of your work."

"I'm not involved in that part of the process."

"It's just that the coincidences seem pretty astounding."

"How can I help you, Mr. Azadian?" Heller asks with a greater dose of formality.

"I thought you might be able to shed some light on all of this."

"As you've seen, I do a lot of my work in the darkness."

Toni's whistle interrupts the silence, probably by design. Dreyfus comes yelping around the corner in response. Excited Sebastian bounds behind in hot pursuit.

"There's a good Dreyfus," Toni says in the universal doggy-baby voice that somehow feels less ridiculous coming from her. "There's my little Dreyfus."

Sebastian's head bobs as he waits impatiently for recognition.

"There's a good doggy," Toni says in the same voice as she reaches over to pull Sebastian's ears from side to side.

Sebastian yelps joyously, burying his head into the fold of her arm.

Looking at Toni and Sebastian, Heller's face softens. "Maybe the two of you were connected in a past life," he says with an impish smile.

Toni chuckles. "I'm sure we were best friends."

Her words seem to delight Heller. "Together forever," he says wistfully, losing himself for a moment in thought. "You know, Antonia, I'm not a young man anymore."

"Oh, bite your tongue, Noam."

"My total life expectancy may be greater than Sebastian's but the question, as always, is starting from where."

"Oh, stop," she says playfully.

"We all live lives filled with uncertainty, but if something should ever happen to me," Heller continues, "I can think of no better home for my dear little companion than with you."

Toni locks eyes with Heller.

"It's a miracle, you know," he says, again shifting gears.

Toni waits for an explanation, rubbing a dog's head with each hand.

"These dogs, like each of us, carry so much with them. All of their experiences, their histories, the story of their four-billion-year journey from single-cell organisms to these precious creatures. They're like a log book of a journey they can never know."

A slightly dazed look comes across Heller's face, as if he's become lost in his own musings. Then he snaps into focus. "There's something I'd like to show you, Antonia. May I?"

Toni nods trustingly as she stands. Clearly there is some kind of extra-verbal communication passing between them, but I, for the life of me, have no idea what it is.

He takes her arm and leads her back toward the room with the jellyfish. I follow.

"I'm sorry, Mr. Azadian," he says earnestly. "It's something I'd just like to show Antonia. Just for her. I hope you'll understand."

I'm unsure how to respond. My every instinct is to trust Noam Heller, but something is happening here I don't quite comprehend.

Toni's eyes tell me it's okay. I take a step back.

"Thank you for understanding," Heller says.

I'm not sure I do, but I look around the lab for ten minutes or so until the two of them emerge from the back room. Toni has a glowing, almost beatific look on her face that I've never seen before, as if she's just seen Jesus. I ask her with my eyes but her message is clear. *Don't ask.*

"Now if you will please excuse me, I need to feed Sebastian and I've got a great deal of work still to do," Heller says politely. "I can't begin to tell you what a pleasure it has been to spend this time with you. Discovery is a seed that, once planted, grows in unexpected and mysterious ways."

The whole experience has been so overwhelming it's hard for me or the still-mesmerized Toni to answer. I take her arm and lead her out to the car. Dreyfus races back and forth behind us, knowing his place is in our car but only reluctantly leaving his new friend Sebastian behind.

I want to ask Toni more about what happened in the back room, even though I already know from her body language she won't tell. I want to discuss the burning issue of why Heller let us enter in the first place and showed us so much. But as I boot up my car, Maurice's video feed cuts off my thoughts.

"Where the hell have you been?" he growls. Maurice doesn't wait for me to answer. "Doesn't matter. Have you ever heard of Tobago?"

"As in Trinidad and Tobago?"

"Yes. The island just off the coast of Venezuela."

"Okay."

"It's a low-tech jurisdiction but still plugged into the Interpol system."

"Okay."

"The NamUS missing persons system automatically plugs into Interpol."

"Okay," I say slowly, the hair starting to stand on the back of my neck.

"Seventy minutes ago the iris scanner in their airport registered the arrival of Benjamin Hart and William Wolfson."

17

I offer to go straight to Maurice's office, but he insists we meet back in our old meeting ground, picnic area C in the forgotten armpit of Swope Park, the massive and once great urban park that has fallen victim to Kansas City's center of gravity, and tax base, moving south to the Kansas suburbs.

I rush to drop off Toni and Dreyfus at her place so she can go to work after her mother picks up the dog, then connect with Joseph and Jerry on my dashboard screen on my way to the park. We discuss what the information from Tobago could possibly mean and I urge them both to start looking for any evidence about how Hart and Wolfson might have gotten there. I arrive in picnic area C but don't see Maurice. Jerry is updating me on his efforts to hack into the commercial flight manifests when Maurice finally pulls up in his gray Taurus.

"Look," he says as I step into the passenger seat of his car, "this still isn't a priority for KCPD. I told you I'd have a look and I'm sharing with you what I've found. Confidentially."

"I really appreciate it, Maurice," I say impatiently. Maurice is a by-the-book kind of guy and sharing information with journalists, even ones like me, is not what the book says to do. "Can you tell me more?"

Maurice taps his u.D and the images appear on his dashboard. "Here are the two images captured by the surveillance camera in the Tobago airport."

The images are a bit grainy and taken from ceiling cameras obviously some distance from the targets. The background is entirely nondescript; just the floor behind them. But neither of the figures looks like the old men I'd seen in their recent photos. Occam be damned—my mind begins to race.

"Hart was in his eighties and Wolfson in his late seventies, yes?" Maurice says.

I nod but am drawn closer and closer to the photographs. I frantically sort through my conversation with Dr. Heller earlier today, see the majestic jellyfish morphing. "This isn't strange enough to inspire you guys to do more?"

Maurice looks at me apologetically. "I'm not saying there isn't something here, only that our overburdened department doesn't have the resources to follow up on every strange occurrence. That's why I'm here, Rich. You asked me to help, and I've helped. I'm telling you what I've found."

"That's it? Case closed?"

"Of course not. But we're not sending inspectors to the south Atlantic. We're having a hard enough time staying on top of things here at home."

"Can you transfer those photographs to me?"

Maurice looks agitated. "I'm not even supposed to be showing you the damned things."

I widen my eyes.

He shakes his head before dictating the transfer from his u.D to mine. It's probably as close to intimacy as Maurice gets.

"One more thing, Maurice," I say.

"Dammit, Rich—"

"If there's anything you can do to get the Tobago police to look into this a little bit more . . ."

Maurice stares at me. It's clearly time for me to go back to my car. I'm burning to speak to Heller again, but there's something I need to do beforehand.

18

I feel jittery waiting for Katherine Hart to come to her door. I'd called to tell her I was on my way and still don't know exactly how I'm going to play this as she ushers me in.

"How are you doing, Dr. Hart?" I ask, not wanting to rush to the purpose of my visit as much as my pounding heart demands.

"I'm still here," she says somberly, "and this is the last time I'm going to tell you. It's Katherine."

Her entreaty is so warm it somehow startles me for a moment.

"Have you found anything?" she asks quietly.

I feel the sweat pooling on my palms. "Do you mind if I show you a photograph?"

Her body stiffens as I tap my u.D.

As I transfer to her screen, a look of wonder crosses Katherine Hart's face.

"Do you recognize the photo?"

"Not the photo. I've never seen it before. It must be very old. Where did you find this?"

I feel a strong urge to tell her about Tobago and Noam Heller but hold myself back. I have a few theories in my head and most of them could only be described as insane. Science has been advancing exponentially for decades, but people are still not jellyfish. The thought of violating her peace with so little information seems unforgivably cruel. "I came across it in my poking around. Do you recognize the person?"

She looks at me like I'm a fool. "Of course I do." A distant smile momentarily surfaces through her grief. "Ben must have been about forty then. Somehow getting a little piece of him like this helps keep him alive for me."

I look at her, forcing myself to stay composed. Blood surges through my veins as I promise Katherine Hart I'll keep looking. I excuse myself, feeling guilty that I'm withholding from her. But I know to my core I'd need a lot more information before jumping to implausible conclusions that could turn Katherine Hart's world upside down.

I crave answers and there's only one person I can think of who may be able to shed some light.

I take the Tesla off of autodrive so I can speed the old-fashioned way toward Heller Labs, calling Joel Glass and sending him a copy of the photo along the way. He calls me back ten minutes later. Mrs. Wolfson, not surprisingly, recognized the person in the photo but didn't remember seeing it before.

The Heller Labs warehouse still looks abandoned as I pull up to its front door, but this time I know better. I honk my horn loudly three times then walk around the building, bang on the back door, and wait.

Nothing.

I do another loop, slapping my palms on the metal grates covering the windows.

Nothing.

I go back to the front door and bang again. The cold metal is thick and imposing. Placing my ear to the door, I can almost perceive the faint sounds of growling and barking.

I bang harder. "Sebastian," I yell. The volume of the barking goes up a notch. I don't know much about dogs, but this seems like a more agitated Sebastian than I'd been with earlier today.

But barking, I remind myself, channeling my inner Occam, is what a dog does. What if Heller just doesn't want to see me? Or maybe he's just gone out for a walk or, for all I know, a taxi's come to take him somewhere else. *I hardly ever leave this place*, Heller had said. I walk toward the river and scan the horizon. No Heller.

I calm myself, get back in my car, and settle in to wait.

As the sun slowly settles over the bending Missouri River, I start to get nervous. Yes, I reason, Dr. Heller might just be taking the afternoon off or he might be at a conference or doctor's appointment, but somehow I had the feeling when we left the lab early this morning that he was going to stay there for a very long time doing his work. And doesn't he eventually need to walk Sebastian?

I wait an hour more and still nothing.

I bang on the door again and still hear Sebastian's faint barking and growling. Is he responding to my banging or is something else going on? I have no idea, but something doesn't feel right. Shards of our earlier conversation begin bubbling up in my mind. *Revolutionary science can transform the world but it often brings danger. . . . We all live on borrowed time. . . . If something should ever happen to me. . . .*

I know I'm being histrionic, but with all the strange occurrences of the past couple of days, I'm already on edge. I keep imagining I'll see Heller coming back from the river after a long walk. I picture myself approaching him like I did yesterday evening. *Dr. Livingstone, I presume?*

My body receives the message from somewhere inside a moment before my conscious mind. What had Heller said when I'd approached him? "So this is it?" I say aloud.

This is what? He had no idea who I was, but something about my sudden arrival frightened him. This is the beginning, the middle? I'm already tapping my u.D as I process the third possibility.

Maurice, staring at me on the monitor after I've made my case, is more cautious. "That's a lot of conjecture, Rich," he says. "If we had to investigate every fatalistic comment every old person made, this city would grind to a halt."

"It feels like more than that," I plead. "We should really have a look."

"So the guy isn't there, and the dog is barking. Do you know how many houses we'd be visiting if that's what constituted probable cause? Do you know how many good explanations there could be that don't require your dragging me from my family at eight thirty at night?"

"All I ask is that you just drop by here for a few minutes. Heller said he had a lot of work still to do, that he was living on borrowed time. And what else can 'So this is it' mean?"

Maurice eyes me suspiciously. "Lots of things."

"Please. I have a strange feeling."

"A strange feeling?"

The silence hangs.

"Dammit, Rich," Maurice says, shaking his head in exasperation. "What's the address?"

Maurice pulls up thirty minutes later, annoyance permeating his every pore.

I bang on the door for demonstration, then look at Maurice plaintively.

He reads my thought. "It doesn't work that way. We have procedures. There is a thing called a warrant."

"Even if you had reason to believe someone could be in danger inside? What if you knew an older person had fallen in the bathroom and couldn't get up?"

Maurice knows exactly where I'm going and finally acquiesces to the favor he's probably come here to do. "Are you telling me you fear the man living in this building has been harmed or that you have reason to believe he is ill and in need of assistance?" he asks without conviction.

I raise my right hand. "I have reason to believe Dr. Heller is ill and in need of assistance."

Maurice glowers back. "You really are a pain in the ass," he mutters.

He walks back to his car and takes a small metal box from his trunk. He approaches the door and starts working. It's a complicated lock and won't budge. Then he goes back to his car and pulls a crow bar and a large hammer from the trunk. "A damn hunch," he grumbles as he sets the crow bar in the crack of the door and steadies the hammer.

The fourteenth whack sends the door flying open. I see a terrified Sebastian racing through the small door in the back of the lab as we enter.

Maurice seems as astounded at the sight of the glistening, light-bathed lab as Toni and I were early this morning, but everything is in order. It looks exactly as we left it. The lights are on, the mice are scurrying, the Bach eternal sonata is still playing.

"Hello, Dr. Heller," I call. "Dr. Heller?"

No response.

"Are we done?" Maurice says, clearly still annoyed.

"Can we just look around a bit?"

"We're not even supposed to . . ." Maurice glares. "Five minutes."

I wander through the lab feeling guilty that I'm violating Dr. Heller's private space. Even the mice seem to eye me suspiciously.

"What's in there?" Maurice asks as I open the massive metal door in the back of the lab.

"It's pretty incredible," I say, leading him in.

As we pass the second door, my gut processes the sight a millisecond faster than my conscious mind.

Noam Heller's half-eaten body floats in a penumbra of blue light in the dark, luminescent tank. The spaghetti of hydra tentacles wrap around him as the remnants of his body are slowly devoured.

19

I stand paralyzed before the horrific sight.

Maurice doesn't have the same problem. He shines his flashlight around the wall until he finds the switch, then flips it, bathing the room in an antiseptic white light. The jellyfish startle subtly from the sudden change but their tentacles remain wrapped around the remnants of Dr. Heller.

"You are *not* going to eat the rest of this guy," he orders in his deep bass.

My senses begin to awaken from their shock. Revulsion gurgles up from the depths of my gut.

"HQ, come in," Maurice barks into his radio.

The radio is silent.

"Base, come in," he repeats more sharply.

My face is frozen in shock but my recovering mind registers the problem. "This room is cut off from communications networks."

Maurice pushes out the door. "Base, come in. This is Deputy Chief Henderson. I'm at 1836 Levee Road. I need a squad car and an investigation team here right now. We have a body. Repeat. We have a body."

"Roger that, DC," the radio operator responds. "Back up arriving in approximately seven minutes."

My brain begins to race through the options. Suicide? Murder? I can't know the answer right now, but my thoughts flip frantically through the growing list of strange occurrences and I feel the desperate need for more information. I push open the door back into the lab and race through.

"Where are you . . ." Maurice yells, his attention still focused on the body.

I hear the words coming from behind me but don't stop. The police will be here and the place secured in a matter of minutes. After that, I won't have access to anything here for weeks, maybe months, maybe forever. There are so many unanswered questions swirling in my head, so many questions pointing somehow at Dr. Heller, that I have to believe there are things to be learned in this vast complex in the few minutes I have.

I push through the white door in the rear of the lab into what appears to be a small surgical ward. The hospital-style bed on rollers stands in the middle surrounded by what looks like some kind of transfusion system, a large helmet connected to a processor by a thick cord, and what seems like a body system regulatory unit of some kind. A well-stocked glass cabinet is filled to the brim with surgical supplies. I race around the room opening all the adjoining doors. One is filled with cleaning supplies. Two others reveal small, simple rooms with beds, IV stands, a couple of monitors, and not much more. I race on.

The fourth door opens into Heller's living space. The large room looks like a good-sized studio apartment, an exposed kitchen on one side and carefully made bed on the other. One wall is covered with bookshelves. I walk through and open another door on the corner farthest away from the lab. The compact space behind it contains eight stacked processors and a wall transformed into a massive screen. A scroll of letters and numbers flows endlessly across. I can't imagine I have much time.

"Come on, Jerry," I say frantically, tapping my u.D to make the call. His voice streams through my earpiece. I have to believe whatever secrets Heller held might somehow be connected to data flowing through these systems.

"I don't have time to explain," I say heatedly. "I'm in a server room and I may only have one or two minutes to figure out what's here. Tell me what I need to do."

"Um," Jerry stutters before his voice focuses, "turn on your video feed and give me a tour of the room."

I tap my u.D and wave my wrist across the room.

"Good," he says, sensing my nerves and praising me like a small child. "Now take your u.D off your wrist."

I separate my universal.Device by pulling apart the two data sticks connecting its loop.

"Now look at the bottom left corner of the bottom processor in the stack. Do you see a small data port that matches the inversion plug on your u.D?"

"I do," I say nervously.

"Plug your u.D in."

I follow the instruction, my hand shaking.

"You need to leave your u.D plugged in for the next ten minutes or so," Jerry continues steadily. "Now, do you see a code in front of you on the monitor?"

I look up and don't see anything. I hear the noise of sirens coming closer. "Shit, Jerry. I don't."

"Are you sure?"

"No, I . . ." A small box pops up stopping me mid-sentence. "It's here," I say.

"Good. Read it to me."

I begin frantically whispering the long stream of numbers and letters. "474bdcx23 . . ."

"Where the hell are you?" I hear Maurice yelling from Heller's living quarters. Frantically pushing a chair in front of where my u.D is plugged in, I jump out of the server room to meet him.

"Sorry, Maurice," I say, calming myself. "I was just looking for the dog."

"This is a crime scene, dammit. You can't just be wandering around."

The sound of the sirens is now deafening.

"I know," I say apologetically. "Sorry. He's got to be around here somewhere."

Maurice takes a step toward me as four police officers come rushing in through the operating room door, pistols drawn.

"Stand down," Maurice shouts.

Their eyes dart around as they place their pistols back in their holsters.

Maurice takes command. "We need to secure the area and establish the entire building as a crime scene. I want the investigation team here now. The body is in the room with the silver door off of the lab. Get forensics here right away. And we need to find a way to stop those damn jellyfish."

The officers fan out to secure the building as more police arrive.

"Now I need you to step outside, Rich," Maurice orders.

I begin to leave Heller's living quarters but then hear a whimper coming from under the bed. I walk over and get down on my hands and knees and see Sebastian, curled in a ball, shaking, and whimpering quietly.

"It's his dog, Seb—"

"Out," Maurice orders in a tone not to be questioned.

"But—"

"Out."

I stand and walk grudgingly out the door, trying to calibrate how much time has lapsed since I left the server room. It's been minutes, but with all the intense excitement it's hard for me to calculate how many.

Outside, I circle the building looking for something, anything, that might tell me more as the KCPD arrives in force. My mind whirls with images of Heller from earlier today, interacting with Toni and the dogs beside the river, inviting us into his lab, standing with us before the immortal jellyfish. It doesn't take my internal Occam to recognize the potential connection between his work, our visit, and his death. I feel the rot in my gut where the thought of Heller being devoured by the jellyfish still resides. Heller and Toni also seemed to have a special connection and I already know how deeply this news will hurt her.

Another police car pulls up. I watch the officer take an empty cage from the back seat and enter the building. I have a good idea what he's here for and rush over as he exits the building a few minutes later.

"Hi there," I say. "Can I speak with you a moment?"

I hear Sebastian's frightened yelp from inside the cage.

"Who are you?" the officer replies.

"Can you tell me where you're taking the dog?"

"We have a facility," he replies, stepping past me toward the car.

"Wait." The word projects more forcefully than I had intended.

It doesn't stop the officer. "You still haven't told me who you are, so if you'll please excuse me . . ."

I jump over to stand between him and the car. "Before you do that, I just need you to call Deputy Chief Henderson to come out."

"He's the one who told me to do this. Now get out of my way, sir," the officer asserts aggressively.

I don't move. "Just call Henderson." I try to project an authority I clearly don't possess.

"Get out of my way, sir," the officer commands with only the slightest hint of politeness, making clear that brute force is the next step if I don't get out of his way. "I'm not going to tell you again."

"What the hell is going on here?" Maurice demands as he walks toward us from the door.

"This gentleman is impeding my way," the officer says, turning toward Maurice. "He told me I need to call you before putting the canine in my car."

"This 'gentleman' doesn't have the authority here to take a piss," Maurice says. "Proceed."

"Wait," I say, still not moving from between the officer and his car. "What are you going to do with this dog? Interrogate him?"

"We're going to put him in the department's canine facility, where he now belongs," Maurice replies, clearly annoyed he's explaining this to me at all.

"Just hear me out for one minute, Maurice," I plead. The images, words, and questions flow through my mind. Toni on the ground petting the delighted Sebastian. Best friends in a past life. Heller telling Toni to care for Sebastian if something should ever happen to him. Did he know this was coming?

Maurice shakes his head. "What?"

"Just let me take him home to Toni. It'll be a far better home for the dog, and if you need him for any reason, I'll just bring him to you right away. You know where I live. What are you going to get from the dog, a confession?"

Maurice's face tightens, then releases slightly. He's just done me the favor of breaking in. But I've done him the favor of finding a body. "What are you gonna use for a leash?"

20

"Baby?" I say, peeking my head through the small crack I've opened in Toni's back door. I'm trying to block the door for a few moments but feel the pull on the string I'm holding in my outside hand.

"What happened?" she asks, responding to the look of concern on my face from her perch beside the kitchen table.

I feel the dog squirming around my leg and through the crack, then let go of the string.

A look of unbridled joy crosses Toni's face as Sebastian approaches, only to vanish just as quickly. "Why is he here?"

I don't respond.

Sebastian jumps up on her lap, pushing his snout into the space between her arm and her chest. "It's okay, it's okay," she says lovingly, rubbing his head. "He's shaking. What happened?"

I get on my knees before her and tell the story.

Toni's eyes begin to tear.

"I'm so sorry," I whisper.

Toni is an intensive care nurse not unexposed to death, but the idea of this vibrant man being consumed by carnivorous jellyfish clearly shakes her. "How could this have possibly happened?"

I place my hand gently on the back of her neck. "Heller said you should take Sebastian if something ever happened to him."

She looks up at me with wide eyes. "Like he knew it might?"

"It's hard to believe all of these strange occurrences are random. Hart and Wolfson disappear from their hospices; we make a connection to Heller; and now Heller is dead. We can't rule out an accident, or suicide, but . . ."

"He said he had a huge amount of work to do," Toni says softly, translating her sadness into tenderness toward Sebastian. "He dedicated his life to his research, to the memory of Yael. He had a puppy to take care of. And how could he have possibly fallen into the aquarium through the slit on the top?"

A nervous synapse fires through my brain. If death surrounds this story, where am I heading by following it? What am I doing by bringing it home?

Toni strokes Sebastian's head. "You poor dear," she says. "You must be so frightened. You must be starving."

She carries Sebastian toward the cupboard and takes out two bowls with her free hand. She fills one with water and the other with a turkey burger left over from the freezerator. Then she places Sebastian on the floor. He laps up the water voraciously. Toni kneels beside him.

"I told Maurice we would look after him for now," I say. "I can't imagine they'll need him for anything but he technically belongs to them."

"Are you okay?" she asks, standing and putting her arms around me. With the quiet tension flowing between us these past months, the gesture almost startles me.

"Thank you," I say, wrapping my arms around Toni. "I think so."

"So what now?"

"I need to connect with Jerry, then I need to speak with Martina. Can I borrow your u.D?"

Toni nods, but I sense in her gesture a slight disappointment that I'm ending our brief connection to get back to work. She leans down to comfort the dog.

I pause a moment, then pick up her u.D from the counter and carry it into the dining room.

"Where are we?" I ask as Jerry's sweaty face pops up on Toni's table screen.

"I'm in at the first level," he says. "This is not going to be easy. It's a compartmentalized ARM server with individual access points and OTP encryption systems guarding each portal."

"I'm not exactly sure what all that means. Can we get past it?"

"I don't know yet," Jerry says, frustrated. "I'm working on it."

"Thank you, Jerry."

He doesn't break his focus on the wall of the screens before him as I tap off.

My boss is harder to reach. It's now after midnight, and I have to wake her up using the emergency special access code.

"What the fuck, Azadian," Martina says groggily and without conviction as she comes on screen. The words are rote for her after repeating them for so long, but she probably knows I wouldn't drag her out of bed for no reason.

As I explain all that's happened, her face wakens. A dead body of a renowned scientist in a hidden lab in the West Bottoms is just the type of local story the new *Kansas City Star* is supposed to pursue.

"I want you on this like a fly on shit," she says.

21

I climb into bed at 1:15 a.m. after filing my story. Toni and I both toss and turn all night. Our few moments of slumber are interrupted by Sebastian yelping and growling in his sleep from the nest he's built himself in Toni's clothes hamper. All three of us are a wreck when the bedroom screen activates itself at 7 a.m., but Sebastian approaches the bed, seeming to intuit that if it's morning some extra attention must be coming his way.

Toni looks over at me. "I think that's your job."

"Oh, no," I say.

"Are you kidding me?" Her look seals my fate. "Use your string as a leash. The plastic bags are under the sink."

I know where the plastic bags are; I've just always been disgusted by watching otherwise civilized humans bending over to grab steaming piles of poo with only the thinnest layer of Price Chopper's plastic covering their hands. A news feed I saw a few weeks ago of the Japanese robot walking a dog down a sidewalk in Tokyo, poop-removal shovel at the ready, flashes through my mind.

I look at Toni a few moments too long and decide not to mention the robot. I'm the robot. I turn toward Sebastian. "All right, you little fucker, let's go for a walk."

The walking part is not as bad as I thought. When Sebastian dives under a bush to do his business, I don't see anyone around to ask about etiquette but assume leaving it there is probably a fertilizing gift to the bush.

But I'm only faintly focusing on the dog. My mind is filled with theories on how Heller might have died and struggling to get the nauseating image of his half-consumed body out of my head.

I walk in the door after ten minutes outside and see Toni putting the final touches on a small barricaded area in the kitchen with a pile of towels in one corner for a bed.

"It's the best we can do for now," she says. "Can you stop by during the day to check on him and take him out?"

"Of course," I say, still ruminating about Heller. If Heller was murdered, whoever did it is out there somewhere. Is it only coincidence that this happened after our visit? Are *we* now on someone's radar? It's not just that Martina ordered me. From deep inside, I know I *need* to be on this story like a fly on shit.

Toni seems to sense my thoughts are elsewhere. "What do you think Heller meant, that we'd come at a serendipitous moment?"

"I've been thinking about that and don't have much of an answer," I say quietly. "He said he wouldn't normally be so forthcoming."

"So why be forthcoming now, why with us?" Toni asks.

"What do you think?"

She bites her bottom lip and folds her wiry arms as she thinks. "He invites us into a place he'd set up to keep people out, says in multiple ways he's facing danger, then winds up dead later that same day."

The loud beep of her Haier Breakfast Deluxe machine puts the brakes on my train of thought. I still don't have an answer but won't find it in Toni's kitchen. I grab the omelet sandwich, wrap it in a paper towel, give Toni a quick kiss, and head out the door.

Pulling into the Hospital Hill parking lot of the UMKC Department of Life Sciences, I am hoping that Franklin Chou can help. One of the country's foremost genetics experts, with a joint appointment in life sciences and the medical school, Chou was introduced to me a couple of years ago by Jerry Weisberg. I haven't done much to keep up the relationship but we have enough history to justify my showing up unannounced.

The department receptionist tells me he's not in his office but admits, when I push, that I might be able to locate him in the lab. I find him peering intensely through a scope at a small glass plate.

"Professor Chou?"

His head and tightly cropped black hair do not move as I approach.

"Professor Chou?" I repeat.

"Not now," he says dismissively, as if speaking to a misbehaving student, still not lifting his head.

"Professor Chou, it's Rich Azadian."

"Rich Azadian," he repeats playfully, twisting a knob slightly to move the plate under his scope. "There must be some serious shit going down."

I can't help but chuckle. "I hate to be so predictable."

He finally lifts his head from the scope and faces me. In his mid-thirties, he seems to compensate for his dimpled, boyish face with his formal bow tie and minimalist top-frame glasses.

"Have you heard of a cancer researcher named Noam Heller?"

"He used to be at Sowers. I haven't heard anything about him in a few years."

"He died yesterday."

"I'm sorry to hear that." Chou does not seem moved. "He was old."

"We found his body in the aquarium in his lab. He was being consumed by carnivorous jellyfish."

Concern registers across Chou's face. "So what brings you here?"

"I was hoping to ask you about the science he was working on."

"Let's go to my office."

22

"Here's what I think," Chou says after I've described the conversation with Heller and all I can remember about his lab. He pauses a moment, then leans forward in his chair. "First, there's no doubt that genetic mutations and targeted molecules can be used to extend the life spans of individual cells. That work has been around for over a decade. We've made steady progress, but everyone keeps hoping for miracles that are probably still decades away, maybe more. It's one thing to make a roundworm live a few extra weeks, even months, with genetic manipulation, but hand washing has done more to extend the human lifespan across the population than genetic manipulations will do for a long, long time."

"But—"

"Second, there are lots of ways to hack a mouse. We've been breeding the transgenic mice for decades. We've starved them and pumped them up with rapamycin, NAD, and this and that, and we've definitely produced some longer-living and stronger and maybe even marginally smarter mice."

I know this from the crash course in genetically enhanced mice I got from US Marshall Anderson Gillespie, the man who saved my life in Norman, Oklahoma, two years ago. "Go on."

"From what you describe, it sounds like Heller was experimenting with parabiosis on the mice. Tony Wyss-Coray and a few others showed years ago that if you transfused blood between a young and an old mouse, the old mouse would get biologically younger and the young mouse biologically older. But this work has been a lot more complicated in humans. Our systems are so much more complex. Would it be conceptually possible to create some kind of parabiosis-plus, not just transfusing blood but goosing the process with other factors? Could we eventually do some sort of autologous parabiosis-plus, using our own stored cells from before our cells had genetically mutated into cancers? Again, conceptually, yes. Practically, probably not very soon with any degree of efficacy or safety."

"Okay."

"Third, you said that Heller's primary focus was on the reversion of cells to their precancerous state. The idea of somehow using genetic manipulations to revert these types of cells has been around for at least four years. It was actually Noam Heller and a few others who put it forward. I think you know that. This is the first I've heard of adding so many other factors to the process. I've heard rumors that some of the preliminary experiments on this have worked with mice. A lot of money has gone into testing. The trials are still in the field."

"Santique?"

"Them and a few others. It's a race," Chou says. "This is huge business. If this approach works, and whoever does it first gets the right global patents, it would mean billions of dollars in added revenues."

"And high stock valuations."

"That's not my field," Chou continues, "but everyone knows the stock prices of the big health companies competing in the great cancer race have been shooting up and that these valuations are what let them keep snapping up the most advanced innovations and treatments coming out of smaller labs and startups."

"But they can't all win the race."

"In life, like in evolutionary biology, there are winners and losers."

"What can you tell me about the equipment Heller had in his lab? Does it indicate anything?" I ask.

"Tell me about the jellyfish tank," Chou says.

I do.

"And you said they were deep-sea jellyfish?"

"That's what he said. From under the Arctic ice."

"Deep-sea carnivorous jellyfish?"

"That's what he told us."

Chou lays his palm on his tabletop monitor then starts dictating commands. "Do you remember the name of the species?"

I wrack my brain but can't remember.

Chou swipes through images of different types of jellyfish before stopping on one.

"Was it *Turritopsis nutricula melanaster*?"

"I think so. I remember thinking it sounded like Count Dracula."

Chou lifts his head in astonishment. "Do you have any idea what it would cost to keep deep-sea Arctic *Turritopsis* like that alive for any significant period of time?"

"Thousands?"

"Millions," he says, his eyes glazing as his thoughts deepen. "Maybe more. Creatures at that depth live in a highly pressurized environment. They couldn't survive in the low-pressure environment of the surface." He begins doing calculations in his head. "Maintaining that kind of pressure in an artificial environment would mean you'd have over a hundred tons of pressure against the aquarium walls. You'd need extremely powerful pumps to get water in and out."

I'd been mesmerized by the jellyfish themselves but hadn't, until now, appreciated how much must have gone into just getting them there and keeping them alive.

Chou digs in. "Tell me exactly how each room was laid out."

I do.

"Very interesting," he says. "It sounds like a mix between a high throughput animal bio facility, a stem cell lab, and a cancer ward."

"What does that tell us?"

"I don't know. Life sciences work is very specific. I'd need to see the lab, look at the specimens, note how the equipment is calibrated. If there are still plates in the screening machines, I can bring them back and sequence the DNA from the samples here. That would probably tell us a lot."

"Can I take you there now?" I say, not sure I can even get Maurice to let me in to the crime scene.

"I wish I could, Rich, but I'm teaching at eleven."

"Can someone else cover for you? This is pretty important."

"It's exam time. I can't do that to my students. They've got a lot riding on it."

"Are you sure?"

Chou nods apologetically. "Just pick me up here at one," he says, leaning back in his chair. "Heller's lab isn't going anywhere."

I speak with Jerry from the dashboard screen as my Tesla weaves its way to the *Star*. He's been working most of the night trying to break through the internal firewalls in Heller's network and is still not making much progress. I don't need to ask whether he'll keep going. The answer is clear from the weary determination in his eyes.

"What do you have?" Martina demands as I enter the newsroom.

"Well, hello to you, Ms. Hernandez," I say cheekily. The story I filed on the murder late last night has already been gaining traction, so I'm feeling I have at least some of my bases covered.

"Don't be a jackass, Jorge."

"I'm not a jackass, I'm a fly on shit."

"I'm putting Halley on the story," she says without emotion.

"What for?" I ask, probably not doing enough to hide my annoyance. First she sends Sierra to the health-care forum I'm already covering and now this? I don't want to be stupidly territorial but I've brought this story from nothing.

"From what you've told me, this is now a health-care story. That's her beat."

"And potholes are an engineering story, but we don't send those stories to engineering."

Martina shakes her head.

I start to wonder if she is somehow getting back at me for my enhanced notoriety or still angry I was offered the editorship, or something even deeper is going on. "And what about the disappearance of Hart and Wolfson?" I argue, my mind focusing simultaneously on Katherine Hart and my future at the *Star*. Is Martina somehow grooming Sierra to take my place?

"You really are a pain in the ass, Azadian. This isn't about you. It's about the nature of the story."

"I'm not giving it up."

"You'll do what I tell you to do." She stares at me harshly but then I see her eyes softening in spite of herself. She shakes her head slightly. "The two of you can work on it together."

23

I know I'm being petty, but I don't see Sierra in the office, so I bend down and make my way as stealthily as possible toward my cubicle.

Arriving, I find the small, iconic turquoise box on my desk and know intuitively who has secured me a new u.D. I can be rough on him sometimes, even ungrateful, but where would I be without Joseph?

I file the minimal update to my story and sneak out the back door of the newsroom without sending Sierra a message. I'm not exactly feeling like taking the first step in reaching out.

I swing by Toni's after stopping at the Brookside Barkery for a leash and some dog food. I'm in a foul mood, angry with Martina and unfairly annoyed at the poor, innocent dog, but as I enter the kitchen Sebastian isn't there.

"Where are you, you little fucker?" I call out. "Dog." I look around the house. I don't hear an answer. "Sebastian."

I find him curled up in a ball in Toni's closet laundry basket. He is shaking.

I can't help but feel compassion. "It's okay, dog," I say, rubbing his head. "It's okay, Sebastian."

Sebastian seems to calm in my presence, which somehow surprises me.

"All right," I say, "how about we go for a little walk? You can do your thing, I'll give you some food and some water, then we're all good."

He looks up at me, not buying it. It's hard not to be a little touched.

"Okay," I say, this time meaning it, "let's talk. Tell me about your relationship *with your mother*."

I sit down on the floor in Toni's closet next to the basket. Sebastian jumps into my lap. "Whoa," I say.

As he burrows into my chest, I put a hand on top of his head and another on his stomach. "It's okay. It's going to be okay. Good doggie. Good Sebastian," I say, feeling like a bit of an idiot.

After fifteen minutes of this, Sebastian is sufficiently calmed to go for our walk. He lets me put on the new leash and collar and we head out. He does his business on the neighbors' lawn. I hold my breath and scoop it up with the Price Chopper bag, which I place in another bag and then another. I feed him and give him water then don't have the heart to put him back in the barricade.

Maybe we should have him stay with Dreyfus at Toni's mom's place, I think, as I finally get hold of Maurice from my car after four attempts.

"It's a damn crime scene," Maurice snaps, "I don't know why you're calling me."

"He's one of the top life sciences experts in Kansas City," I argue. "At least he can give us a better read on what was happening at Heller's lab. He knows how to understand the calibrations of the equipment. He says he can sequence the DNA of the cells being read in Heller's machines to tell us exactly what Heller was working on. Heller had to have been killed in some connection with his work. How else are you going to get that kind of specialized information? An expert who won't cost the department a dime. Come on, Maurice."

"We've got science people at KCPD."

"At his level?"

"You can't just waltz in to a crime scene."

"Which is why I'm calling you."

The silence lingers.

"Dammit, Rich," Maurice says exasperatedly. "When?"

"Thirty minutes?"

"Make it twenty," Maurice says. "I need to be back in less than an hour. This is going to be quick."

"Yes, sir."

Annoyance defines Maurice's face as he taps out.

As I pull into the parking lot of UMKC Life Sciences, I instruct my new u.D to deliver a message to Sierra in an hour. *Martina wants us to work together on my story. When can you meet?* Sometimes I can't help myself.

"How was class?" I ask as Chou opens the door to my car and gets in. He's carrying a silver container that looks like an overgrown lunchbox.

"Nice car," he says, ignoring my question.

I feel a little embarrassed.

"I've been thinking about your disappearing scientists," he says as the Tesla turns itself down Paseo.

I look over at him. "Yes?"

"It's obviously strange they disappeared and that the iris scanners picked up both of them around the same time, but I'm a scientist and I tend to not go for the fantastical when simpler options can do the trick."

"Occam's razor?"

"Something like that," Chou says. "Based on everything I know, the only way two old guys with terminal cancer could show up thousands of miles away looking a lot better than they did before is for two things to have happened."

"And they are?"

"First," he says, "their cancer needs to have been cured."

"Second?"

"They need to have seen an excellent plastic surgeon."

It's the first that catches my attention. "And if someone had come up with a cure for cancer that worked that well . . ."

"Exactly," Chou says as we merge onto I-35 North. "You don't need to overcome mortality to be a hero. Curing cancer would be an absolute game-changer."

"So let's just say they were cured. Why would someone want to whisk them away? Why not just highlight that they'd been saved?"

"I don't know." Chou ponders as we circle back under the bridge and turn left onto East Levee. "Maybe they—"

My car levitates as a blast screams through our ears.

"What the—" I shout, my heart pounding. I jam my foot on the brake as the Tesla's emergency protocol kicks in. The brakes lock in three quick pumps, skidding the car sideways to a long, screeching halt. Emergency warnings flash across the windshield. Every muscle in my body tenses. My hands dig into the steering wheel.

"You okay?" I yell at Chou.

"I think so," he pants, his eyes darting down at his body and around our untouched car.

"Then what the fuck just happened?" My body twitches. As I begin to relax my death grip on the steering wheel, my eyes focus on the fireball rising a block away. Foreboding overcomes me. "Oh, shit."

My body is shaking, overcome by a single thought. My mind frantically calculates the minutes as I slap the driver control icon and desperately jam the gas to full throttle, racing toward the smoke. The Tesla transforms into the rocket it was built to be. It's been more than twenty minutes.

The Tesla screams to a stop in front of the building. Fire is raging. Debris sprinkles down from the choking air. Two empty police cars are parked out front, their sides charred from the blast.

My heart thumps, my body rocks, but only one thought fills my head.

Maurice.

24

I jump out of the car and run toward the flames, waving my hands trying to keep the smoke from my burning eyes. The smoldering heat feels
like it's about to peel the skin from my face. I race around the building
hoping to find an opening in the spreading wall of flame. Nothing.

The remnants of the door are burned off its hinges. I kick it open.
A wave of heat sears across me as I peer in. The vast mouse cart
smashes to the floor. I gasp for air. Sparks fly from the machines.
Burning debris is crashing. Ash floats everywhere. An overpowering
wall of smoke fills the room and begins to enter my lungs. "Maurice,"
I shriek. "Are you in there?" There's no way my voice can penetrate
the din of the roaring flame. "Maurice."

There is only one option. If he is inside, I need to find him. I scan
desperately for something to shield my body but find nothing.

Taking a deep breath to store oxygen, images of Toni and my
mother, Maya and little Nayiri flow through my head. I take off my
jacket and hold it over my head. "I'm so sorry," I say out loud, preparing to rush in.

"Stop." Maurice's shout reaches me the moment before he tackles
me to the ground. "What the hell are you doing?"

I look over at him in wonder. "I thought you were—"

"I was late," he gasps, "but I have two men in there."

"Let's get 'em," I shout, the adrenaline still pumping through me.

Maurice's face flows from defiance to resignation to dejection,
displaying a range of emotion greater than I've ever seen before. "It
doesn't work that way, Rich. There's no access point."

"We can—"

The whir of sirens overwhelms my voice.

The three massive fire trucks pull to a stop. The battle-ready fire-fighters start pouring out.

"I have two men in there," Maurice shouts, running toward them.

Within two minutes the firefighters are shooting water and chemical retardant on the flame. In eight, they've created enough of a corridor to send three men in. They return, choking, fifteen tense minutes later with nothing, and no one, in their arms. The incident commander looks at Maurice. He doesn't need to say a word.

Maurice tilts his head forward and presses his eyes closed for a moment. He takes a deep breath. "Get your chief on the line. We need to set up a joint command."

"Roger that," the tall commander replies between barking out his orders.

Maurice begins the frenetic exchange on his radio, calling in the KCPD teams and coordinating with his chief.

With the firefighters battling the unyielding fire and the police arriving in force, I take a step back from the flames. Franklin Chou is still rattled but okay. I gaze into the fire, trying to pull together all I've seen, to understand what lies below the smoldering surface.

The vibration of my u.D pulls me out of my trance. I tap in the audio feed.

"Have you heard about the explosion in the West Bottoms?"

"I'm here now, Martina."

"Oh, fuck," she says. "The same place?"

"Yes."

"Jesus. Are you okay?"

"Yeah."

"Azadian, I asked if you're okay. Do you need anything?" Martina can be pretty tough most of the time, but her care generally breaks through when it really matters.

"I'm okay, Martina," I say sincerely, "but it looks like two police officers were killed in the blast."

"Shit. What's happening now?"

"KCFD is fighting down the blaze, and PD is setting up a perimeter. It's a bit chaotic."

"What do you think?"

"Unless Heller somehow committed suicide and set a timer to blow up his lab the next day, I have to believe he's been murdered. Whoever did it must have wanted his body to be completely devoured. Maybe they wanted to destroy all the potential evidence, not just about the murder but also the work Heller was doing."

"We'll need more. We've got to own this story. We've got to own it starting now. Have you connected with Halley?"

"Not yet."

"Do it and get me the story of the blast, the death, and two policemen."

"Yeah," I mumble.

"You sure you're okay?"

"Yes," I say more firmly before tapping off.

25

The great Sir Isaac Newton realized toward the end of his life that were the universe not infinite, gravity would inevitably crash all the stars into each other. As I stand mesmerized before the tragic, majestic infinity of the billowing blaze, I feel my world unbound and pulling apart.

But three people are now dead and my mind veers toward a burning set of more finite interrogations. Who would do such a thing? Why? What connects the explosion to Heller's death? Is something being covered up? What evidence is being destroyed? I shuffle and reshuffle the deck of my mind, searching for answers.

Nothing has come together twenty minutes later as I put Franklin Chou into a taxibot home. I know I need to reach Toni before she hears this news from anywhere else.

My call reaches her just as she's stepping in to help intubate a newborn, so I give her the story as quickly and efficiently as possible. Explosion. Two police officers killed. I am fine.

"Oh my god, honey," she says. "Where are you? I'm coming right now."

"Sweetheart, you have to trust me that I'm okay. I need to be on this story now. I just wanted you to hear it from me first, to know I'm safe."

I hear Toni breathe in deeply. "No more scaring me like this, Dikran Azadian," she says. "Those poor souls."

"I spent some QT with Sebastian this afternoon," I say after a pause, trying to divert Toni's attention.

"How's he doing?"

"I think he's still traumatized. It might be nice to have him spend some time with Dreyfus."

"You were thinking that?"

"I'm not that bad, am I?"

"Do I have to answer that question?"

"Dinner at your place at around eight?"

"*Bacheegs*," she says. "Please be safe."

I smile fleetingly, but the lift I get from Toni melts as soon as I refocus on the scene before me. I catch the incident commander as he tours the perimeter of the receding fire. "Any idea what could have caused this?"

"We'll issue a report."

"I know you will, but can I ask if this looks like something that could happen accidentally?"

"Anything can happen accidentally."

"Off the record, can you tell me, in your personal opinion, not for attribution, does this look like an accident?"

"Personally, off the record, I'm not speaking for the department and I'm not even speaking for me," he says. "It looks like a combined electrical and gas systems overload, but we'd still have to do an investigation to find out."

"How can you tell?"

"I can't fully, but the initial sparks look like they came from two different places on two different lines."

"And that means?"

"You'd have to ask the power company about that."

He steps toward the building, signaling me not to follow.

"Hey."

I hear the familiar voice and turn to face it. In dark denim and a form-fitted red sweater, Sierra looks as if she's stepped out of the J. Crew catalog. In spite of all the politics with Martina, I'm happy to see her. "Hey."

"It's all right you bagged out on our coffee," she says.

I smile for a fraction of a second until I remember that Sierra is my competition.

"So." She pauses. "Martina filled me in on the background. I guess we're working together."

"Guess so."

"And?"

I realize I need to take control of this conversation to keep the story in my hands. "I'm heading back to file, but I need you to start digging on which big health companies are competing to produce a miracle cure for cancer."

Sierra seems to suspect what I'm up to. "That's a pretty broad topic, don't you think? I don't mean to be in your knickers, but if you turn around you might see there's a smoldering building behind you."

"Thanks," I say, deadpan, trying to maintain momentum. "I hadn't noticed."

Sierra stares at me.

"The link to the cancer treatments could be crucial to this story," I continue. "There are four or five firms who are part of this race. Santique Health funded Heller and is one of them. I can focus on the explosion, but I need you to look at the companies. Can you do it?"

She nods suspiciously.

"Good," I say, sealing the deal. "We should talk at least once a day starting tomorrow."

I walk over to my car feeling somehow empowered that I'm approaching a Tesla XY instead of my old Hyundai clunker.

It's almost six when I march into the newsroom and over to Joseph's cubicle. "Anything?" I ask.

He looks up at me with his thousand-year-old eyes. "Martina said you weren't harmed in the blast." Even through his reserve, it's abundantly clear what he's actually saying. *We've worked together for almost three years and I have to hear that you haven't been hurt from someone who acts most of the time like she doesn't give a damn about either of us?*

"I'm glad she told you. I'm fine, but I can't say as much for the two officers who were inside."

"How can I help?"

"I'm going to write the preliminary story now. Can you get some background on the two people who were killed?"

"Do we have their names?"

"See if you can figure it out." Joseph is peerless when searching vast fields of data from his cubicle, but I need him to be a little more assertive using human contacts to help with this story. "Can you do it?"

He looks uneasy. "I can try."

I turn to walk away.

"I did get information from the flight manifests in and out of Tobago," he adds.

"And?"

"No record of anyone going by the names of Benjamin Hart or William Wolfson."

I thank Joseph, then fall into my swivel chair to begin dictating my story. As the words splash on my cubicle wall, I massage them around with my hands until they feel right. My entire body still smells like smoke. I try to weave that sensory experience into the words.

But in the end it's just a story about a death and an explosion and two police officers killed. And I have an uneasy sense I'm still missing the real story.

I tap in Maurice. His face appears on my wall.

"I just wanted to check in with you."

"I appreciate that, Rich," he says sincerely, "and I appreciate you were willing to run into a burning building to try to save me."

"You'd have done the same for me."

"There was no entry point, so you would have been killed instantly," Maurice adds, "but I appreciate the gesture. I want you to know that." Maurice is straining at the far end of his intimacy spectrum and it means a lot to me.

"Have you spoken with the families of the officers who were killed?"

"Are you asking me as a reporter?"

"I won't release anything you tell me not to."

"The chief and I just came from their homes. The chaplain is with them now. It's the worst part of this job."

"I'm sorry." I work to keep my voice steady. "If you think it would help the families, we'd like to do meaningful obituaries at some point."

"Yeah, Rich," Maurice says, "just not right now. We'll be releasing the names later tonight, then you can connect with the press officer."

"And you?"

"Two of my officers are down, and I'm going to find out why."

I tell him of my conversation with the incident commander and ask Maurice if he can get the records from Kansas City Power and Light. He doesn't commit, but I sense he'll do it. I resolve to surreptitiously ask Jerry to see what he can dig up as a backup.

"How could it be," I ask, trying to lure Maurice into the broader story, "that all of this happens at the same time? Two scientists disappear, then Heller is killed, then the explosion."

He doesn't take the bait. "I don't know, but my first focus right now is on my men and the second focus is on Heller. Anything beyond that is off my radar."

"But Benjamin Hart—"

"Off my radar right now."

"Have you heard anything back from the Tobago police at least?"

Maurice shakes his head, looking slightly annoyed.

"Could I possibly ask you to follow up?"

26

Compared to the vast expanse of the 4.5 billion years of this planet, or the nearly four billion years it took life to morph from a single-cell organism into the hundred trillion or so cells I lug around today, each of our presences is but a blip.

Blip, actually, is too strong a word.

We are a pimple on the nose of a speck joy-riding on the blip's ass.

In other words, we are small.

But each of us is the hero of our own little play, endowed with enough narcissism to believe our lives, our presence here on Earth during the estimated five billion more years our blue marble has left to twirl, somehow counts.

Faced with death two years ago in a musty hotel room in Norman, Oklahoma, I realized that as small as our lives may be in the grand scheme of things, loving another person is our tiny ripple in the universe, our song into the vastness of space announcing the inexplicable artistry of our one true creation greater than ourselves.

But over the past two years I've gradually lost hold of this insight. Perpetually overthinking life, I seem to have reverted to my ongoing dialectical battle between—and I'll be the first to roll my eyes whenever Jean-Paul Sartre is referenced—being and nothingness.

In the last three days I've learned of two men's disappearances into thin air, come across the body of a genius I'd just met being grotesquely devoured by jellyfish, and essentially witnessed the deaths of two police officers caught in a massive explosion. No wonder my grip on reality—whatever that strange concept actually means—is feeling tenuous as I pull into Toni's driveway.

She's running back and forth in the kitchen waving her arms as I enter through the door from the garage. An easy smile blankets her face. "Come on, Sebastian, come on," she says in her silly baby voice.

The dog leaps in circles with delight.

"Look who it is!" she says to the dog in the same voice. "It's Daddy."

I turn as if to see if someone is standing behind me. Toni seems to forgive my poor attempt at humor and crawls toward me.

She swats my left shoe back and forth, which the dog recognizes as placing my foot on the edible list. Sebastian darts in with what looks like an irrepressible smile and I'm reminded, as if I need reminding, which I probably sometimes do, just how special Toni is.

Maybe the dog knows on some level he's now an orphan, maybe he doesn't. But right now Toni has delivered him into a momentary trance of joy.

I drop to my hands and knees and lower my head to face Sebastian. He leaps and I roll him over, rubbing his stomach.

"Look at you," Toni says.

I spring at Toni and bite her playfully on the shoulder, now rolling her over and catching her in my arms.

"I was worried about you," she says with sudden seriousness, staring me in the eye.

"I know, baby," I say, feeling reconnected. "I'm okay. How are you feeling?"

"Just happy to be off the hormones. My eggs are resting comfortably in liquid nitrogen."

I smile at Toni, not quite knowing what to say.

The dog must read the change of energy because he suddenly launches himself between us.

"There's a good Sebastian," Toni coos. "There's a good Sebastibasti."

Sebastian yelps, but his excitement stops in its tracks the moment the Kitchenette bell rings. He lifts his head in panic, his body starts to shake, he leaps off us and runs up the stairs with Toni and me in hot pursuit.

We follow him into Toni's bedroom and find him burying his head under the clothes in her laundry basket.

"It's okay, it's okay, Sebastian," Toni says as we kneel down. Her voice could melt butter.

Sebastian is shaking.

"If only he could talk," I say.

"We could bring him with us to couples therapy."

Ouch.

Toni's eyes train on Sebastian. "He's such a puppy but he has an old soul."

"An old soul?" I ask, not a lot of room for reincarnation in my hard-won atheism.

"I just get the feeling he plugs into energies."

Something about her words, about the way she says them, triggers a thought. I close my eyes to process it. "What did Heller say about the dog when we were with him yesterday?"

"What do you mean?"

"Something about the dog containing our history. Do you remember?"

"Yeah. He said that dogs carry their entire history in their cells," she says, still unsure why I'm asking.

"Right," I add, my mind struggling to piece together the ill-fitting shards. "Like a log book of a journey they can never know."

Toni scrutinizes me, not sure where I am going.

I feel a few shards starting to shift together. "And what about his name? Sebastian, as in Johann Sebastian. The eternal sonata, where each melody contains the mathematical formula guiding the whole." I lean my back against the closet wall and cover my eyes for a moment with my hand. "Doesn't that sound a bit like a genome?"

Toni raises an eyebrow.

"It's almost like Heller is saying something with the name," I continue. The idea seems crazy even to me, but I can't escape the strange logic. "Do you mind if I take Sebastian for some tests?"

Her body stiffens. "What kind of tests?"

"Lab tests?" I say contritely, realizing as the words leave my mouth how poorly they will be received.

"Does 'over my dead body' mean anything to you?"

"There's a lot at stake here," I plead softly.

Her stare tells me she's not willing to sacrifice the dog on the altar of my hunch.

"How about if you come, too?" I add, trying to strike a more palatable deal. "I won't do anything with Sebastian unless you give the green light."

Toni is unmoved.

"I promise?" I add.

Calling her expression suspicious would be a vast understatement.

27

I call Franklin Chou from Toni's bedroom and describe my theory, wanting to make sure that Toni, and in some way maybe even Sebastian, hears what I am saying. Toni listens apprehensively, cradling the dog in her lap.

I sense what she was thinking. *It's taken this long to make Sebastian feel at home and now you want to take him to a strange place where he'll be poked with needles? Is that what you call taking care of something?*

It's probably typical of us, I think as I help the two of them into the passenger seat of my Tesla; Toni processing the interaction based on emotion while I float somewhere in the philosophical stratosphere of my head. But Heller didn't seem like a person to use language lightly. If he said the dog told a story and that each individual melody contained a key to the complexity of the entire sonata, how could I not follow that trail, test the hypothesis?

Maurice's message arrives on our way. *Tobago police sent photo of men getting into the car. License number didn't match anything in their records, probably a fake. Searched the island. No trace of car or three men.*

He obviously doesn't want a dialogue or he'd have connected by video.

Three? I respond.

The two who matched the scan and their driver.

Anything on the driver?

Irises didn't correspond to anything in their global database.

I'm still processing this new information when we find Chou, still shaken from the explosion earlier in the day and suspicious of my request, but now engaged enough to have put on a pair of jeans and headed back to his lab so late at night.

Sebastian, on the other hand, senses something is amiss. He'd resisted getting out of the car and dug his head into Toni's arms as she'd carried him into the elevator. He now growls furiously as Toni and I hold him down and Chou uses a small metal instrument to extract a series of skin grafts and takes blood with a hypodermic needle. "It's going to be okay. It's going to be okay, Sebastian," Toni coos to no avail.

Chou carefully examines the blood samples on glass plates under his scope while Toni sits in a swivel chair with Sebastian sleeping in her lap.

After about ten minutes, Chou looks up at me with a strange, nonplussed expression. "Has Sebastian been around any other dogs recently?"

"I really don't know," I say. "We brought Toni's mom's dog over yesterday. The two of them played together."

"How old is that dog?"

"Dreyfus is about three," Toni whispers, not wanting to rouse Sebastian.

"It couldn't be him, then. Has Sebastian been out of your house in the last twenty-four hours or so?" Chou asks.

"Just when I've taken him out."

"Did he interact with other dogs then?"

"No."

"Are you sure? He's not been out of the house alone?"

"I'm certain."

Chou turns his head and looks back into the scope. "I'm looking at the cells from the skin graft," he says slowly, moving a small lever to shift the glass plate. "About seventy percent of the skin cells are exactly what I'd expect to see from a puppy. Good, normal, healthy skin cells."

"And the other thirty percent?" I ask, suspecting I may already know the answer.

"That's what strange. The other thirty percent are the kind of dead cells being shed, cells you would expect on a very old dog."

My mind flows with images of blue-hued jellyfish. "Are you sure?"

"I've taken grafts from five places on Sebastian's body. It's hard to imagine cells rubbing off from something else could be so evenly distributed. I've never seen anything like this before."

"So the dog is young and old at the same time. Exactly what Heller was experimenting with."

"I'm a scientist, Rich. I can't go off into flights of fancy, but this is certainly very strange."

"How can we test the hypothesis?" I ask excitedly.

"That's what the blood's for," Chou says, "and we're going to need more of it."

I cringe at the look of pain on Toni's face as we approach. "I'm so sorry, baby," I say softly.

Toni recognizes the need, but that doesn't make her empathy for Sebastian any less acute as the needle punctures the dog's restful sleep.

"Sorry, Sebastian," I say, trying to be comforting.

Wrapped in Toni's arms, he still shakes.

"We've got to take him home," Toni orders.

"How long will this take?" I ask Chou as we stand to leave.

"Tomorrow late morning at the soonest, and that's if I'm here all night. It'll take at least twelve hours to run the sequence through a genome-wide association algorithm."

"Anything we can do to speed things up?"

"Sorry, Rich."

"You'll call me when you know something?"

Chou lifts his eyebrows. "Goodbye, Rich."

"Thank you," I say sincerely.

He makes a sweeping hand gesture for us to leave.

It's after midnight and we're both exhausted, all three exhausted, as I drive home.

"It's just so incredible," I muse. "I don't want to get ahead of myself, but it's hard not to imagine . . ."

Toni is not focused on my hypothesizing. "You poor dear," she says to the still shaking dog. "I'm sorry we put you through this. We're almost home. It's okay, Sebastian."

As the car slows into Toni's driveway, Sebastian somehow senses he's almost home. His head lifts. He looks around expectantly.

"That's right," Toni coos. "We're almost there."

Sebastian leaps from Toni's lap and through her outstretched arms as I open the passenger-side door. Toni jumps from the car to follow.

"You did it, Sebastian," she says, turning her key in the front door. "You're home."

The pressure of Sebastian's head pushes the door open enough for him to slide in the crack. Toni swings the rest of it open, and Sebastian sprints up the stairs toward his laundry basket haven.

"That's right . . ." Toni says, stepping in after him.

The faint smell hits me first. *Did we leave the freezerator door open? Did we leave the groceries out? Did we drop eggs?*

From somewhere deep within me a massive alarm bell sounds.

A violent energy surges through my body.

"Toni," I screech at the top of my voice.

Her startled body jerks to face me from halfway up the stairs.

I bound up the stairs toward her in two leaps, grab her waist, and pull her back with all my might.

"What are you doing?" she shrieks as I yank her out the door.

She begins to realize. "The dog—"

It happens in a fraction of a second.

I race around my car and throw her to the ground. I dive to cover her body as the deafening blast obliterates the last remnants of a fragile peace.

28

My body shakes uncontrollably as I wrap myself around Toni.

I feel the heat flowing across the back of my head. My heart is pounding. Innate impulses from somewhere deep in my evolutionary past take over.

"Baby," I shriek, looking down at Toni as my conscious brain struggles to reboot.

She looks up at me, unable to speak.

"Are you okay?" I shout through the din.

She swallows, as if the physical gesture can help her mind consume the reality of what is happening. Her eyes vacillate between blank and bewildered.

I feel the heat flashing across my face, hear the debris smashing into the car, its windows shattering. The burst of light turns night into a terrifying facsimile of day. "We need to get farther away from the flames," I yell, my body still trembling but my mind beginning to command my emotions.

Toni nods vacantly.

I grab her gently by the shoulders. "We need to move," I say with as much focus as I can muster.

Her eyes lock with mine.

"We're going to keep low and run across the street behind that truck. Do you hear me?"

She nods.

I put my hand on her forehead, trying to project a calm I don't remotely possess. "It's going to be okay. Are you ready?"

Toni affirms.

I take her hand. "One, two, three!" I pull her up and push the first few steps from behind before she finds her feet. I follow her as she runs, trying to remain between her and the billowing flame. Small debris filters down from the choking air.

We dive behind the truck, gasping for air.

"We can't stay here," I yell over the deafening noise of the fire. "We're going to run behind that house on three." I hold Toni's shoulders and look into her dazed eyes, then point her in the direction of her neighbor's house. "Are you ready?"

She nods.

"One, two, three."

I push her in front of me and we run.

It's only when we're leaning against the back of the house across the street that I see full recognition arriving in Toni's eyes. It's only then I feel the terrifying realization arriving in my own head.

"Sebastian," she whispers.

I take her in my arms. Her body is beginning to regain its agency. "I'm so sorry."

My heart is pumping wildly, but the dog's name kicks my mind into overdrive. Two explosions in one day. What connects Heller's lab and Toni's house? The dog? Us? My story? I suddenly feel existentially vulnerable. If someone is after us, are they here now? I pull Toni more tightly into me as I nervously scan the area around the burning house.

The distant swirl of the sirens amplifies to a scream as the police and firefighters descend.

Grabbing Toni's hand, I run with her toward the first of the police cars to arrive. "I need someone to stand with her."

The policeman hardly notices me as he reports into his radio.

"She may be in serious danger," I plead more forcefully.

"We're all in danger until this fire is out," he barks.

"You don't understand—"

"What's going on here?"

That voice. I turn to see Maurice running toward Toni and me.

"What the hell happened?" he shouts, placing a hand on each of our shoulders.

"We were just coming back," I pant. "We opened the door and I smelled gas. I pulled her out just before the explosion."

Maurice's face goes pale. "Are you okay?" He looks into my eyes, then Toni's, then places a hand on each of Toni's shoulders. "Toni?"

She looks at him, stunned, then nods tentatively.

"Gas at Heller's earlier today and gas here," I add. "Whoever is doing this is after something."

Maurice lets go of Toni and faces me. "What do you think that is?"

"I don't know. Maybe the dog, maybe Toni, maybe me."

"Why?"

"I don't know." I gasp, frantically reviewing the options. "It looks like the dog was genetically hacked in some way."

Maurice stares, taking in what I'm saying. "What the hell?"

"I need you to give Toni protection," I continue, "at least until we know what we're up against."

"All right," Maurice says solemnly. "You may both need it. All I can spare is two twelve-hour shifts of two men each. Where will the two of you stay?"

Do I send her to her parents' house in Independence? Should we both go there? Could that put her parents in danger? Does it make sense for us to split up? At least if I keep her at my place I'll be able to keep an eye on her. "My house," I say, looking over at Toni.

Her face is recomposing. She confirms the decision with her eyes.

"Can you have KC Power and Light shut off the gas lines leading into my house and maybe also the electric?" I ask, still only beginning to fathom that Toni and I just came a moment away from being killed.

"Will do. We're in touch with them now. It looks like the blast in Heller's lab came from a cyber-infiltration of the KCPL system. I'm guessing this one, too."

I turn toward Toni and wrap her tightly in my arms. "I'm so sorry," I repeat, feeling betrayed by the inadequacy of my words. I hold her as we watch her photos, her diaries, every vestige of this physical space, the memories, my Tesla, and the corpse of poor Sebastian broil in the massive inferno.

"He was a good little dog," she says wistfully.

He was, I think to myself, maybe so much more.

"I should call my parents," Toni says, breaking our private silence amid the deafening roar of the flames, sirens, and yells of firefighters coordinating their attack.

I hold her as she does, and for another hour as we watch the fire slowly die, the flooding lights illuminating the smoldering ruins. As the heat subsides, the November chill reaches ever deeper into our bones.

It's nearly 3 a.m. when the first two police officers assigned to protect Toni and me deliver us to my place in Hyde Park and take up their positions at the front and back doors.

As we walk into the kitchen, Toni screams and grabs me.

"*Okaerinasaimase, ureshiigozaimasu,*" my Haruki 2300 personal service bot says, his expressive eyes opening wide over his shiny, white, round face. He places his hands on his thighs and bows deeply from the waist. "*Gobujini modorarete ureshuugozaimasu.*"

"That scared the bejeezus out of me," Toni pants. "I thought that thing was out of juice."

"Me too," I say, wrapping my arms around Toni. I'd quickly grown leery of Haruki after it started linking to my u.D and appliances and following me around asking hundreds of questions during its initial LifeSync set up last year. When Haruki had gotten stuck, unable to navigate his four feet of shiny white carbon fiber through the clutter of my house to get to the recharging dock, I'd felt almost relieved. I'm just a bit embarrassed that only now, with Toni in such a fragile state, has Haruki suddenly found a burst of energy somewhere and reverted to his Japanese factory settings. "It's okay, baby," I say, tightening my grip. "Let's go up."

Haruki has run out of steam at the bottom of his bow and returned to his inert state. I roll him aside and lead Toni up the stairs, then prepare a bath and sit beside her as she bathes. When she invites me in, I take off my clothes and join her. Melting into each other's arms as the smell of ash slowly recedes, we drift off to sleep.

29

The thought has somehow fought its way through the dreamy meandering of my subconscious. The electricity is still on. My body jerks awake.

I don't know how long we've slept, but the last hints of warmth in the water tell me it can't be more than half an hour. I pull Toni into me.

"Baby," I whisper, trying to not convey concern.

Her body wiggles slightly, then folds into mine until it begins to recognize the discomfort of the cool water and with it, everything else. Her eyes open with a start.

"Come on, sweetheart," I say softly, helping her up and wrapping her in a towel. She's half awake, and I'm hoping she'll be able to go back to sleep. I lead her over to the bed.

She stops halfway there. "I was having a crazy dream," she murmurs.

"Go back to sleep, baby," I whisper. Any dream is better than this reality. I lift the comforter and ease her in. "Everything's going to be okay."

I say the words but am not convinced. How can everything be okay when someone willing to kill has not been identified or stopped?

"I dreamed there was—"

"Just close your eyes, sweetheart," I say, placing my hand on her head. "Get some rest. We'll talk more in the morning." I wrap her in the comforter, already rehearsing my conversation with Maurice.

She moans slightly, then rolls over to her side.

When I'm sure she's asleep, I strap my u.D on my wrist, push in my earpiece, and head into the hallway.

"It's not even 5 a.m.," Maurice grumbles.

"I know," I say. "I'm sorry."

"How's she doing?" he asks, getting his bearings.

"I'm not sure it's all sunk in yet. She's still asleep."

Maurice lets the silence rest. It's clear this is not why I'm calling.

"Maurice," I say, still feeling like an idiot for neglecting this last night, "the power and gas are still on. I'm really sorry to bother you this early, but I thought those were getting shut down immediately."

"KCP&L was supposed to shut off those links last night. I'll make a call right now."

"And I may need an additional patrol car to take me to work. Until we know what we're up against, I think it's probably best to be careful."

"I don't disagree with your logic, my friend, we just don't have that kind of capacity." Maurice pauses. "But maybe we can get one of the department's retirees to drive you around and keep an eye on you. You'll need someone to actively drive the car in this kind of situation. The self-driving protocols are too predictable. It might cost you a few bucks. What time would you need it?"

"Would it be too much to be picked up at seven?"

"Probably," Maurice says. "I have someone in mind for the job, one of the retirees, Tom Callahan. You can negotiate the terms when he gets there."

"Thank you, Maurice. I really appreciate it."

I tap off the call, then tap my u.D to shut off the wi-fi transmissions from my appliances. As I race around the house double-checking, I pass inert Haruki still bowed in the corner of my kitchen. Grabbing a modafinil from the back of the cabinet and popping it in my mouth, I vow to never again let my guard down like I did last night. Then I step into the garage and set up the generator.

A few minutes after seven I hear the car pull up. I walk quietly upstairs and back to my room. Toni is wrapped cocoon-like in the comforter.

"Baby," I whisper, trying to find a tone that wakes her enough from her sleep to hear what I have to say but not so much she won't be able to go back to bed. "I need to go to work."

As the words leave my mouth I realize how poorly they've expressed what I'm trying to say. Of course, I need to file a story on the explosion and fire at Toni's house and update the one I filed yesterday on the destruction of Heller Labs, but if that were my sole motivation I would not be leaving Toni alone after everything she's been through. I need to go to work because I am terrified that whoever killed Heller and triggered the two explosions is still out there, because we're all in grave danger as long as that's the case, because I have very little faith that the Kansas City Police Department will have the capacity or drive to understand in any meaningful way how the many strange and disparate data points all fit together.

She rolls her head slowly to face me and opens her eyes halfway. "Really?"

I place my hand gently on the crown of her head. "Go back to sleep, baby. Believe me, I'd rather stay with you. The police are outside the door. Your parents are coming by in a couple of hours. The coffee is in the pot. Just sleep as long as you can."

A brief flash of wakefulness crosses Toni's face. "Are you sure?"

"I won't be long," I whisper, knowing and feeling guilty on some primitive level because I should be staying here.

Toni's look asks me if I'm confident I know what I'm doing.

"Go back to bed, sweetheart. I won't be long," I repeat.

She leans her head back grudgingly.

As I head out to the blue Lincoln parked in front, Tom Callahan steps out to greet me. He's a bit short with graying hair parted on the side, an unkempt mustache, and a paunch, but I get the sense he can still pack a punch when he needs to. I reach to shake his hand. He takes mine to guide me into the car.

"The key is to minimize your exposure to the unknown as much as possible," he drawls. "I'll get you where you need to go in the quickest way possible. Big boss says we need to keep you safe."

"No argument from me," I say. "I just hope the guys at the house feel the same."

Callahan observes me in the rear view mirror waiting for his reply. "I'm old school," he says.

I'm not exactly sure what he means but the idea that there's old and new school somehow makes me nervous.

The feeling of guilt is still with me as I step into the newsroom at 7:15 a.m. The entire floor is silent. I turn the corner and see Joseph waving his hands as he shifts the scores of documents across his cubicle's digital wall.

He jumps up and rushes over when he sees me approach. "Boss," he says. The small word overflows with concern.

We stand facing each other awkwardly. It's as close as Joseph comes to a hug.

"Thank you, Joseph," I say, responding to the words he would have expressed verbally if Joseph were that kind of person. "Toni's okay, I'm okay, but someone seems to have wanted the dog or us dead and we've got to find them."

Joseph nods slightly, understanding the implications of my words. "The police?"

"I just don't trust they're trying to pull all the pieces together."

"And no one else—"

"I don't know, Joseph," I say. "Not anyone I know of."

A quiet determination defines Joseph's face. "Let's do this, then."

We walk to one of the small conference rooms and tap the icon to turn the glass walls into four frosted electronic whiteboards. I dictate the text for each category—Hart, Wolfson, Tobago, Santique, other big health companies, Heller, Heller research, Heller Labs, Toni's house, Sebastian—then move each to a different section of the walls with my hand. Then Joseph and I start filling in the spaces around each of these data points. I dictate from my notes, and Joseph weaves in the information and files he's collected. The data hubs around each of our big categories are filling, but no matter how much we add, it's clear the narrative spokes connecting them are missing.

"What's going on here?" The angry voice disrupts our trance-like focus.

Joseph and I turn, surprised to see Sierra in her blue blazer and khaki slacks looking like she's just come from playing polo.

"I could've sworn we agreed yesterday we're working together on this," she says, her eyes scanning the walls.

An embarrassed look crosses my face. "You're right, I'm sorry," I fumble. "It's been a bit of a rough night and I . . ."

Sierra places her hand on my arm. "I understand," she says. "I heard about the second explosion. I'm glad no one was hurt."

"Only the dog," I say.

Sierra looks at me, surprised. She squeezes my forearm firmly. "But if I'm on this story, you can't freeze me out. Got it?"

I nod.

It's not enough for Sierra. She looks me straight in the eye. "Are we good?" she repeats, waiting for my verbal response.

"We are good," I say, noting Joseph's interest in Sierra's assertiveness out of the corner of my eye.

She lets go of my arm.

"So what have you learned about the health companies?" I say.

"I thought you'd never ask." She taps her u.D and her files splash onto the wall. "Five of the biggest health companies in the world are competing with each other to develop the miracle cancer cure people have been saying for years is just around the corner. All of them are investing hundreds of millions or even billions of dollars in finding it, all of them spending heavily in Washington, London, Brussels, and Tokyo to tilt the regulatory environment in their favor. All of them spreading rumors that a major breakthrough is imminent to drive up their stock prices and increase the pool of capital available for acquiring smaller businesses, superstar researchers, and specialist research labs."

She moves her files into the space around the "other big health companies" section on the wall with a few waves of her hand, the virtual data folding around the title like a mosaic. "And it looks like each is waging a pretty consistent campaign to subtly—or sometimes not so subtly—undermine or even sabotage the progress of the others."

She flips open stories of companies working in the middle of the night to have laws changed to thwart their competitors, stealing star researchers from other companies, and even hacking into each other's networks to sabotage particularly promising research data.

Santique is one of the corporations, but nothing other than the connection to Hart and Wolfson is unique. The disparate data points float, remaining disconnected.

Sierra, Joseph, and I mull together before the wall, sometimes silently, sometimes asking each other unanswerable questions, sometimes moving pieces of data from one category to another.

I feel the vibration, then tap my wrist. Franklin Chou's massive face appears over the data on our wall. He's wearing the same clothes I saw him in last night. His furrowed face radiates a seriousness I've never seen before.

"You've got to get here immediately," he orders.

30

The armed university guard stops us at the door to Franklin Chou's lab. "And you are?"

I give him our names. "Can you tell me why you're asking?"

"We need to know who's coming into the lab," she says.

Chou sees us through the window and steps out to greet us. "It's okay," he says. "They can come in." He ushers us in nervously.

Chou already knows Joseph, but I introduce him to Sierra.

The lab, even at this early hour, is already a symphony of activity.

"What was that about?" I ask.

"University security found someone dressed in black with a face mask trying to get into the lab at 3 a.m. When they approached him, he tasered the two guards and ran. They couldn't track him. Now they insist on having guards here twenty-four seven."

"Are your guys in touch with KCPD on this?" I ask anxiously.

"Yes," Chou says, "but you should probably follow up."

I feel a surge of insecurity. "Someone is putting together the pieces as quickly as we are collecting them. I'm sorry."

Chou has already moved on. "That's not why I called you." He stands in front of a massive wall screen, letters and color codes scrolling across. "This is one of the most incredible things I've ever seen."

We stare at him expectantly.

"I hope it's okay I've brought in more students. When I saw the preliminary data I knew I needed more firepower. You have no idea how significant this is."

Chou takes a deep breath.

"Because the skin graft yesterday showed skin cells of both a young and an old dog, the first thing I did was look for those kinds of markers in the cells taken from the blood sample. It didn't take me long to find signs of decay in the mitochondrial DNA, suggesting a much older dog than Sebastian."

"Confirming," I say, "that Sebastian was young and old at the same time."

"Or young but had once been old. I ran a full genome analysis, then compared Sebastian's genome to the standard genome for a brown Labrador Retriever in the National Center for Biotechnology Information database. Canine genetics are notoriously complicated from all the breeding, and there really is no such thing as a fully standard dog genome, but sequences that were off the norm were segregated into a separate file."

Chou looks soberly at the three of us before resuming. "Some of the differentiations were exactly what you would expect in different dogs of the same breed."

"But—" Sierra jumps in.

"Others weren't," Chou cuts her off. "My next thought was that few dog breeds are pure and this might be just a remnant of interbreeding, so I ran those sequences through the full set of canine genomes at NCBI. Again nothing."

I have a growing premonition where this is going.

"The next logical step was to run sequences through the entire NCBI database, so I had one of my guys plug us in to the university system for more processing power. It took two hours for the rough match to come through."

I stare expectantly at Chou.

"Your Dracula jellyfish," he continues. "*Turritopsis nutricula melanaster*."

"So the dog has young cells with old genetic markers and sequences inserted from the genome of immortal jellyfish?" My mind races through images of Heller's roundworms and mice, Benjamin

Hart and William Wolfson. "He's named after Johann Sebastian Bach, lived in a home where the Bach sonata is programmed to play forever, and morphs back to youth like a jellyfish returning to its polyp stage? Is that even possible?"

"Before this morning, I'd have said no," Chou says. "Now I'm not so sure. We also found heightened levels of nicotinamide adenine dinucleotide in his mitochondria."

"What's that?" Sierra asks.

"NAD," Chou answers. "A molecule that regulates oxygen levels in cells, it's—"

"Heller mentioned NAD in his lab," I interrupt.

"High levels of NAD can trick cells into thinking, and acting, like they are younger than they are," Chou says.

Even amid the symphonic hubbub of the lab, the sense of mind-bending wonder descending on the four of us is palpable.

Chou continues, "But that's not why I needed you to be here right now."

You've just described potentially one of the most significant biological transformations in history and that's not why we're here?

All three pairs of our eyes plead him onward.

"I told you I've been looking at Sebastian's mitochondria," he says.

None of us move.

"You probably know this," Chou adds, "but mitochondria are filled with proteins, ions, and sugars. Mitochondria also have their own DNA, mitochondrial DNA."

"And?" I say, trying to push him along. This is no time for a biology lecture.

Chou looks around the lab at his students in full motion, then focuses on the three of us to make sure we are following. "But when I examined Sebastian's cells under the electron microscope, I saw something strange inside his mitochondria."

"Strange in what way?" Sierra fires.

"Not natural," Chou responds, "as if a piece of synthetic DNA had been inserted."

I feel my heartbeat quickening.

"So we extracted it," Chou continues, "and ran it through the sequencer."

"And?" I say, exasperated at the professorial pace of Chou's explanation.

"At first, it looked like a mishmash of unreadable code, but then one of my postdocs ran the DNA sequence against the UniProt protein sequence database, which gave us an essential clue. What do you know about DNA data storage?"

My urge to complete the story is far greater than my desire for a tutorial. I hold myself back.

"You need to understand this," Chou says. "It's important. DNA has been the greatest data storage medium in human history, far greater than silicon, graphene, phosphorene, or anything else. About a decade ago, scientists at the European Bioinformatics Institute had the idea of using synthetic DNA to store data. They've made uneven progress since then. Our DNA sequencing machines are run on a binary system of ones and zeroes, like most computers. That's why the synthetic data initially came out jumbled. The EBI system is ternary; it uses zeroes, ones, and twos to encode data into synthetic DNA for biostorage, so it takes a ternary analysis system to decode the data."

I'm desperate to know where this leads.

Chou reads the frustration on my face and presses on. "One of my postdocs—Hee Chung Park—knew how to reset our newest Illumina sequencer from binary to ternary. We were running the sequence and just starting to see the data when I called you this morning. I've only seen a few fragments."

I can't take this any longer. "What does it say?"

Chou looks across the three of us one more time and takes a deep breath. Pushing the air out, he lifts his wrist and speaks into his u.D. "Open Heller DNA Read File."

31

It takes a few moments for my mind to recalibrate. I am simultaneously focused and dazed, processing the new information and stunned by it at the same time.

"The files were chopped into thousands of individual pieces," Chou says. "We had to reorder them based on indexing data contained in the files themselves. We—"

"What did the files say?" I can't wait any longer.

"One looks like it's a letter from Dr. Heller to whoever unlocked the message. It's just completing defragmentation."

"And the second?" Sierra asks expectantly.

"The second looks like a sophisticated encryption access key."

"Can we just open the letter?" I plead.

Chou glances over at one of his students. She nods back. He then dictates the command into his wrist.

Sierra, Joseph, and I glance at each other nervously as the words flow across the wall.

Then we begin reading.

August 27, 2025

If you are reading this letter you have already come a long way. I am presuming, perhaps only because I have no alternative, that I can trust you. I also recognize that if you are reading this I may in fact be dead.

Although DNA data storage is potentially unlimited, I am

writing a short message to increase the likelihood it can be accurately decoded. It looks like that was a good bet.

Ten years ago, I began focusing all of my efforts on cancer research after that terrible disease took my beloved wife, Yael.

Four years ago, I hypothesized an approach for reverting cells to their previous, precancerous state through a combination of molecular vectors, genetic manipulations, and integration of a critical number of cultured cells taken from the host at an earlier stage of life before the cancer had taken root.

With the financial support of the Santique Health Corporation, I began extensive research and animal trials to prove this approach. After the cancer treatment protocol proved successful in mice, additional research was needed on a higher-level mammal.

Sebastian, the dog carrying this message, had been a gift from Yael just before she died, given to help me through her loss. Sebastian became my friend and only real companion after I moved into my laboratory space in 2022. By early 2024, Sebastian had developed multiple lymphosarcomas and was in the last stage of his demise. At that time, I decided that Sebastian would be a suitable candidate for the next stage of trials of this highly experimental cancer treatment technique.

At first, his cancer receded exactly as it had in the mice. Within a few months, however, it became painfully clear that the response to the treatment in the dog did not track with that in the mice. After significant analysis and additional testing, I realized that because the overall complexity and resilience of the dog's entire system was far greater than that of the mice, the dog's cellular ecosystem was more quickly responding to and rejecting the introduction of the specific inputs designed to revert the cancer cells.

As Sebastian's death became imminent, I took a step back, first theoretically and then in my research. If the complexity of the dog's system was too great to allow for sustained change among a small group of cancerous cells, the two options were to change the way I was treating the individual cells or to somehow alter the overall system which was rejecting them. I tried the former first, but this approach was a dead-end. It was then I began experimenting with the latter.

In my extended additional experiments with mice, I finally came upon the exact formula of genetic change induced through a precise combination of specific chemical compounds infused with specific levels of differentiation factor eleven, nicotinamide adenine dinucleotide, mononucleotide, telomerase, rapamycin, and N-acetylglucosamine molecules, along with CRISPR-inserted daf-2 and daf-16 mutations of cells extracted from the specific mice at earlier stages of their development. It took many thousands of different trials of these factors in different ratios to find the best ones, but even these trials never succeeded completely. The reverted mice emerged as poor versions of their earlier selves. It was only when I isolated and inserted specific strains of the Turritopsis nutricula melanaster *jellyfish gene into their genomes that the mice successfully underwent total cellular reversion to earlier versions of their physical selves.*

When I placed these reverted mice into the mazes they had learned to navigate before their reversion, I found they were no longer able to remember what they had learned. When I tried the same experiment where they had learned one maze before their cells had been initially extracted and one maze after—but before their reversion treatment—the mice were able to navigate the former but not the latter. This led to the inevitable conclusion that the mice were becoming younger but they were also losing all of their memories since the moment their original cell samples had been taken.

As Sebastian's cancer progressed rapidly toward terminal status, I made the decision to do my first higher-level mammal trial on my beloved companion. As you almost certainly have figured out by now, this process worked.

While I was doing this research in isolation, I was also receiving considerable pressure from senior executives of the Santique

Health Corporation to begin human trials of the cancer treatment protocol. Although Santique was not, by my design, aware of my total organism cellular reversion research, they were well aware of the progress I made in cellular reversion as a potential treatment for cancer and had begun additional research in their corporate labs based on my preliminary findings. Independent of me, Santique made the decision to go forward with experimental human trials in early 2025.

If I am dead, I imagine you are asking how I knew I might be in danger and what has happened to my formula for the total cellular reversion of complex organisms or, more colloquially, the formula for eternal life.

I have always believed that revolutionary science by definition brings with it danger. This perception has only grown through my experiences in South Africa, Israel, and the United States. Given the monumental societal and global implications of this work, and how many lives have been lost over the millennia chasing the ever-elusive fountain of youth, it was only prudent to believe that knowledge of my work could have profound and potentially deadly consequences.

I have reflected at length about the potential global implications of my discovery. Unless properly controlled and regulated, this innovation could lead to mass chaos. People would very likely line up to be reverted to earlier physical states irrespective of the fact that they would be signing up to erase all of their memories, including those of their families and friends. Many would do whatever it took to bathe in this irresistible rejuvenation.

I had first seriously considered destroying the research and euthanizing Sebastian once I realized what I had achieved. After a great deal of thought, however, I came to believe over time that this work has within it the possibility to cure most diseases that have tortured our species for the entirety of our existence. To achieve this, it must to be managed responsibly outside the control of any specific government or even governments at all.

The only entity which I believe has the potential to be entrusted with this knowledge is the Council of Elders of Scientists Beyond Nations, and I cannot say I even trust them completely.

The data file embedded in addition to this letter in Sebastian's mitochondria contains an unbreakable encryption code that can, when paired with its parallel key, unlock access to my network in which my research files and other notes and records are located. The second encryption key code required to unlock this access is currently possessed by the SBN Council of Elders.

Obviously, I could have given SBN the entire code, but I have divided the encryption key in the hope that whoever accesses the code embedded in Sebastian will have a level of sophistication to assess conditions in the aftermath of my presumed death. In light of the magnitude of my discovery and its potential economic and even national security implications, I do not trust any one entity enough to give them sole access or responsibility. This perception has been borne out by very strong recent indications that my fear and caution are not misplaced, which is why I have taken the step of encoding this message. Because you are reading this, I assume my worst fears for my safety may have been realized.

But, as you are now presumably beginning to grasp, the knowledge contained in these files is far more significant than my life. It carries the significance of life itself.

Only when the two encryption keys are matched will the total cellular reversion process, the formula of eternal life, be revealed.

I am counting on you, whoever you are, to do all in your power to maximize the potential benefits, and minimize the dangers, of this revolutionary advance.

32

We stand motionless, the limited vessels of our minds unable to fully absorb the enormity of Heller's words.

Sebastian's cells told a story we had conceptually processed by the parameters of the world we had known. If Heller's words are to be believed, that world—a world of life and death, of limited time, of Adam and Eve begetting begats then returning to ashes, of noble lives and tragic deaths, the world of our parents and their parents and on and on since the beginning of our species, the world of human mortality—is on the verge of being transcended. The possibility of eternal life opens—magically, hubristically, tragically, dangerously—before us.

"Who wouldn't kill for that?" The words leak from my mouth.

Sierra doesn't seem to even hear me. "If the dog can be rejuvenated, we live in a different world."

All of us are lost in our own private, unfolding mazes.

"*Samsara*," Joseph utters.

"It's just a letter." Chou breaks the collective trance. "It's going to take a lot more than a letter and some strange cells to make the case Heller's somehow conquered death."

I know on an intellectual level that Chou is right, but that's not where my head is operating. The vague idea, more like a fantasy, had already crossed my mind when Maurice passed me the photo of Hart and Wolfson from Tobago, but the puzzle pieces now form and re-form in my head with compounding velocity. "If Heller knew he was in danger, why wouldn't he have said who he feared?" My mind jumps back to Toni asking why Heller let us into his lab, why he said he wanted her to have the dog if something should happen. Did he see us as his last chance to get his message out?

"Maybe he didn't know specifically," Sierra says. "Maybe there were different groups of people who wanted what he had or to stop him."

Joseph rubs his face, as if willing himself out of the trance. "Maybe he wanted to make sure the knowledge survived in the hands of people he trusted."

Images of Heller's instantaneous bond with Toni flash through my mind, but my thoughts jump to a more immediate question. "What more can we learn about Scientists Beyond Nations?"

"Great scientists on a ship in international waters—"

"We're going to need a lot more."

Joseph nods, perhaps slightly annoyed I've cut him off. But we all know that for the past five years, Scientists Beyond Nations, SBN, has been the quiet alternative to the sometimes raucous global debate about how to apply the radical scientific advances that have so deeply divided the world's governments and paralyzed the United Nations.

The news is always shrouded in mystery, but most people have a vague sense that SBN's mothership, a refurbished old Soviet aircraft carrier, has been stealthily roaming the high seas outside of national jurisdictions and periodically threatening to fire upon any vessels that might possibly approach.

Bringing together scientists from around the world committed to conducting their research outside the control, regulation, or political pressure of national governments, the ship may be all but invisible but the occasional pronouncements of their Council of Elders are anything but. Their releases announcing controversial new techno-logical innovations arrive simultaneously at major health research institutes and media organizations around the world, as if out of thin air. When all countries have the new information, few have been able to resist the pressure of their populations to test the science and make available whatever treatments it indicates.

Breakthroughs in Alzheimer's treatment were a case in point after SBN researchers discovered a single rhesus monkey gene that could cure the terrible disease in humans. Not everyone was comfortable with editing monkey genes into humans, but fewer people were comfortable with Alzheimer's.

"Adam Shelton," Sierra interjects.

Joseph and I turn to face her. Shelton is not exactly a household name, but most informed people have heard the rumors that the reclusive Cuba-based billionaire is funding SBN's operations.

"I'm a business reporter. Follow the money," she continues.

"And?" I ask.

"If we're digging on SBN, we've got to dig on Shelton."

"Can you do it?"

Her lifted left eyebrow squashes the question.

I turn back to face Chou. "Can you transfer these files to my u.D?"

He hesitates. "We have no idea what all of this means, on a scientific level. This could have huge implications. All of my students have committed themselves to complete confidentiality in our work—"

I lift my hand. "We need to be careful but there's no way this can end here. Three people have been killed, two are missing, and more could be in danger. We have no idea who is behind it all. We're just going to have to trust each other."

Chou stares at me for a moment before lifting his wrist to transfer the Sebastian files to my u.D.

As we drive back to the *Star*, voices float through my head: Plato and Aristotle debating the immortality of the soul, Epicurus charging that only life's transience makes it meaningful. What would it mean if we humans became as immortal as our invented gods, I wonder.

But the images dominating my thoughts as we rush up the stairs are far more prosaic: Toni at my house and still in danger, her own house smoldering in the ashes; Heller's half-devoured body floating in the jellyfish tank; Katherine Hart's quiet dignity as she sits, head in her hands, in her living room. Yes, I think to myself, this may be among the greatest discoveries of all time, but it still doesn't tell me who blew up Toni's house, who killed Heller, and where Hart and Wolfson are, if indeed they are still alive.

Martina is waiting for us in the conference room as we rush in.

Joseph boots up the wall and starts folding in the new data as I bring her up to speed.

"*Ay, Santo Dios*," she mutters.

Jerry's face pops up on the wall, brought in through the video link by Joseph.

"We've got to own this," Martina declares.

I've been fighting with Martina for seven years to print all sorts of stories I thought were important and that she dismissed, but now, faced with the most important story of our time, perhaps even our history, I channel Heller's warning and suddenly feel a surge of caution. "Own?"

She turns toward me, the tilt of her head challenging me to justify my suspicious tone.

"We haven't yet proven the science," I say gingerly. "Heller wrote that we need to be extremely careful because of the implications. Maybe Chou is right. We can't just say death has been defeated with nothing more than some dog cells and a letter. Maybe it's true, maybe it's not, but we know what will happen if people get even a sniff of the idea that immortality could be real. You saw what happened in Buenos Aires."

Martina's face softens slightly as she takes in my words. A small pharmaceutical company in Argentina announced last year it had developed a pill that could add ten years to people's lives. It turned out to have been a marketing stunt—the pills were a mix of caffeine, turmeric, and tadalafil—but that didn't matter. Within an hour of the announcement, the clinic was besieged by a mob of thousands. A couple of hours later, the crowd broke the police barricade and rampaged through the clinic looking for the pills. Eight people were dead and the clinic was in flames before riot police finally restored order. Ironically, death has always followed humanity's quest for immortality.

"We still don't know who killed Heller and who tried to kill Toni and me last night," I continue. "We still don't know what happened to Hart and Wolfson. We still don't even know who all the players are in this. And what happens to the handoff to Scientists Beyond Nations if this story comes out now?"

"Do you know?"

"No," I say, "but I can think of a lot of bad options."

"This is bigger than us now." Martina says resolutely. "I hate to say it, but we probably have a legal responsibility to give these files to the police. And if they have them, we may as well publish what we know before someone else does."

"You know this is bigger than the paper. Of course we have to tell the police about anything connected to the murders, but people's lives are at stake here."

"I don't need a lecture from you on responsibility."

"I know. You're right. I just don't trust—"

"Stop." Jerry's word throws a temporary barrier between Martina and me.

I take a step back and face Jerry's image on the wall.

"You need to give the police information about the murders and the general information," he says softly and with an authority I've never before known he could possess.

"But—"

Jerry cuts me off. "You don't need to give the police the encryption code or access to all of the scientific files. I have an idea. I think we can add a rider, a virus, to the encryption key we have, so that when SBN connects the encryption code we give them from the dog's DNA with the one they already have, we might be able to get a window with full access to Heller's system. I've been trying for almost forty-eight hours to get in some other way, but I really think it can't be done."

"Can it work?" I ask. Heller's database is the central pillar of the vast matrix covering our conference wall. Access to it is the key to everything else.

"Theoretically, yes," Jerry says, "but we can only know by trying."

I turn back to face Martina. "What do you think?"

She furrows her eyebrows, and I realize I need more.

"We have the potential to write the greatest story of all time," I add. "Not just the limited, unconfirmed story we have now. The real story, the full story, backed by all the data. All of it."

Martina steps forward to fight, but then her face softens. "Don't patronize me, Jorge. Obviously we're not going to charge forward half-assed, but we can't hold on to this forever. A story like this never stays quiet, and if someone's going to launch it, it ought to be us. Two days," she declares, clearly regretting the words as they leave her mouth. "That's our target. Forty-eight hours."

It's not a lot of time but I know Martina well enough not to argue. "Done." The clock in my head starts ticking. "Jerry, what do you need to do to build the rider on the encryption key?"

"Send me the file," he says.

"How long will it take?"

"I can probably get something by tonight," he says, already messaging with Joseph on the download.

"Joseph?"

"Boss?" he asks, not turning from the data wall.

"I want everything you can find on SBN. No detail is too small."

"On it," he says.

"Sierra."

"Yes, *kapitan?*" she says in an exaggerated voice I am probably right to translate as *who the fuck are you to be giving me orders, but I'm willing to do what you say for now.*

"Can you find out how we can connect with SBN?"

"Aye-aye," she says, half saluting and half swatting me away with the back of her hand.

"And Adam Shelton. We need to be up his—"

"I'm going to climb up his bum with a ladder and an ice pick," she says, pivoting mockingly and goose-stepping out the door.

I turn to face Martina.

"You are not about to give me orders, Jorge."

I revert to the old me. "Will you please join me to go speak with Maurice Henderson?"

33

"Look," Maurice says, halfway between angry and apologetic, "I've got a team investigating the Heller Labs explosion, I've got a team on the Antonia Hewitt explosion, I've got six people protecting you and Toni, I've gotten you the information you need from the Atlantic island, and I just don't have the resources to keep throwing people at every hunch."

Martina and I stare at Maurice, both annoyed.

I've rarely met Maurice in his office and never done it in such a formal way with my editor beside me. "It's more than a hunch," I say.

"Yeah," he responds, "it's some cells and a letter. I get it. If it's true, it's a very big deal. I get it. But this is the Kansas City Police Department, not the National Institutes of Health. You're in the wrong place. My job is to find out who killed Heller, killed my men, and blew up the two buildings."

"I can't believe you're being this narrow," I say, trying to contain myself. "Hart, Wolfson, the iris scans, the strangely rejuvenated dog. There's something going on here much bigger than this city."

"You may be right, Rich. That's what I'm telling you. It's just not my jurisdiction."

"Even if there's a connection between all of this and Heller's death?"

"We don't know that and until we do we have to carry out our investigation, not just dive at the first theory that comes our way. If I had unlimited resources, believe me, I'd do it. But I'll pass this to the FBI and suggest they discuss it with NIH."

The approach feels needlessly bureaucratic and useless at best and dangerous at worst. I wonder if sending this information up the food chain could even somehow encourage whoever is threatening us to step up their game.

"Okay," Martina says, her annoyance only barely contained. "Just remember we told you."

"You've got to do more, Maurice," I say.

"I'm sorry. This isn't the only thing happening in this city. We've got kids getting hooked on synthetic hallucinogens, others going nuts from jacked-up electrical pulses at brain stimulation raves. We've got gangs on the east side killing each other over meth, federal warnings coming in every day about threats from the Middle East . . . I'm doing what I can."

"But—"

Martina cuts me off. "Let's go." She stands and turns toward the door.

I look at Maurice pleadingly.

"I'm doing what I can," he repeats, still seated behind his desk.

I try to balance my gratitude for all he's done with my displeasure he's not doing more.

"Let me know what you learn," he says to my back as I walk out.

Outside, the sky's gray matches my mood. If KCPD won't explore the big-picture story connecting all the disparate pieces, and Maurice's only idea is to pass information up the bureaucratic chain, I have the sinking feeling that until somebody else wakes up the only ones really taking Heller's warning seriously are me and my desperately inadequate group of friends.

We drop Martina back at the *Star* before I have Callahan take me back to my place.

"New school," he grumbles as we drive up and see the police guard mumbling into his u.D at the back door. I assume he conflates "new school" and distracted, which makes me nervous. I walk through the garage door and into the kitchen and find Toni and her mother scrubbing the place down with latex gloves. Dreyfus is at their feet, wagging his tail as if this is the most exciting activity ever.

"You don't have to do that. I can . . ."

They both give me the same look, as if the facial expression for pitying my ineptitude has somehow passed genetically from mother to daughter.

"Can I at least help? I've got a robot that can—"

"We've got it, honey." Toni walks over and kisses my cheek.

Toni's mom, Elizabeth, glances sympathetically over at Haruki, still inert and face-down in the corner.

I know they are engaged in some kind of mother-daughter bonding experience as they prepare this new nest, but I get the sense that the destruction of Toni's home and being here in my imperfectly maintained space has also forced the conversation between them about where Toni and I are heading. I'm pretty confident Elizabeth likes me, and I know she appreciates the bond Toni and I share and how we've grown together, but that probably doesn't change her mind about the basic facts of our situation. She must be telling her daughter some very polite, Midwestern version of, "What the hell are the two of you doing?" It might even be what I'd do in her situation.

"How was work?" Elizabeth, who would never, of course, in a million years use the word "hell," asks.

But it's hard not to interpret a criticism in the question. I feel the urge to explain that I've gone to work to protect her daughter, but I sense the sentence won't translate. "I'm trying to find out who could have done this."

"Isn't that what the police are supposed to do?" Elizabeth asks.

"It depends on what you mean by 'supposed,'" I say, my words sounding overly legalistic, even to me.

Her polite nod suggests she may not be following my logic.

"How are you feeling?" I say, turning toward Toni and taking her hands in mine.

"Still a bit shocked, I think. I don't really care that much about the stuff." She stops and corrects herself. "I probably do care about some of it but I know it's replaceable. I just feel awful about Heller and Sebastian. I'm not sure I've accepted that I no longer have a home."

My head lifts slightly.

"I didn't mean it like that, Rich," she adds. "You know what I mean. And it's still worrying that Heller's lab and my house were blown up the same day."

"That's what the police guards are here for," I say, still not fully convinced they are enough.

"Do we know anything more about the explosions?"

"I was just with Maurice. He says it's looking like a computer hack led to a gas and electricity surge, exactly the same as with Heller. Jerry Weisberg suspects the same thing from his poking around the KCP&L network."

"Are you and Antonia okay staying here?" Elizabeth interjects.

"I hope so," I say, probably unconvincingly. "We're off the gas and electricity grid and getting all of our power from the generator and solar panels."

"Can the police track down who did it?" Toni asks.

"They're trying, but anyone sophisticated enough to do something like that may be sophisticated enough to keep their identity hidden."

Toni and I pull together.

"Have you eaten?" Elizabeth lobs into our embrace. "Can I make you a sandwich?"

"There's not much in the freezerator . . ."

"Oh, we know," Elizabeth says. "Believe me, we know."

Her words are probably as close to an insult as she can get, making me feel even more inadequate as a homemaker. I obsequiously roll Haruki toward the charger.

Toni, her mother, her father—who wanders down from his nap in my den—and I spend an hour eating food bravely assembled from the historical depths of my freezerator. We talk about the insurance claims, having some groceries delivered, getting Toni new clothes.

The conversation feels abnormally normal, like the family I once had before it was changed by my sister's tragic death, the loss of my father, my mother's descent into an obsessive focus on me, and my slow pulling away. I think of Maya and Nayiri living comfortably with my mother in Glendale and I start to see the outlines of something that feels almost like an extended family in its own particular sort of way. My always-whirling mind begins to slow, as if fewer rotations might give me the time and space to look around and see what I actually may almost have.

And then my u.D vibrates.

I tap my wrist and Sierra's glowing face pops up on my freezerator door.

"Rich," she says, "you need to be at Wheeler Airport at four."

Toni eyes me warily.

"Sierra Halley," I say, "this is Toni Hewitt and her parents, Elizabeth and Owen."

"Nice to meet you," Sierra says tersely. "I'm very sorry about your house."

"Thank you," Toni responds. I can tell from her face she has questions about the attractive young woman on the screen.

"Wheeler Airport at four," Sierra orders.

"Tell me more," I say.

Sierra rolls her eyes, annoyed I'm even asking. "Adam Shelton is sending a plane for you."

34

Joseph arrives at my house first with the dossier on Scientists Beyond Nations. "I could do more if I had time," he says breathlessly, "but here's what I have."

The impending arrival of Shelton's plane has compressed our timeline.

Quickly scanning the file, I realize I hadn't fully appreciated the magnitude of SBN's efforts. Its transponder disabled and only connecting rarely via satellite using an electronic cloaking device, the SBN ship is all but invisible to the outside world. The microwave-absorbing stealth technologies wrapping it apparently make it almost impossible to track. Although reporters have looked, no one has figured out how scientists wanting to join SBN get transferred to the ship. When SBN needs to announce a new discovery, the messages just suddenly appear in the inboxes of health ministries and media organizations around the world, the supporting background data unexpectedly materializing in the untraceable SBN digital data room.

On board, scientists pursue unbridled science, following their inquiry in sensitive fields like synthetic biology, biokinetics, and human systems engineering with a great deal of freedom and virtually unlimited resources. It's all under the guidance of the SBN Council of Elders, a group of the most senior scientists on the planet who have dedicated the rest of their lives to the pursuit of pure science and SBN's mission.

There have been, of course, calls from the Vatican and Wahhabi Mecca to hunt down the SBN floating laboratory, but the major powers have remained somewhat ambivalent and have never coalesced around a plan. Until they do, SBN's behemoth glides stealthily across the high seas, periodically sharing transformative discoveries with the world and shaking up the global scientific establishment.

"Do you have what you need on this?" Joseph asks. I sense an impatience I can't quite place.

"Looks good," I say. "I'm sure I'll have more questions along the way."

"Jerry will meet you at the airport before you go," he says.

I get the feeling Joseph is making sure I'm okay and at the same time somehow relinquishing responsibility. "Is there something else?"

Joseph's eyes betray a hint of surprise. "Martina put me on the Brain-Pulse story," he admits after an uncomfortable pause.

I feel a twinge in my gut.

Brain-Pulse, a hot new company selling headbands that send electrical pulses into people's cranial nerves, thought it was designing a way to give people a little extra energy. But some enterprising kids in California figured out how to hack the system and multiply the electric current a hundred times. Brain-Pulse raves have quickly become legendary across the country, not slowed by the increasing number of kids literally going nuts from the overstimulation of their sympathetic nervous systems.

I get that covering the next dangerous epidemic victimizing Kansas City's young people could be a defining opportunity for Joseph to emerge in his own right as a reporter. I also worry what I'll do without Joseph's full support. "That's great news, Joseph." I swallow. "Just ace it."

Joseph and I are facing each other, trying to acclimatize to our new power structure, when Sierra rushes in the door.

"Not sure what's happening here," she says, "but we've got to get you to the airport now. The plane needs to leave no later than 4:30. Ready to roll?"

Toni walks into the living room.

"Toni Hewitt, Sierra Halley," I say, making the introduction.

"Very nice to meet you in person, Toni," Sierra says, "but we've really got to go."

Toni nods politely, but I sense there's a lot more happening under the surface.

I feel the urge to invite Toni to come with us to Wheeler Airport but know it's not practical to have her join. She's taken a leave of absence from work and is safer at my place with the police guards, at least until we can get her house situation sorted out and figure out what's going on. Toni and I embrace fiercely, but I sense an uncomfortable hesitation between us as I walk toward the Lincoln with Sierra. Whatever my motivation, my justification, my cause, I am leaving.

As Tom Callahan speeds us to the airport, Sierra walks me through Adam Shelton's incredible story. Born in Boston in 1970, graduated summa cum laude from MIT at eighteen, completed his PhD in data systems engineering three years later with offers to teach at Harvard, MIT, Cal Tech, ETH Zurich, and National University of Singapore, but instead moved to Israel and started a small data systems engineering company, IntelliData Systems. IDS has long been one of the key backbones of the global metadata network—in other words, the world—making Shelton one of the planet's wealthiest people.

And the most reclusive.

With no family to speak of, he apparently spent the first quarter century of his career running the company from his top-floor apartments in the IDS co-headquarters in Tel Aviv and Singapore. Ten years ago, rumors emerged that he was afflicted with some kind of degenerative illness. As the IDS stock dipped, investors demanded that the mastermind behind the company's unbridled global success make his personal information publically known. Instead, Shelton passed the CEO role to his former operations deputy, gave up his chairmanship, dropped off the board, and moved to Cuba, where he has scarcely been heard from since.

Still the largest shareholder of IDS with a wealth estimated to top fifty billion dollars, Shelton allegedly used twenty billion to seed

SBN and still had plenty to spare. No one knew exactly why he did it, but Sierra's preliminary research unearthed a rumor that he was willing to spend whatever it took to cure the mysterious disease ailing him.

Crossing the Broadway Bridge, I am not surprised to see the spotless A419 waiting on the tarmac. But I'm not ready to board. I ask Callahan to drive us to the general parking lot on the highway side of the municipal airport and wait.

At 4 p.m. I am edgy; 4:15 nervous; 4:25 hardly able to breathe. At 4:27, Jerry's Mahindra Neo comes sputtering toward us and screeches to a halt.

Jerry jumps out the door and shuffles toward us with the data stick in his hand. I get out of the car to greet him.

"Here it is," he says breathlessly.

I look down at the small, nondescript device. "Will it work?"

"I hope so," Jerry mumbles. "I didn't have time to test it. I hardly had time to do it." He takes my u.D off my wrist, then plugs it into the data stick. A small green light activates.

"What do I do with this?"

"I'm passing the file to your u.D. Just transfer it to Shelton's u.D from yours. Tell him it's for the SBN Council of Elders. Let him download it to their system. The rest is in the code."

I inhale deeply. Life, if I've learned anything so far, is in the code.

"But if he suspects anything," Jerry adds, "they'll go through this bit by bit. I've camouflaged the virus as much as possible, but nothing is perfect. A general scan won't pick it up. At least I don't think it will. I can't know for sure without testing."

His words hardly reassure me as I climb the stairs and board the plane. I've been on corporate jets a few times in my life but never one with gold-plated paneling and priceless art on the walls, or enhanced reality screens covering so much of the surface area; never one with its own gym and full bedroom; never one where I was the only passenger.

The attendant, a formal, modelesque British blonde in her twenties, introduces herself as "Ms. Paige Newmark" and welcomes me to my seat. The seat feels more like a reclining sofa than any chair I've ever occupied in a plane. She offers me a hot towel and a drink. I politely refuse both as the plane taxis. In minutes we are off the ground. I close my eyes and think of Toni and Heller and Maurice, of Katherine Hart and Joel Glass.

I tilt the chair back and try to sleep without any success. After twenty minutes or so, I sit up and rifle through the articles projected onto the plane's digital wall. When Ms. Newmark brings dinner by, I try to enjoy the grilled scallops, cooked to perfection. Nothing makes the slightest dent in my nervousness.

I assemble and reassemble in my jittery head all the data we've been collecting. The virus stored on my wrist feels like it's entering my bloodstream. I am anxious to keep moving, but the flight seems to take forever.

Every cell in my body is on edge as the Airbus finally begins its descent. Looking out the window, I see the distant glow in the night sky of what I assume to be the Havana waterfront. I've never been to Cuba, but since the death of the Castros, the end of the embargo, and the arrival of billions in casino investments from Macau, the sin city of the Havana Riviera is said to have come back with a vengeance. That's certainly what the flashing lights look like from here. Inland, I see a few disparate points of light from what I assume to be lonely farmhouses and dilapidated shacks, the remnants of the island's glorious revolution.

But my plane doesn't turn toward Havana. Instead it banks left toward a small airfield I see in lights out my window. My heart is pounding as the plane evens out and touches down.

As our taxi nears its end a few minutes later, Ms. Newmark strides over. Even in heels on a moving plane, her walk maintains its placid grace. She speaks softly in her perfectly crisp British accent. "Welcome to Xanadu, Mr. Azadian."

35

I breathe in the salty, humid, tropical air as the door opens. The light from the runway barely permeates the immense darkness of the surrounding trees. The sound of crashing waves merges with a symphony of chirps, tweets, and croaks oozing from the dense rainforest.

Ms. Newmark leads me down the stairs and to the black Mercedes sedan parked nearby. "*A la casa principal*," she instructs the driver in elegant Spanish as we get in.

After about ten minutes of driving, the road through the thick forest begins to be punctuated by small lights. Brightening as we progress, the lights accent an incredible array of perfectly manicured bushes, exotic flowers, and sprawling banyan trees.

As we turn right around a corner, the breathtaking floodlit mansion comes into view atop the hill. Dominating the space around it, the colossal yellow Spanish-style estate is divided into five sections with turrets rising from each side and a gargantuan wooden veranda floating over a large central entryway. Light refracts off the crests of waves breaking in the distance.

"It has quite a history," Ms. Newmark says, responding to my widened eyes. "Dr. Shelton may choose to tell you about it."

Something about the reverent way she references Shelton unsettles me.

The car rolls to a careful stop in front of the house. Ms. Newmark walks around the car and opens my door, pointing me toward the main entrance. As I approach, the massive wooden doors open electronically.

Lined with polished mahogany, the wooden buttresses lattice the entryway's vaulted ceiling. The floors are a complex mosaic of blue, green, and white marble.

I wander into the first room through a narrow pathway lined with quartz and enter the immense atrium.

Four ultra-modern, white L-shaped sofas complete a large square around the near perimeter of the room. The center area is dominated by an elaborate chandelier hanging down from what must be a fifty-foot ceiling. A tall cylindrical table stands in the middle of the room with a single glass of white wine on it, which I presume is for me. Large Chinese-looking murals of warriors on horseback line the walls to my right and left and facing the water. I stand staring at one, trying to figure out what story it's trying to tell.

"In Xanadu did Kubla Khan a stately pleasure-dome decree."

The words are recited so calmly they don't startle me, even though I hadn't heard anyone come in. Perhaps he was here all along. I turn to see Adam Shelton standing motionless behind me.

"Samuel Taylor Coleridge," I say without thinking, momentarily annoyed by Shelton's canned introduction.

He gives me an appreciative nod. Short and compact, his brown hair is shaved to half an inch. His blue suit fits tightly over his gray shirt and articulated muscles. His sharp metallic-blue eyes focus over sunken cheeks. He scrutinizes me intensely for a moment more than feels comfortable. "I trust your ride here was satisfactory?"

"Do I need to answer that question?"

"Money can buy many things, but it can't buy everything."

"Was it John or Paul who wrote that?" I say. "I never can remember."

Shelton keeps his eyes tracked intensely, and uncomfortably, on me. Augmented Retinal Display lenses may be the latest gadget among the digerati, but I still can't get used to their robotic transformation of the human eye. I wonder what sort of data Shelton is currently being fed as I search for a hint of humor on his face or evidence of his rumored ill-health but see neither. "Thank you for agreeing to meet me on such short notice."

"We both know the stakes are high. There was no other choice."

I stare back at him, waiting for him to reveal something, anything.

"We have important business tonight. Let me show you around the house and give you time to refresh before dinner," he continues. "We can talk then about why you are here."

Shelton leads me out a side door to the veranda at the back of the house. I hear waves crashing into the cement breaker below.

"Nature's majesty," he says.

I let the comment settle. Few things highlight our smallness more than the vast ocean. "But left to nature we'd all live disease-ridden lives to die at forty."

"I read your book," he says, shifting his approach. "You have a lot to be proud of."

"Thank you."

"Four billion years of mother nature and now our evolution is up to us. It's an enormous responsibility."

"In part," I say, "increasingly. So why are you here? Why retreat to this isolated place?"

He looks out across the ocean void. "Is this not enough?"

I wonder what more he is seeing through his ARD lens. "I guess that depends on the scope of a person's ambitions."

"I can assure you, Mr. Azadian, I am quite content in that category." He scrutinizes me as if taking my measure. "The house was built—"

"House?"

"Was built by Irenee DuPont, just before he retired as chairman of one of the biggest chemical companies in the world. He chose this spot on the San Bernadino crags, imported the best of everything to build his Xanadu."

"His choice of name?"

"Of course. For my generation it's a trashy Olivia Newton-John song and an ill-fated mall in New Jersey."

I smile nervously.

"But it's still an interesting choice. Xanadu was Kublai Khan's summer palace. The Mongols had ruthlessly conquered China and needed a place that felt more like home than Beijing."

"So this is where you come after the whoop-ass?"

"DuPont was a powerful man and also a fascist sympathizer who supported Hitler in the early years." Shelton pauses reflexively. "Ironic."

I assume he means it's ironic that DuPont's palace is now owned by a Jew, but I can't be sure.

"He wanted to inject young men with special chemicals to turn them into eugenic supermen," Shelton adds.

I pivot to stare straight into Shelton's eyes. "And the world comes full circle?"

36

The strangeness has been growing from the moment the plane touched down, but it multiplies as Shelton leads me around the immense mansion.

The building is a hundred years old, but it hardly feels it. Shelton describes the painstaking refurbishment process he began eight years ago after buying the old Varadero Golf Club. He restored the mansion to its original splendor and repurposed the golf course. Part of the grounds became his private airport, part lavish gardens, and the rest was transformed into a rainforest and indigenous wildlife preserve.

Every detail of the building is perfect, every fixture a reflection of its original in form but fully modernized in function. The crystal candelabras lining the walls gradually brighten as we enter each room and dim as we exit. The thick mahogany doors slide gently apart as we approach and slip back together after we've walked through. Although I see the faint shadows of black-clad guards outside, I see no people, no staff, no attendants other than a few Robotic Home Assistants docked at their stations, but I know that invisible workers must be making the mansion spotless. It's hard to imagine Shelton scouring the place with a bucket.

The isolation, storied past, and mysterious present of the estate and the enigma of Shelton are mesmerizing, but as he leads me through the vast grounds I keep reminding myself why I'm here. Heller is dead, two policemen are dead, Hart and Wolfson are missing, Toni is in danger, and the narrative of human mortality is on the verge of revolution. Focus.

"Shall we call you for dinner in an hour?" Shelton says as we approach a closed door apparently not yet instructed to open.

His question is not meant to be answered.

"You'll find everything you need," he adds, tapping his wrist to open the ornate door. He walks away as I enter.

The corner room is larger than an entire floor of my house, the ceilings at least twenty-five feet high. Massive windows on two sides overlook the vast darkness of the ocean. Shards of light bounce off the crests of breaking waves. The marble floors are immaculately polished, the enormous bathroom filled with every conceivable item a person might want; the bathtub is larger than a whirlpool and filled with fresh flower petals.

Some other time it would be easy to be intoxicated by the scene. I imagine Toni and me taking a vacation in a place like this someday. But this is not that time. I find myself gently rubbing the u.D on my right wrist. *Learn what you can, pass the file, go home.*

I prepare a bath and settle in to think.

In the calm of the hot water, images of the past five days flash restlessly through my brain as I struggle to put the pieces together. Vast synaptic gaps still separate the data points.

I get out of the water and put on the lush bathrobe and slippers. As I shave and comb my hair, the mirror tracks and expands the reflection of my hand movements, making me feel strangely like Cinderella getting ready for the ball. The collared shirt and sports coat in my closet are, disturbingly, exactly my size.

At precisely an hour from when Shelton left me, I hear three sharp knocks on my door and open it.

"Good evening, sir," Ms. Newmark says formally. "Will you come with me?"

She walks me up a flight of stairs to a vast open deck surrounded by Alhambric columns. The room is empty but for a long, thin rectangular table in the middle. The sound of rolling waves crashes through the room. Two place settings are set across from each other. Shelton is standing at the far wall gazing out over the ocean darkness. Ms. Newmark guides me to him.

"I can stand here for hours," Shelton murmurs, without turning toward me.

I sense he means what he's saying, but the artificiality of our interaction again grates on me. He may be someone who strategically maps out every word before he speaks but I don't have the patience for theatrics right now.

"This place is magnificent," I say, "no doubt. But, if you'll forgive me, I'm here because people are dead and people I care about deeply are in danger. Scientists Beyond Nations is part of the story, and you are the story behind SBN."

He turns and looks at me sharply. His stare is unsettling, even through the ARD lenses. "I know that, Mr. Azadian," he says. "Please tell me what you know."

"There's a lot I also need to learn from you."

"As I believe you already know, I'm not one who readily parts with personal information."

"Then this may be a short dinner."

His eyes remain locked on mine. "We can talk."

Shelton presses a button on a small device resting on the table. The glass doors slide gently shut as a roof rolls out slab by slab, turning the exterior space interior. The sound of the crashing waves vanishes.

I hear the faint din of classical music that sounds like Bach. Again, Bach.

"May I ask what inspired you to establish SBN?" I say after an awkward pause.

"It wasn't only me. I was what they call 'present at the creation.' A lot of incredibly important science was being suppressed by governments. Look at what's happening in the United States. Alvarez and King are clawing each other's eyes out over health care, and you can't even have a decent debate. It's no better in other countries. The Chinese are hijacking science for the state; the Russian kleptocrats are feeding the illicit market in human organs. It's not pretty. A lot of great scientists were peering over the horizon into the future and didn't have faith their work could be protected from government interference or attacks by fundamentalists of every stripe. A lot of people feared that science fueled by profit or ideology or national security interests instead of a careful consideration of the future of our species and our planet could wind up taking disastrous turns. The fears already existed, the scientists already existed. I helped give them a framework, a ship, and the funds to secure their future."

"Not a small contribution," I say, "or a small ship."

"As you can see, I am not a man of small things."

"Some would say government regulation serves a purpose, that unregulated science can lead to grotesque outcomes."

"And they would be right. We know all too well what the Nazi doctors did, the unmoored competition to alter the human genome you described in your book. Science detached from morality is the world's greatest danger; in service of it, it is our greatest hope."

"But who decides what is moral? You?"

"It's fair for you to ask," Shelton replies. "That's why we created the SBN Council of Elders. No single person, no single nation, is capable of making that decision. The United Nations is useless. Perhaps the best we can do is empower a select group of wise people to help guide us. It's not a perfect answer, but it doesn't need to be perfect. It only needs to be better than the alternatives. The science is not going away. As a matter of fact, it's progressing at an exponential pace difficult for most people to fathom."

"Can you tell me more about your connection to the Council?"

"I have a connection," he says guardedly. "For reasons you can appreciate, I can't say more."

"But you are able to reach them?"

"When absolutely necessary, yes."

"And the rumors about your illness? Fabrications?"

"These issues are bigger than any one person." Shelton's eyes lock onto mine, and I realize my line of questioning is done.

"Tell me about Noam Heller," he continues.

I'd prepared for this question but still feel the knot forming in in my gut. I can't say I trust Shelton but I know to my core that sharing information with him is my best hope. He waves me through all of the background, which he seems to know far better than I.

"I met Dr. Heller only three days ago," I say, hardly believing how much has happened since. "I'm not sure 'met' is the right word. I approached him outside his lab and he told me to go to hell."

Shelton's eyes show a hint of life. "Why were you there in the first place?"

I describe my interaction with Santique and my search for more information about the experimental cancer protocol.

Shelton stops me in the middle of my explanation. "You've come a long way to speak with me. We both have a lot at stake here. From what I understand, your friends in Kansas City could be in a lot of danger."

My spine stiffens and body reflexively pulls back from the table.

"Let me be clear," he adds carefully. "I know nothing about the incidents in Kansas City other than what my people have told me. Of course, I have my own information network. You may have no way of trusting this, but I give you my word I was not involved with that violence in any way. I don't know who was. I know no more than you."

Shelton's words seem sincere but I feel out of my depth struggling to evaluate them.

"But it's obvious," he continues, "that something connected to Heller is triggering all of this. My hope is that you and I can figure out what's behind it. Maybe even help each other. But doing so will require a modicum of trust on both sides."

I weigh the options in my head, picturing the electronic wall at the *Star* with its missing links. I am sitting in front of one of the greatest data engineers in history. I don't fully know his motivations but somewhere deep inside I recognize I may have no choice but to trust him. I lean forward.

"Last Tuesday," I begin, "I went to a hospice in Kansas City looking into the disappearance of a scientist named Benjamin Hart . . ."

It's late. The seven courses of our exquisite meal have long since vanished, and we are on our fourth cup of coffee. We've gone through every word of Heller's letter on the screen embedded in the dining table. After securing my promise to not publish what he tells me that cannot be verified from public sources, Shelton has given me additional background on SBN and its intricacies. He described the ingenious encrypted communication system he created to provide periodic secure communication with the SBN ship.

"So I presume you have it," he says, once again focusing his intense gaze deep into my eyes.

"Of course."

"And you will give it to me?"

"It was what Heller wanted," I say, trying to mask the beating of my heart.

Shelton nods slightly.

"But I need something from you," I add.

"What?"

My mind flips through everything I might need to protect Toni, provide closure to Katherine Hart, even take care of Maya and Nayiri. All of the options are vague and only uncertainty ties them together, but I sense I have only one shot to get a commitment from Shelton. I need answers more than anything else. "I need you to put me in direct touch with the SBN Council of Elders."

Shelton stares at me coolly through his ARD lens. "I've already given you more access to me than most anyone else in the world. I can't and won't go further."

A flash of anger passes through me. I'm not surprised by Shelton's response; I just want more. Even if my actions here have been anything but pure, I'm not willing to leave empty-handed. I scan my brain but can't come up with the right ask. So I punt. "I want your word I can call on you if I need anything in the future."

"'Anything' is an ambitious ask," he says ironically, "but I will do my best within reason."

He puts out his hand. I stare at it for a moment before lifting mine, reluctantly, to meet it.

My heart is pounding. The frenetic energy pulsing through my brain reminds me I'm about to pass a virus to one of the great computer engineers of all time. I sit back in my chair and take a deep breath before speaking into my u.D. "Transfer Heller Encryption Key Access File 110925."

37

I've always thought of my capacity to be alone as a great source of strength, but lying in the ridiculously large canopy bed in my immense room in this colossal estate, I toss and turn and think about being home in my queen-size bed with Toni. I picture her wrapped tightly in my down comforter without me.

Thoughts of Jerry's virus worm through my synaptic neurons. It may or may not be already infiltrating the handshake between the two encryption keys. What chance does Jerry Weisberg from frigging Kansas City have, I keep asking myself nervously, of his viral rider going undiscovered by someone as sophisticated as Shelton?

I'm already wide awake when the u.D alarm vibrates at 6:30 a.m. A typed note has been slipped under my door in the night. *Breakfast outside your door. Wheels up 7:30 a.m.*

I roll in the cart. The freshly baked croissants, tropical fruit plate, scrambled eggs, juice, and French press coffee would be a joy on any other day. Today, all I can handle is the coffee.

Paige Newmark is waiting for me at the bottom of the stairs. "Mr. Shelton has been called away. He asked me to tell you how much he appreciated your visit."

Called away? When? By whom?

"He wanted me to give you this."

She hands me a small card. "It's his private u.D access number," she says as if sharing a unique and precious gift.

As the chauffeur drives us to the runway, the rising orange sun reveals the spectacular manicured gardens I had been unable to fully appreciate last night and the boundaries of the dense surrounding forest. It is difficult to imagine that this jungle could have possibly been a golf course just eight years ago. Perhaps, I reflect, Hobbes was right. There is a jungle waiting to swallow each of us the moment we let our guard down.

Ms. Newmark anticipates my question as we approach the tarmac. "Mr. Shelton's plane is currently in use, so we'll be taking the Cessna. It may not have all the amenities but it can certainly get you to Kansas City."

She waits at the bottom of the stairs as I climb aboard the small corporate jet but does not follow me up. I watch her standing beside the airstrip, erect and unmoved, as we taxi and take flight, then I collapse into a deep sleep as the small airplane climbs.

Only the captain's announcement of our descent into Kansas City pulls me from my coma. I train my groggy eyes out the window, somehow both warmed and alarmed by the sight of the familiar downtown skyline, the nautilus-like shells of the Kauffman performing arts center, and the meandering Missouri River. Callahan is waiting for me in the Lincoln, parked in the lot just beside the runway.

"You need to get over here," Jerry says excitedly when I call him on my u.D from the car. "I've been trying to reach you. It's happening."

The possibilities surge through my brain. "I'm on my way. We need the whole team."

I feel guilty as I make my final call to Joseph before my quick drop-by to check on Toni. Brain-Pulse may be very important for Kansas City, but Heller's files have the potential to mean exponentially more to the world.

Dreyfus finds me first as I run in my back door. *Oh boy, that guy's back. Maybe he'll play with me. Oh boy. Really? Really?*

I give him a perfunctory pat on the head as I pass, desperate to get in and out as quickly as possible.

Haruki glides over energetically. "*Okaerinasaimase ureshiigo-*

zaimasu," he says, bowing vigorously. "*Gobujini modorarete ureshuu-gozaimasu*."

"Not now, Haruki."

"*Goyouken wo omoushitsuke kudasai-mase, ureshiigozaimasu?*"

I have no idea what he is saying and only want him out of the way but realize in face of his expectant round eyes that the path of least resistance is engagement. "Speak English, Haruki."

"Yes, master," Haruki says. "Welcome home. How may I be of service?"

"Um," I mutter, looking apologetically at Toni and her suspicious parents, who have now entered the kitchen, and feeling the need to be back at the *Star* as quickly as possible. "Just go stand quietly in the next room."

"Yes, master," Haruki says, rolling away with a look in his eyes that almost seems like disappointment.

"And no need to call me master," I add, a bit embarrassed by the interaction in front of Toni's parents.

Haruki pivots back to face me and leans his head slightly forward at an angle, as if favoring the ear he does not have. "What shall I call you, master?"

I begin to open my mouth but Toni steps forward and beats me to it. "Call him Dikran," she says with a wink in my direction.

I contort my mouth to counter, then override with the recognition that doing so would make me look even more foolish.

Haruki bows. "Yes, Dikran-san." He turns toward the dining room.

"Hi, baby," Toni says, wrapping her arms around me. "How was your trip?"

I want to grab her and draw her into me but too much stimulus is overcrowding my brain. "It was an unbelievably bizarre experience. A lot of things are happening." I give her the thirty-second version of the story as I begin leaning toward the door. "How are you holding up?"

"How was the play, Mrs. Lincoln?"

I stand straight. "I'm sorry," I say more presently, placing a hand on each of her shoulders. Whatever I've been doing, I feel bad that Toni's the one whose house has been obliterated and I've not been around. "Are you okay?"

She looks at me and smiles, piercing me with her green eyes. "I just wanted you to ask. I'm fine, all things considered. Still sad about Heller and Sebastian, having strange dreams. I'm more worried about you. You look awful, you know."

I hadn't thought about it, but I probably do.

"Now get the hell out of here," she adds with a gentle push and mischievous grin.

I feel like I should say something but don't. My words have been sharpened for decades on the hard stone of ideas, but I sometimes feel like a flailing butter knife when it comes to emotions. "I'll be back later," I declare over my shoulder.

Rushing into Jerry's basement hideout, I am overwhelmed by the multitude of files splashed across the four digital walls, data codes streaming like sparks of light across the top. Jerry, Franklin Chou, and Sierra are each waving their hands as they pass through the vast stream of files.

"We're getting it," Jerry announces excitedly, not looking in my direction, "We're pulling this down as quickly as we can. Whoever is accessing this data stream right now will reconfigure the codes as quickly as they can once they get the full download."

"How much do we have?" I ask.

"I'm not sure," Jerry says. "It's a huge amount of data. We're running a searchbot to pull out any files with our keywords and have divided the labor of going through what comes up."

The numbers from the large wall refract off of Chou's glasses. "This is some of the most incredible research data I've ever seen," he murmurs, mesmerized.

"Franklin is reviewing the data, Sierra is looking at the language files, I'm focusing on the download." Jerry still has not taken his eyes off the screen. "I have no idea if there are any poison pills in the data, so we need to download and start reviewing the content as quickly as possible."

"And Joseph?" I ask.

Joseph looks over at me. I still have a hard time reading his face.

"Hart and Wolfson," he says, steadily waving his hands to circulate the files. "All of the documents are here—the tracking records of their cancers, the failure of the cancer treatment protocol, the assessment of their suitability for total cellular reversion, the procurement of their blood samples from four decades ago from cryopreservation, their procedure at Heller Labs, their departure . . ."

I'd known there was a possible link between Sebastian's cells and Hart and Wolfson's retinas scanning in at Tobago, but my surging aortic valve announces what my mind is only beginning to absorb. The story is almost too vast to consume.

"It's not just them. Three other scientists were also included in the program: Dr. Ephraim Ungar from Palo Alto, Professor Michaela Bernstein from Chicago, Solomon Marcus from Boston," Joseph continues.

"All Jews?" I say, thinking back to the Wolfson's mezuzah.

"I hadn't thought of it, boss," Joseph says.

"Who's taking them? How are they getting there?"

"That's what I'm on." Sierra's words are sharp and focused. "I'm only speeding through the documents, but it looks like Heller did some kind of deal with Scientists Beyond Nations. They bring him the human subjects, Heller does the reversion, then SBN whisks them away."

"To where?"

"I don't know yet," she says, "but there's at least one obvious possibility."

"And if you're getting these rejuvenated scientists to a ship, wouldn't it make sense to leave from a remote place in the middle of nowhere, an island maybe?" I turn toward Chou. "Can you tell if the science works?"

"It'll take time to analyze the data," Chou says as if through a fog, "but the alterations of genomic sequences of the five scientists seem to track exactly the patterns I saw with the dog."

"With jellyfish DNA?" I ask.

"That and the other factors in Heller's formula. If that data is correct, and I'm not prepared to say it is, it appears the scientists were reverted to the age of their previous cellular samples, about forty years or so for each of them. If this is real, they would have woken from the transfusions missing the memories of forty years of life."

"So let me get this straight," I say solemnly. "There may now be two groups of people in the world who possess the secret to eternal life?"

Joseph, Sierra, and Chou all turn from their respective walls to face me.

"I'm not so sure," Chou says.

"Not sure?"

"I'm still going through the data. There's way too much here."

"But?"

"I can't confirm if it actually works, but it looks like the reversion process requires a very specific set of CRISPR-induced genetic manipulations, molecular transfections, and chimeric alterations of nucleotides within the genes during an enhanced autologous parabiosis process."

"What are you even talking about?" I say impatiently. "In English, please?"

Chou looks annoyed. "This is extremely complicated science, Rich. The forced expression of very specific genes during the transfusion. It must have taken literally tens or hundreds of thousands of trials—not just of the genetics but also of the added molecular compounds—for Heller to find the right formula, if he did at all. I'd only know if I replicated it in my lab."

"Could he have made that kind of progress alone?"

"That's the genius of this. He seems to have developed a bioan-alytical ternary model that crunched the data based on the cellular samples taken from the organisms in his lab."

"English?"

Chou stares at me intently, as if weighing his words. "Maybe."

"So is the formula in the files?"

"That's what I'm looking for," Chou says, waving his hands fran-tically. "I can't seem to find it."

"The window is closing," Jerry shouts.

We turn to face him.

"They're reprogramming the access portal."

"How much of the data do we have?" I yell.

"I think most of it," he says, "at least as much as we are going to get."

"Shit, Jerry, can we speed this up?"

"This is an unbelievable amount of data coming through a very narrow filter. It's not us, it's . . ."

The parade of code stops in its tracks, the numbers and letters halting on the wall in mid-stream.

"That's it," Jerry whispers, collapsing into his Exemplis swivel chair.

Chou, Sierra, and Joseph turn back toward their walls.

"I should build a firewall to try to protect this data," Jerry adds.

"*Thayoli*," Joseph mutters, gaping at the wall in front of him.

I have no idea what the word means but it doesn't take much to recognize it's probably not something good Malayalees say in mixed company. "What?"

As Joseph reads from the end of a language file he's uncovered, I imagine Heller dictating the words in his illustrious accent.

"'Of course,'" he says, channeling Heller, "'I fully recognize the magnitude of my discovery and have therefore taken one final precau-tion. The formula for total cellular reversion described in my notes can only work if an additional catalyst is added during the transfu-sion process. This catalytic compound consists of small molecules and uniquely folded proteins found only in nature that cannot be reverse-engineered using any tools existing today. Although I have provided SBN a frozen vial of my catalytic compound and retained one in my lab, it will be impossible to successfully reproduce the biological age-reversing enhanced autologous chimeric parabiosis process without either one of these vials or the specific formula describing how to produce this final but essential component. The formula for doing so is not included in this electronic file.'"

"Genius," Chou utters.

We all turn to face him.

"So even after he's divided the keys for access to the reversion formula itself," he continues, transfixed, "he's added one final piece of the puzzle, even more deeply hidden, the catalytic compound with its own secret formula and only two vials of it in existence. He's broken the process into parts and concealed each separately."

"What does that mean?" Sierra asks.

"It's the ultimate insurance policy. He was extremely nervous the secret process for age reversion might get into the wrong hands," I say. "Unless the catalytic compound formula can also be found, the only reversions possible will be using the contents of those two vials."

"I need to get back to my lab," Chou says feverishly. "It means that our impossible job just got a quantum leap tougher."

38

My mind swirls as I strain to assimilate the massive amount of data on Jerry's walls.

If there are two existing vials and a secret catalytic compound critical to unlocking one of the greatest secrets of all time, who wouldn't kill to possess them? Heller must have known that, which was why he took so many precautions and had so many compartmentalized layers of hidden information. Whoever killed Heller must have been searching for the vials and trying to get Heller to reveal the formula. Did they get it? It's impossible to know. If they got what they needed from Heller before killing him, why go back later to destroy the lab? To cover their tracks? If they were covering their tracks, why not destroy the lab when they killed him? Or did they worry someone else might get the information? If so, where else might they look? My gut twists as I come up with only two options: Sebastian and Toni.

And Sebastian is already dead.

The idea begins to expand in my mind.

With my constant motion, I'd almost overlooked the few moments Toni spent with Heller in the darkened jellyfish room in the back of his lab. He said we'd arrived at a serendipitous moment. She'd come out of the room with a beatific look on her face and an expression that made clear I was not to ask. Could Heller have delivered some kind of message to her in those moments, told her something about access to the formula? Could that explain why her house was targeted? But who could have known, other than me and Heller, that she'd been in that room with him alone?

You are such an idiot! The message screams from the depths of my subconscious. Hadn't Heller said the jellyfish room was its own little world, the only place where he could truly be alone, that my u.D couldn't connect to the network from inside? Didn't Maurice's radio not work there? Is there some connection between Heller's private meeting with Toni and the fact that his dead body was found in the same room hours later?

My mind darts back to Heller's words in his letter encoded in Sebastian's DNA. He said he had strong indications his anxiety was not misplaced, fears for his life and safety. Could he have feared his lab was being monitored somehow and seen the jellyfish room as some kind of communications safe room where outsiders couldn't spy on him?

I'm tempted to race back out to Callahan and the Lincoln, but something stops me in my tracks. If I run home to Toni, what will I do? I'll get every piece of information I can about her private time with Heller. And then what? Will she be any safer? I need more backup. I call her on my u.D as the Lincoln speeds toward KCPD headquarters.

"Baby, are you okay?" I say breathlessly.

"Yeah," she says cautiously, reading my nervousness. "We're starting to go through the insurance claim forms."

"Are the police there?"

"Of course. What's going on?"

"I need to ask you a question. It's incredibly important."

"Go on."

"When we were in his lab last Friday, Heller invited you into the back room with the jellyfish tank and asked me to stay out."

"He did," she affirms slowly.

"I need to know exactly what happened in that room, every detail."

Toni pauses. "I'm not sure I can share it."

I don't know what to make of her words. "Baby, you've got to. This is incredibly important."

"I'm not hiding anything from you, it's just that my memory is blurry. I remember walking into the room and Dr. Heller asking me to look deeply into the bell of the jellyfish," she says, "to tell him what colors I saw and the shapes that contained them."

"To stare at the medusa. And?"

"I started to describe the colors and the shapes. They were fluorescent and reverberating. He told me to look deeper." Toni stops speaking.

"Go on."

The line is silent.

"Baby?"

"I'm just thinking about these strange dreams I've been having," Toni continues after a pause. "I hadn't really thought of it before now, but the neons of the dream are reminding me of the colors of the jellyfish."

"But can you remember what happened in the room?"

"I can't. Even focusing on it now, I don't seem to remember."

"What do you mean?" I ask impatiently.

"It's like time stops. I remember walking in, I remember Heller asking me to look deeply at the jellyfish, and then I remember walking out of the room and seeing you."

My mind races back to Joseph's briefing notes on Heller. The specifics had added up to my impression of him as an incredible Renaissance man, but had I focused sufficiently on the details? I tap my u.D and scroll through the notes. *Expert in computer science, biology, psychology, advanced mathematics.* Psychology?

"Do you think he might have hypnotized you?"

"Maybe. I just don't remember. It's really weird. It's just that the colors of the jellyfish and the colors of these dreams seem to be the same and—"

"Tell me about your dreams."

"It's more like fragments of dreams," Toni says contemplatively, "like floating colors."

"Anything more you remember?"

"No, baby. Nothing specific."

"Can you keep trying?" I say, recognizing that hope, rather than science, is guiding my words.

"I guess," Toni says tentatively. "Hard to make any promises about remembering dreams."

My mind shifts up a gear in the quiet moment following her words. Could Heller have sensed danger and somehow planted a seed of something in the depths of Toni's mind? Is that what the dream fragments might represent? I can't know, but the possibility that Toni could be carrying some kind of secret in her brain that someone is willing to kill for shakes me to my core. "Just don't go anywhere. Don't leave the house. Stay away from the windows."

"What's going on?" Toni demands. "What aren't you telling me, Rich?"

"I don't know. It looks like Heller was keeping a secret someone wanted. Your house got blown up for a reason and one possibility is that people may think he somehow transferred that secret to you."

"Well, that would kind of suck."

"This is serious, baby," I say soberly. "Just please stay away from the windows."

I'm still thinking of Toni as I race into KCPD headquarters.

"We've confirmed the cyberhack on the gas and power lines," Maurice declares as I enter his office. The pervasive fake dark wood paneling absorbs the light from the one small window on this already cloudy day. I pull the door closed behind me and begin my update.

"What have you heard from the FBI and NIH?" I ask impatiently.

"FBI says they'll send someone in the next couple of days." He pauses, then says derisively, "They say right now this looks local."

"What the hell!" I explode. "Local? You've got to be kidding me."

"Calm down, Rich." Maurice is unruffled by my theatrics. "They said the three people who've been killed, Heller and my two men, are from Missouri, killed in Missouri."

"That makes no sense. Every death happens somewhere. What

about everything we told you about the dog's cells, Heller's science, Scientists Beyond Nations, Adam Shelton?"

"I told them that," Maurice says. "They said it sounded like an interesting theory they would discuss with NIH."

"Which they probably won't do until they send someone here?"

"I don't know."

"That is bullshit. So the only ones looking into this are KCPD and the *Star*?"

"For now, yes."

My heart sinks. The lineup seems pathetic given the magnitude of the stakes. "So what are you guys doing?"

Maurice hears the criticism in my tone. "I've lost two men. There's nothing I take more seriously. We've got a dedicated team working on this. But we are a police department. We have procedures, methods, limitations, and our first priority is the local incidents."

The mention of methods and procedures only makes me feel, even more depressingly, that KCPD doesn't have the imagination to put the pieces together and that I and our little team are all alone. "Let me tell you more," I add quietly.

Maurice listens intently as I describe my experience with Shelton in Cuba and what we just learned from the data file.

"It's an unbelievable story. I get it. I'll reach out to the FBI again. We're doing what we can. You have to trust me," Maurice says.

I look into his eyes a few moments before speaking. "I do trust you, Maurice," I say earnestly. "It's just not nearly enough."

39

I rush home from KCPD to check on Toni. We excuse ourselves from her parents, go up to my room, close the door to keep Dreyfus out, and lie in each other's arms as I tell her about Cuba and Heller's files.

"You look frazzled," she says. "I'm starting to really worry about you."

"I probably am more than a bit frazzled," I reply, squeezing her closer.

"I know this is a dirty trick to make you feel better, but . . ."

Before I object, she taps her u.D and the box opens on my digital wall. A few seconds later, Maya and Nayiri's faces appear in my bedroom.

"Well, hello to you," Maya calls cheekily. "Sure we're not finding you, um, in the middle of something?"

I can't help but smile nervously.

"Auntie Toni, Uncle Dikran," Nayiri cries.

"She's growing so fast," I say.

"She sure is," Maya responds proudly, turning her loving eyes toward the baby. "Aren't you, my little amazing?"

The four of us talk warmly but my mind is still elsewhere. "Just let us know what we can do," I say a bit absent-mindedly before we tap off the call a few minutes later.

"Okay," Toni says, reading the undiminished tension on my face. "Don't say I didn't try."

My half smile feels forced.

Toni doesn't give up. "But you have to admit Nayiri is just incredible, a miracle, really. I'm not sure I understand everything Gillespie and his team did, but . . ." My eyes lift, but Toni articulates the thought before I get there. "You don't think . . ."

"He was at the center of the US government's work at the intersection of intelligence operations and radical science," I say. "You'd have to think he might know something."

"And he kind of owes us one, you know," Toni adds.

Anderson Gillespie had been, to me, the menacing face of government threats two years ago until I'd realized there was a lot more to him than met the eye. He'd sent a message a while back letting us know he'd been discharged from the Department of National Competitiveness and sent us his contact information for a cabin he'd moved to, somewhere in the Ozarks. And there it rested.

Until now.

My hands tremble slightly as I tap my u.D. His face appears on the wall of my media room. His skin is as gaunt as ever but now seems even more sallow. His hair is as short-cropped as it was, black giving in to the first hints of gray. But his penetrating harshness remains unabated.

"Dikran Azadian," he says, eyeing me guardedly, his voice betraying not a small bit of surprise.

The sight of him still unnerves me, resuscitating the memory of what it felt like to be on the wrong side of his aggression.

"And Antonia," he adds, looking at her, in a far warmer voice.

"How's the fishing?" I say.

"That's what you're calling me to ask?" Gillespie says. He appears to be sitting in front of a large blue shower curtain, as if trying to eliminate any clues about his surroundings.

Toni redirects my bumbling approach. "We're happy to see you, Anderson," she says tenderly. "We think of you often."

Gillespie closes his eyes for a brief moment.

Toni reads the small gesture. "What's past is past, but there is always the future," she says.

Gillespie's face softens, and I jump into the breach. "We need your help with something."

I feel Toni digging her fingernails into my leg.

The familiar scowl returns to his face.

"We'd like to ask you for your help, Anderson," Toni repeats in a gentler tone. "It may be very important."

"Go on," he says warily.

"It's a long story."

"I can assure you I've got nothing but time."

I hesitate a moment, unsure how much I should say, but this is not a time for caution. "Last Tuesday—"

"Stop," Gillespie orders.

I look at him expectantly.

"I'm sending you an SSL file through your u.D," he continues.

"I already have Silent Circle encryption on it," I explain.

He looks at me like I'm an idiot. "Activate the SSL and we'll be secure."

I follow his instructions.

Gillespie confirms our security level. "Go on," he instructs.

Gillespie's eyes have been continually narrowing, fraction by fraction, for nearly an hour as he's taken in every word I've said, asking penetrating questions along the way. "And those idiots know this and are doing nothing about it?" He shakes his head.

"Looks like it."

"Morons," he adds.

I get the impression his own betrayal is folded into the word.

"So what do you need from me? You know I'm retired." Gillespie raises his hand. "Let me rephrase. I've been discharged and am living on disability."

I don't answer immediately. Gillespie is lucky he's not in jail.

"What do you need, Azadian?"

"Adam Shelton and Scientists Beyond Nations."

"I'm listening."

"I'd imagine US intelligence services track people and organizations like these."

"I'd imagine so."

"And you are part of that community."

"I was. I could have sworn I spoke ten seconds ago about being discharged."

"You're not discharged from your brain, from your relationships."

"Want to bet?"

"I wouldn't be calling you if I weren't desperate, if we weren't desperate. This story has huge implications."

"Story?" he asks.

"I misspoke. It's not about the story. You know how much havoc the idea of immortality has wrought in human history, how many people have died in search of it."

Gillespie does not look convinced. "What is this, a history lesson?"

"Match that with revolutionary genetics and it has the potential to be a pretty toxic mix," I point out.

"Anderson, we need you," Toni interjects as it becomes clear my arguments are failing to hit their mark. "Rich may be in danger. I may be in danger. And if we're in danger, Maya and the baby could even be in danger."

Gillespie tilts his head back and widens his eyes.

"Whoever killed Heller clearly understands the stakes here," I add, following Toni's lead. "I have no idea what they know, whom they are after, when they will stop. I've got to figure out what's happening before—"

"There were rumors about Shelton."

The sharpness of Gillespie's words startles me. "What kinds of rumors?"

"Unsubstantiated ones. He was a boy genius who chose to leave the United States to start his company."

"Yes. He moved to Israel," I say.

"Why?" Gillespie asks. "Silicon Valley is here. A lot of capital is here. Israel is a mess. The whole country is in danger of being wiped out, especially if the security dome gets taken away, the jihadis rush in, and the crazies start lobbing tactical nukes."

"But they have an amazing technology sector."

"There were rumors that IntelliData Systems was launched secretly under the auspices of the ISS."

"What's that?"

"The Israeli Scientific Service."

I straighten in my chair, surprise smeared across my face. "Who are they?"

Gillespie looks at me like I'm a fool. He blows a burst of air through his nose then shakes his head. "A top secret branch of Israeli intelligence, the Mossad."

40

There must be some limit to the absorptive capacity of the human mind.

If we time traveled an average *Homo sapien* from twenty thousand years ago to today, his brain would be exactly like ours, but he would probably go temporarily insane as he struggled to take in all twenty thousand years of progress all at once. Our minds are not designed for massive leaps.

As the startling revelations have come fast and furious over the past week, I've felt my overtaxed neurons struggling to keep up.

"Why would . . ." My brain doesn't let me finish the sentence.

"I'm just a guy in a cabin in the Ozarks," Gillespie says. "Don't you follow the news?"

I look at Gillespie, unsure if he's even capable of telling a joke. "But why would the ISS be involved in this?"

"Why exactly? Only they can know."

"How about not exactly?" I'm grasping for any thread of logic. "Why possibly?"

"Think, Azadian. Why would Israeli intelligence want to build a global data systems behemoth that provides the underlying code for the complex systems underpinning global communications and commerce? Is that your question?"

Gillespie's formulation makes me feel slow. "So Shelton founded IntelliData Systems and he also funds Scientists Beyond Nations. Does this mean Israel controls Shelton's company and SBN is a front for Israeli intelligence?"

"Who knows. Some people in the community were looking at that a few years back, but I never heard of anyone confirming anything before I was out. I wouldn't have known everything anyway."

"What would be the motivation?" My mind races as I begin to formulate hypotheses.

"Your guess is as good as mine," Gillespie says, "but how does the saying go? Desperate times beget desperate measures."

"Like using the science developed on the SBN ship for military applications?"

"Could be," Gillespie says, his tone suggesting he's not convinced. His cold stare reminds me of the old Gillespie I used to fear.

"Think about it," he continues, throwing me a bone. "You can't escape the news from the Middle East even if you try. Most of the Arab countries are just fictional lines on an antiquated map, swept up in the chaos of the great Sunni–Shia war, the roving bands of jihadis and ethnic militias, and the vast swaths of lawlessness. The United Nations protective dome is under threat, the tiny Gulf states are armed to the teeth and sucking in everyone's money, there's an open revolt in the United Nations against the deal the US made with the Chinese. Not many countries want the UN to protect Israel, even if doing so was the price America extracted from China for protecting the installations pumping China's oil. Missiles are getting fired at Israel every day and the UN dome is a big part of ensuring so few of them get through. If you were Israel what would you do?"

I can think of a lot of answers. "I'd probably lobby the countries who want to cut me off."

"Not sure what world you've been living in, but they've been trying that for a long time. Americans may feel some kind of moral commitment to Israel, but the rest of the world is simply doing a cost-benefit analysis and seems to have decided the cost of blood and treasure of protecting Israel just isn't worth it for them. It was probably only American pressure that got them to agree to the dome in the first place. With America's politics looking chronically unstable, a lot of countries are reconsidering that bet."

"So, what, SBN is some kind of insurance policy? How would that work?"

"I have no idea. This is all conjecture, informed by a few brief conversations years ago, but I can think of at least two good reasons Israeli intelligence might want to help create something like SBN."

"Like?"

"Like feeding new, revolutionary technologies to Israeli companies and the Israeli government. With so many of the best and brightest Israelis leaving for safer places, Israel might want to double down on revolutionary research, even research outside the bounds of what the other countries of the world are comfortable with, to obtain a technological edge."

"So why not just form their own think tank, why go through all the subterfuge of creating SBN and outfitting the ship?"

"You'd have to ask them. But would the most free-thinking scientists from around the world rally to support the Israeli government like they've rallied to join SBN? Seems like that would be a pretty good deal for Israel."

"What's the second reason?"

"Again, this is just conjecture, but what if they came up with something so revolutionary every person and every country in the world wanted it—something they could control—that could give them a lot of leverage, maybe enough leverage to guarantee the continuation of the protective dome, maybe even guarantee the future security of their country?"

It's an audacious idea that somehow makes sense. "And Shelton could be a great vehicle for making this happen. The American boy genius could be a perfect cover."

"Now you're thinking, Azadian."

I roll on. "Could that explain the incredible success of IDS? Shelton had an army of Israel's most gifted programmers behind him and then he vanishes to Cuba just when SBN is being created, escaping the global spotlight and avoiding any probing questions."

"I'm an intel guy," Gillespie says, changing tack. "I don't trust any theory just because it makes sense."

The jigsaw pieces are flying across my mind. "Heller spent a chunk of his career at the Weizmann Institute in Jerusalem. His wife was Israeli."

"You told me Heller gave the other half of the encryption key to SBN, correct?"

"Hart and Wolfson and the three other scientists who vanished— all seem to be Jews."

Gillespie focuses his sharp gaze.

"Would the Israelis want to shut down Heller if they had a connection to him and feared he might expose them in some way?" I ask.

"Why would you think that?"

"Someone got to Heller."

"Maybe that would be one explanation, but if all this is true, I'd imagine there are a lot of other options," Gillespie says.

"At least that might explain why Heller was so secretive? If Israeli intelligence is behind SBN, do we assume Heller would have been aware of it?"

"We shouldn't be assuming more than we have to," Gillespie says. "Right now, we don't have answers."

His use of the plural pronoun somehow comforts me. "Or maybe someone else discovered this connection, some enemy of Israel, an intelligence service, someone who wanted to sabotage the whole thing."

The feeling rises from my gut. What if this is the work of a hostile intelligence service? If I have to consider all of the options, at least one of them has to be that someone may want something from Toni. And if someone that sophisticated wants Toni, what use are the two "new school" guards from the KCPD at my front and back doors? How much am I doing to protect Toni if the only ones looking into this case are my little group and a few half-assed inspectors from the forty-fourth largest metropolitan area in the United States?

Gillespie has never struck me as intuitive, but somehow he reads my mind. "It's unbelievable those idiots aren't doing more to look into this."

"It's not unbelievable," I say, a plan beginning to rapidly gel in my head, "it's terrifying. Can you help us?"

"I'm retired," he says cynically before correcting himself. "Forcibly retired."

Somehow I don't trust his words. I stare at him without flinching.

"Anderson, we really need you," Toni interjects.

He glares through the screen but then his eyes soften slightly. "I'm cut off these days. My old partners can get into big trouble for even speaking with me."

I feel no choice but to throw down the trump card. "You know better than anyone what the stakes are here."

Toni kicks me surreptitiously. Referencing how the US government's secret plan to seed the American population with genetically enhanced children ended up getting nine pregnant women killed and causing a national crisis may be my way of pressuring Gillespie to cooperate, but Toni's style, as usual, is different.

"It's not about that, Anderson," she says softly. "This is about the future, about protecting people. We know you're no longer in the government, but we'd be so incredibly grateful if you could please—"

"I can't promise anything," Gillespie fires, then breathes in deeply.

I pounce on the opportunity with as much gentleness my impatient mind can muster. "Gillespie, I need one thing from you. I know you understand how big of a deal this all is, how many people might be in danger. I need your help."

His body stiffens. His eyes narrow. Annoyance blankets his face. But I still sense Gillespie affords Toni and me grudging respect from our Genesis Code experience and recognizes he owes us one. "I'm listening."

"I need you to tell me where I can find the Scientists Beyond Nations ship."

41

I splash my driver's license from my u.D to the guard's screen before marching into Franklin Chou's lab feeling like I'm racing against a clock I can't even see.

The lab is once again a hive of activity with laser-focused students manning their battle stations in front of the massive wall screens. Large glass cabinets filled with agar plates are assembled in the middle of the room.

"If this is real, it's one of the greatest discoveries of all time," Chou states meditatively as I approach.

"What do you mean 'if this is real'? I thought Hart and Wolfson proved it."

"Much of what we're doing hinges on the science being verifiable. Those records prove only what someone wrote down, not what's confirmed to be true. They almost gave the Nobel Prize to Hwang Woo Suk in Korea before people figured out he was making up his genetic research. They reported you could live forever if you consumed enough resveratrol and red wine until someone tried it and only wound up drunk. I'm a scientist. For me it's only true if it's replicable, and that's what we're trying to do."

"How big of a job is it?" I ask.

"Huge, but ours is a lot easier than Heller's was. He had to make everything up from scratch. All we have to do is follow his blueprint, at least what we have of it."

I move toward the cabinet of agar plates. "Roundworms?"

"That's where he started and that's where we have to. I had this rush shipment delivered earlier today. We're trying to speed things up by keeping the incubators at twenty-five degrees Celsius and also using the digital simulation of the *C. elegans* from the OpenWorm network. I've got four hundred transgenic mice coming tomorrow from Jackson Laboratory."

I'm not sure I'm fully following Chou so I cut to the chase. "How long will it all take?"

"I really have no idea. We have some of the pieces but we're missing the capstone. Heller's formula called for integrating genetic material from an earlier phase of the organism's life, a few short sequences from the *Turritopsis nutricula melanaster* jellyfish DNA, and the specific factors for the chemical compounds and molecules. The lifespan of the roundworms is so short and their reproductive cycles so quick, it's easy to get the first, and the protein sequences for the jellyfish DNA are in Heller's lab notes, but we don't have any of Heller's catalytic compound and don't have the formula to make our own. There could literally be millions of options."

Chou's words depress me. I hadn't fully realized the odds were so bleak. "Millions?"

"I'm afraid so. I've got a lot of graduate students, an unlimited supply of roundworms, and a good amount of computing power, but to say that we're looking for a needle in a haystack would be a vast understatement."

"You'll keep trying?"

Chou ignores my question. It's midnight and the lab is still buzzing. His face is lined, his bowtie crooked, and he's wearing the same shirt I've seen him in for two days.

"Rich," he says with a flicker in his eye, "if you can get me a vial of Heller's catalytic compound or the formula for how to produce more of it, it might speed up our process considerably."

"I can try," I say, fighting dejection. The first of the two vials was either destroyed with Heller's lab or gone before it blew up. My chances of tracking down the second may be entirely in Gillespie's shaky hands. And even if I can somehow find the vials, I still have no idea where to find the actual formula for the catalytic compound, without which the secret for replicating the reversion process once the vials are used or gone will be lost forever.

I stumble out of Chou's lab feeling the exhaustion catching up with me. Fueled by a toxic mix of adrenaline and caffeine, the days seem to blur into each other. Less than twenty-four hours ago I was at dinner with Shelton in his mansion. Now that world feels like a scene from another life.

The newsroom is mostly dark when I arrive, but I find a glow coming from our conference room where Joseph and Sierra quietly plug away. The four digital walls are filled to the brim with recently color-coded files, but the data still doesn't tell us the full story. I brief them on my conversations with Gillespie and Chou. Another data hub, for the Israeli Scientific Service, gets thrown up on the wall.

Joseph and Sierra look like they're about to drop. I tell them to go home so I can spend some quiet time in the conference room.

"Remind me again who you are to tell me to go home?" Sierra asks.

Joseph looks at her admiringly then turns toward me. "Not going home, boss."

I look at Sierra, then Joseph, and shake my head slightly. "All right then," I say, "let's go through this again."

We move the data around but something essential is still missing, the armature connecting the disparate pieces. I lean back in my chair and close my eyes. Nothing comes.

Then the feeling of warm drool on my hands wakes me. I lift my head with a jerk. Joseph is running on fumes as he waves his hands to move files back and forth across the wall. Sierra has somehow maintained a dose of her perkiness, but the limits of human physical capacity seem to be weighing on even her.

"Look who's awake." Sierra grins.

I look at my u.D and feel a twinge of shame. It's 3:22 a.m., and I've been asleep for over an hour.

"Why don't you go home so I can spend some quiet time in the conference room?" Sierra says dryly, taking a slug of coffee.

Touché.

"I need to go check on Toni," I say awkwardly. "Let's all get a few hours of sleep. There may be some kind of magic formula out there, but we sure as hell don't have it now and we'll all kill ourselves if we keep going like this."

Joseph looks at Sierra as she weighs my words.

"Let's meet here tomorrow morning at 8 a.m.," I say.

Only Haruki is awake to greet me enthusiastically as I enter my kitchen through the garage. He bows deeply. "Welcome home, Dikran-san—"

"Not now, Haruki," I exclaim, feeling little energy to interact with anyone or anything, including the ever-perky robot.

"Yes, Dikran-san," he says, his eyes dropping as he turns to follow my march past him on my way up the stairs.

"Please just go to the next room and power down," I say, not looking back.

"Yes, Dikran-san," he says.

Is it just my state of mind, or do I perceive sadness in his voice? I hear the wheels rolling against the tile floor as I walk up the stairs. Then I stop. "Haruki," I say quietly, turning.

Haruki is facing me at the bottom of the stairs. He tilts his head slightly and leans forward, waiting for me to speak. His eyes are bright and alert.

I freeze a moment, unsure if Haruki, in spite of all his advanced hardware and software, is more like a toaster, a dog, or a person.

Haruki lifts his head then tilts it forward again, beckoning me to speak.

More than a toaster, less than a person. "I need you to do something for me."

"Yes, Dikran-san," he says eagerly. "Please explain."

"I want you to keep an eye on Toni. Do you understand?"

"I believe you are asking me to surveil Ms. Antonia Hewitt, am I correct?"

"Something like that, yes, Haruki."

"I will do my very best, Dikran-san."

Looking into Haruki's wide, dilating eyes, I almost see cognition and wonder for a moment what our species' future is going to look like. But then old-fashioned human exhaustion catches up to me. I turn, walk up the stairs, gently open the bedroom door, climb into bed, and slide toward Toni. She pulls me into her accrued warmth, and I sink into her embrace for the fraction of a second before unconsciousness overtakes me.

It feels like the night hasn't happened at all when my u.D vibrates me awake at seven-fifteen.

"Baby," I say, whispering gently into her ear, "I've got to go. I'll be back later." I again feel guilty for leaving her when she's lost so much.

My words rouse her from her sleep. She sits up quickly, puts a hand on each of my shoulders, and looks me in the eye. "Wait a moment," she says softly. "How are you holding up?"

"I'm good," I say, feeling the urge to get back to the *Star* conference room.

"Good?" Her eyes focus sharply on mine.

There are a lot of things I want to say—that I'm afraid, that the world we've known is feeling shaky, that I need to protect her but don't even know what we may be up against—but most of those urges direct me back to the conference room. The others I suppress.

"Any more dreams?"

"No. I'm sorry," she says. "How important is it?"

"I don't know," I say quietly. "There may be no link at all, but if Heller's hypnotized you in some way and you're having dreams with the colors of floating jellyfish, maybe there's something in your sub-conscious trying to get through."

"Want to have a look?" she says with a smile, opening her mouth.

I place my palm on her forehead. "Don't I wish."

Toni rolls her eyes. "I'd probably be afraid to learn all that's going on in that overactive head of yours."

My distracted smile betrays my scattered thoughts.

"But if you think there could be something important lodged somewhere in my brain," she continues, "I'll continue looking."

She's only half mocking me, but somehow the strategy makes strange sense.

42

Joseph Abraham lied.

I step groggily into the conference room at 8 a.m. and find him in the same clothes with the same look of exhausted determination on his face as last night. An empty mug with three used tea bags stuck to its side rests on the table beside two empty SaladBar wrappers. I fight the urge to tell him he needs sleep.

"I haven't found much of anything," he says when he sees me walk in.

The rest of the wall is filled with stacked digital files. The area around the hub for the Israeli Scientific Service remains almost as unpopulated as it did last night.

"There are a lot of minor references," Joseph continues, "a lot of people raising questions in online forums, but almost no real information. It's kind of incredible."

"Incredible there's so little information? Or because it's so well hidden?"

"Probably both. All I can find is the most basic information and even that is contradictory. One site says ISS was created in 2008, another in 2017. I found one reference saying it was the brainchild of former Israeli president Shimon Peres after his ninetieth birthday but another claiming it was started by Israeli venture capitalists coming back from the failed Lebanon invasion in 2006. There's nothing definitive, certainly nothing at all put out by the Israelis."

"What the fuck, Jorge."

My spine stiffens. I turn to watch Sierra Halley put three large cups of coffee and the muffins she's brought in on the table. "Not you, too," I say wearily.

She looks up at the wall and the airiness of her Martina Hernandez impersonation dissipates. "Not much there, huh?"

"Joseph's been here all night and hasn't found much," I say. "Jerry Weisberg's working on it, too."

"No surprise it's tough gathering information on an intelligence service," Sierra says, "at least one other than ours."

"What the fuck, Jorge." This time it's the real Martina marching in.

"Good morning, madam," I say politely.

Martina is not looking at me. Her eyes focus on Sierra. "No more of that. Do I make myself clear?"

I would expect Sierra to shrink a few inches after having been caught out by Martina, but Sierra is not me. She holds her ground and nods.

I would also expect, based on all my past experience, for Martina to exact a pint of blood, but instead she turns back to me. "End of today is forty-eight hours. Where are we?"

"We're heading somewhere, Martina," I say, "it's just not exactly clear where."

"Tell me."

The three of us fill her in on what more we've learned.

"I don't think we're ready to go to print," I say as we reach the end of our summary. "We probably can't even imagine what the implications of all this might be."

"Forty-eight hours," she repeats.

"I hear you, but I just think we need to be mindful—"

"Good thing it's not your decision."

I've learned the hard way to never make a frontal assault on Martina's intransigence. I take a step back and begin working the flank. "I get that we need to cover the component parts of all this," I say. "My stories are already out about the explosions at Heller Labs and at Toni's house. We've already done profiles on the two police officers who were lost. For what it's worth, the story I filed on the disappearance of Professor Hart from the hospice is out there, even if nobody's reading it. I just don't think we're ready to cover the big picture. We still have no idea how the pieces fit together. We don't know if the science works; Chou is checking that. We don't know what the connection with Scientists Beyond Nations means. We don't know if this potential Israeli connection is real and what that says about anything."

Martina's momentary silence gives me the impression she's absorbing my comments.

"Where do you think you're working, Jorge? This is the *Kansas City Star*, not the global journal of scientific and international affairs. We don't have to prove scientific validity to report something. We don't have to crack some kind of crazy global intelligence operation. Our job is to learn what we can about things that affect Kansas City and report that."

"This isn't just about us," I fire back. "If we tip our hand before we have any idea what we're dealing with, we could be stirring a hornet's nest without any plan for what we do next. And you know the implications. Heller warned of the dangers and look what happened to him. If people believe this science is real, the whole country, the whole world could become like Buenos Aires or worse."

"How many times do I have to repeat myself? We are a news organization. Hello."

My back straightens as I prepare to push back. "If there's—"

"We *are* a news organization," Sierra says, cutting me off and looking at Martina. "Of course we need a story. Of course we need to beat our competitors to it. Whatever the implications, this all is not going to stay quiet forever. It's too late for that."

I'm again amazed by Sierra's impudence.

"We can't hold out forever, but we also can't come out before we've nailed down the basic facts. We've come a long way. Look at this wall," Sierra continues, shifting her gaze around the conference room, "but we're not there yet."

Martina's muscles tense as if she is about to pounce.

Sierra turns toward me. "What more information do *you* think we need to be ready to publish?"

"We . . . we," I stutter, thrown momentarily off-balance by Sierra's mediating between Martina and me, "should know if the science is real, what's the link with SBN, who killed Heller and blew up Toni's house, and where are Hart and Wolfson."

I can almost see the internal debate raging within Martina. "We can't just sit on this forever," she says.

"How about three more days?" Sierra says to Martina before looking briefly at me with an expression I assume to be both asking if I can live with that and telling me I'd better accept whatever she negotiates.

Martina retakes command. "I'm giving this two more days."

"Okay," Sierra says. "In forty-eight hours we put out whatever we have."

A painful silence fills the room while Martina deliberates.

"I want every detail along the way," Martina says after the pause, clearly already regretting her brief moment of compromise. She turns and walks out.

"I hope you know what you're doing, Rich," Sierra says after the dust settles.

The panic on my face can hardly be assuring. Even if the science isn't real, this story has the potential to make waves around the world. If it is real, it has the potential to alter one of the fundamental premises of our existence.

We each wander around, trying to assess the elusive connective string tying the disparate data points on our digital wall together.

My hand moves reflexively to meet the vibration on my wrist.

Gillespie's face appears in a box on the wall. "I need to speak with you," he says. "Alone," he adds, looking around the room.

"These are my colleagues Sierra Halley and Joseph Abraham," I say. "They are working closely with me on—"

"Alone," Gillespie thunders.

I hesitate a moment, then give Sierra and Joseph an apologetic shrug. They both seem rightfully annoyed in their different ways as they leave. Joseph closes the door behind them.

"Now switch to secure with the link I send you."

The message arrives and I do.

Gillespie charges forward. "US intelligence doesn't seem to be looking into anything involving Dr. Noam Heller. My contact didn't even know anything had been referred to the FBI."

"That's encouraging," I say sarcastically. The possibility briefly crosses my mind that Maurice never passed on the information. I reject the thought.

"Most of these idiots couldn't boil water."

"What about the ship?"

"The SBN carrier travels in international waters with no transponder and no readable digital footprint. It also uses the most sophisticated stealth technologies and masks its heat signature with radar-absorbent materials. That makes it extremely difficult to track."

I don't know Gillespie well enough to read where this introduction is going, but he's not the kind of person who would call me and ask me to be alone to tell me he's found nothing.

"But the laws of physics still apply, and we're talking about the United States government doing the tracking. A ship like that displaces a lot of water, which can be calculated into surface flow analyses using a sophisticated quantum interference algorithm. This only works when the SBN ship is moving, and it doesn't tend to move much, probably for this reason. But if they know close enough where to look, even a stealth carrier has a heat signature that can be tracked by satellite thermal imagers."

"And?" I say impatiently.

"Nobody in the intelligence community wants to do me any favors these days. In their minds I've already cost them enough. They think they're still cleaning up my mess." He lets the words sink in. "But I still have one or two people who owe me and haven't forgotten."

"Can you just please tell me—"

"Last Thursday, the SBN ship was tracked at approximately 56° west, 11° north."

"I'm not exactly an ancient mariner," I say, annoyed. "Can you just tell me—"

"Just outside the territorial waters of Tobago."

"So Hart and Wolfson's retinas trip the scanners in Tobago, they exit the airport with an invisible man not known to any database, and leave no trace on the island just as the SBN ship is passing by."

"Looks like it."

I close my eyes and inhale. "Do we know where the ship is now?"

"As of this morning, it seems to be resting at 25° north, 69° west."

"Can you just please—"

"International waters on the Atlantic Ocean side of Cuba."

43

"I've got to get there," I say softly.

Martina, Sierra, and Joseph join me staring at the digital map on the conference room wall.

"If Hart and Wolfson are on the ship and the vial is there, the answers have got to be there," I continue.

"What about Shelton?" Joseph asks.

"We already knew there was a connection. This confirms it."

"What are you going to do, Jorge," Martina says suspiciously, "climb aboard with a scaffolding hook?"

"I don't know."

"Why don't you just call Shelton?" Sierra adds. "The guy gave you his contact information."

"If I tip him off now," I say, "won't that increase the odds the ship just moves away? If he wanted me on that ship he could have invited me any time. It wasn't that far away when I was in Cuba. If I have any chance of getting on, it may need to be a surprise."

"What are you talking about?" Martina snaps. "This is not the fucking CIA. What's your plan?"

I weigh a set of feeble options. "I could hire a boat and approach the SBN ship."

"Where and with what money?"

"Miami, Haiti, Dominican Republic. Cuba even."

"You've come a long way, Jorge, but this is now far above your level, maybe above the *Star*'s level, too, certainly far outside the scope of the local stories we're supposed to be focusing on."

"Fuck the new business model."

"Fuck it all you want," she says calmly, "but you still won't be able to fuck the funds for an unplanned naval assault out of it."

My mind struggles to calibrate options.

"I've given you forty-eight hours," she says, turning toward the door. "The clock is ticking."

The uninspired plan is becoming clear in my mind. It has no genius, but I'm starting to believe it's the best I can come up with. I describe it to Sierra and Joseph after Martina leaves the room.

"So you fly to the Dominican Republic or Haiti or Cuba, find a boat and a captain who will take you, and then approach the SBN ship, if it's even still there?" Sierra asks dubiously. "It's a refurbished aircraft carrier, a warship. How are you going to do this without the *Star*, and what makes you think you won't be blown out of the water as you approach?"

I think of Heller's formula and the power and danger it contains, of Heller floating in the tank, of Toni in my home, of her house in ashes. "I'll handle the money," I say, already mentally subtracting the forty-six thousand dollars languishing in my bank account as I shift into gear, "and I'll need you to get back in touch with Shelton at the last minute to try to get them to not shoot. We need to coordinate exactly what needs to happen as I approach the SBN ship."

"*If* you approach the ship," she replies.

I'd love to have a better plan, but this is the best I can come up with.

"Joseph, can you to find me some options for where I can charter a boat and how I can get there?"

"Okay, boss," he says unconvinced, turning toward the wall.

I rush home on my way to the airport. It's 11:30 a.m., and Toni is uncharacteristically still in bed. Her hair is a mess, the air in the room stale.

"Baby, what happened?" I say.

She looks up at me, exhausted. "I did a little research last night on remembering what happens under hypnosis. Apparently sometimes hypnotic memories can be triggered from images. I've been looking at photos of jellyfish through my u.D. Light sleepers also seem to recall their dreams a lot more than deep sleepers. I figured I'd have a better chance if I set my u.D to keep waking me up every hour to write down what's in my head."

I love Toni's tenacity but don't have much confidence in the process, and I hate seeing her this exhausted. "You've been through a lot these past few days, sweetheart," I say, placing my hand gently on her forehead. "I'd hate for you to feel even worse by not sleeping."

"We've both been through a lot, and if there's some strange message hidden in my brain . . . I just still can't remember what happened after Heller had me look into the jellyfish medusa."

"What do you have in your notes?"

She reaches over to grab her pad. Not much. Colors. Fluorescent pinks, purples, yellows, greens. Jellyfish even, looking like long mushrooms, swallowing each other. "I can't make much of it, but it definitely seems somehow linked to my experience with Heller."

I lie on the bed beside Toni. She burrows her head into my chest.

"Maybe don't put so much pressure on yourself," I say. "Maybe memories need to work their way up from somewhere."

"There's something else," Toni adds after a silence. "I'm going nuts here."

"I'm so sorry," I say quietly.

"I know you just want me to be safe, but this is still *your* house. I've been working and looking after the kids in the hospital for most of my adult life. It's part of who I am. And even if there is a danger, it's not entirely clear I'm better off here than at the hospital. I can't be cooped up here forever. This isn't me, waiting around your house all day, filing insurance claims. I need to go back to work."

The idea makes me nervous. "I hear you, but at least here we can control some of the variables when you are here. Why don't we wait a few more days until we can learn more about what we're facing? I'm not sure it's safe for you to be out. Here we have guards at the doors. I'm hoping we can get to the bottom of all this soon."

"I know you're hoping, but can you honestly tell me you have any idea if you'll succeed? I work in a major hospital. There is security everywhere. The police officers will drive me. I'm going back to work."

I don't have an answer.

"Exactly," she says after the silence. "Settled."

"But—"

"It's really not your call, baby," she says gently. "I know you're concerned. That means a lot to me. But I need to go back to work."

I take a deep breath. I know Toni well enough to understand my chances of countering her are near zero.

"It's not just that," she continues. "I'm figuring out what I'll do with my house. I guess I'll rebuild, but there's a big question mark in my life that seems to block a lot of things."

It's probably as gently as she could have raised the issue, but it's abundantly clear the destruction of Toni's house has forced forward a set of questions that should probably have been addressed long ago. My mind scrambles for words. *I know? I understand? Let's talk when I am back?* None of the options seem worth saying.

"Which probably means you're about to tell me you're going somewhere," Toni adds.

"I'm catching a flight from KCI at two," I say quietly.

A part of me senses that giving Toni too many details might only put her in more danger. But I also know I can't head out without providing her any explanation of where I'm going and why. I fill her in on what I've learned and the plan.

She shakes her head after I finish my short explanation. "I don't like it."

"You're not alone," I respond apprehensively.

"But you're not going to budge. Are you, Dikran?"

I place my hand on her arm.

"Please don't," she says softly, looking down. "I know you're working hard, I know you're committed, I know this is important. But life can't be just about ideas and missions, it has to be about people, too. If we're going to be together, it has to be about us."

I know she's right.

"But if you need to go, go," she whispers.

44

I'm anxious on my Delta flight from Kansas City to Atlanta and jittery as I join the excited tourists and exuberant Dominican Americans filling the plane heading from Atlanta. It's nearly ten at night when we touch down in Santo Domingo, eleven when I clear customs and pass through the dilapidated airport arrivals hall. There are only a few ramshackle minivans still left at the airport. I suspect the three hundred dollars I pay to get me to the port of Arroyo Barril, on the finger jutting out from the north of the island, will be cause for weeks of celebration.

The two-and-a-half-hour drive from Santo Domingo seems to pass through an endless blaring merengue party along the pothole-ridden roads. The taxi lurches through an obstacle course of dancing, music, and drinking flowing through the streets as if the roads are just an extension of people's living rooms or some kind of omnipresent nightclub without walls. If this is what the Dominican Republic looks like after midnight on a Tuesday, it's hard to imagine how things are when they really get going.

I bang on the door of the Atlantis Hotel in Samana for almost ten minutes before I'm let in and shown to my threadbare room. Pulled awake by my u.D at six, I find no one stirring in the hotel. I look around the parking lot until I discover a man asleep in a beat-up, burnt orange Datsun F-10, the first Datsun I've seen in decades. Fifty dollars and twenty minutes later I arrive at the port of Arroyo Barril looking for my charter.

But no one is here and nothing is doing.

The waves splash against the cracking concrete of the dock. Two wooden guardhouses creak in the blowing wind, paint peeling from their sides. A few broken-down fishing boats sway back and forth, screeching the Styrofoam of their makeshift bumpers against the mooring.

I tap my u.D for Joseph. It's 5:15 a.m. in Kansas City, and this time he's asleep.

"It's supposed to be there, boss," he mumbles.

"All I can say is I am literally on the dock at Arroyo Barril and I don't see anything."

"I don't know what to tell you," Joseph repeats, waking up. "It's supposed to be an 'ocean-worthy vessel with room for six passengers.' Let me call up my notes."

I hear rustling in the background.

"I have a telephone number for the captain. I'm calling it now."

"I don't see any—"

The sound of a ringing cell phone stops me mid-sentence. I rush over to the fishing boat with Joseph still connected through my ear-piece.

"There's no answer," Joseph says.

I grab the side of the docked boat and jump aboard. The wood panels are weathered; the boat smells like rotting fish. This isn't what I'd imagined an ocean-faring charter to be. Following the ringing, I open the screeching wooden door to the small navigational room and find a rotund black man asleep on a mattress.

"What did you say the name of the ship's captain was?" I ask Joseph.

"It says Juan Jose Flores."

"Juan Jose Flores?" I repeat. Somehow the man sleeping in front of me seems neither Ahab, Stubing, nor Picard. "Are you Juan Jose Flores?" I say loudly, tapping the side of the mattress with my foot.

"*Sí*," he says, not opening his eyes or moving in any way.

"I'm Rich Azadian. My colleague spoke with you yesterday. We're supposed to be chartering a boat. I hope it's not this one."

"*Si*," he says again, cracking open his eyes and sitting up. "Is this one." His face is fleshy and broad under a balding head, his khaki pants stained and faded, his sleeveless undershirt a memory of white.

"Are you sure this boat is ocean worthy?"

He rubs his eyes. "In ocean now." He grabs a Coke from his small cooler and flips the lid.

"I mean the open ocean," I say.

"*Si*," he says slowly, taking a long sip as if that ends that. Captain Juan Jose Flores doesn't seem easily roused.

I don't know much about boats but I'm pretty sure this pile of scrap couldn't pass even the most cursory inspection. But my concern far exceeds my rudimentary Spanish. I aggressively tap my u.D. "We were told we were chartering an ocean-worthy vessel. This is not one by any stretch of the imagination. I demand we find a better boat."

My u.D sings out the words: "*Nos dijeron que estábamos fletando un buque marítimo digno. Este no lo es en ninguna extensión de la imaginación. Exijo que encontremos un mejor barco.*"

Flores is unimpressed and answers me in Spanglish. "We *vamos?*"

I take a deep breath as I scan the rest of the dock. Some of the other boats look even worse. What other options do I even have? I swallow. "Yes."

Flores rubs his face with his right hand then uses his left to push himself up. "Four thousand dollar one day. Two thousand now."

I look around suspiciously. It's highway robbery. "Do you have food and water, enough fuel?"

"*Tiene comida y agua, suficiente combustible?*" the u.D translates.

"Señor," he says slowly, ignoring the voice coming from my wrist. "You hire La *Perseverencia*, you hire *Capitan* Juan Jose Flores."

"Does the radio work?" I ask. "We'll be outside of cellular range, and I may need you to contact someone for me."

"*Funciona la radio? Vamos a estar fuera del área de cobertura del celular, y es posible que necesite a alguien para contactar a alguien por mí,*" my u.D translates.

Flores swats away the u.D language like it's a fly. "Si," he says grudgingly, "*banda lateral única*. For *emergencia* only."

"*Si se puede?*" I say, raising my fist toward the sky.

Flores looks at me and smirks. "We go?"

His humorous gesture is somehow comforting. "We go," I parrot.

"Two thousand dollars."

I hand him the cash.

"Where?"

I tap my u.D for the coordinates. "22° north, 60° west."

"*Vamos,*" he says with a nonchalant confidence.

45

The engine sputters as Flores steers us out to open sea.

"No problem?" I ask nervously, pointing at the engine.

"*Sí*," he says.

I have no idea if he means *sí*, a problem, or *sí*, no problem, but I get the feeling asking again won't clarify things. I also wonder if we're even capable of getting to the coordinates I've provided him given the antiquity of the few pieces of equipment on board.

"You have family?" I say after a long silence.

"*Sí*."

I wait for more. "Children?"

"*Sí*," he says again, focusing his gaze on the open ocean.

With not much to glean from further conversation and momentarily comforted by the thought Flores has something to lose, I step to the front of the boat and sit on the wooden deck. The briny air flows through my hair as I look out at the vast expanse around me. Growing up in Glendale I've been out on the ocean before, but the experience somehow hits me differently now.

The rawness, the smallness of our boat, the relative insignificance of our individual lives, play with my mind as we sputter forward. We understand so little about the brain and yet we've not been able to help ourselves from genetically selecting our next generations to be smarter. We comprehend next to nothing about the complex ecosystem of the oceans and yet we fish them to death and dump our waste into them as if they are inexhaustible. We hardly know what makes our lives meaningful when lived eighty years and yet our species may now be on the verge of extending them in perpetuity. Our creaky boat plods blindly along.

I think about Toni's parting words. Running to the Dominican Republic may make me an honorable person, a responsible person, a loyal person. I'm not sure it makes me a present partner. As if on cue, my u.D vibrates. I hadn't realized we were still in range. I pop in my ear piece and tap my wrist.

"Baby, it's me," Toni's excited voice says in the message. "I woke myself in the middle of the night and the pieces suddenly were clearer. I think I'm starting to remember parts of what Heller told me. Something about a place. The message is in a place. I don't have any details, but I'm remembering. Call me."

I tap, but the u.D does not respond. I tap it again frantically. Nothing.

"*Recepción?*" I yell at Flores, pointing at my u.D.

"*Non, señor.*"

"There's got to be reception. I just received a message. If there's no reception here we need to turn back to a place where we can get it."

The u.D is silent. I tap it to translate mode and repeat my sentence. Nothing.

"*Non recepción,*" Flores repeats.

"Can you make a call on your radio?"

"*Non call, señor, banda lateral única.* For *emergencia* only."

"We turn back for reception?"

"*Non, señor. Recepción* far away."

"But I just received a message."

"*Non, señor. Recepción* far away."

I have no way of assessing Flores's words. Maybe Toni's message arrived a while ago but hadn't registered on my u.D. Maybe it had but I'd missed it during my meditations on the deck. "We turn back for reception," I repeat.

"*Recepción* far away," Flores says again, this time more forcefully. "*Dos horas.*"

With all of the stratospheric balloons and solar drones circling the globe to provide Internet access, how could such swaths of the open ocean remain uncovered? "It can't be two hours. I've just received a message."

"If turn back now, no arrive today. Come back *mañana*."

I feel myself almost physically pulled in two opposite directions. But as the struggle plays out in my mind, I recognize my triage with increasing clarity. I'm desperate to know what Toni has learned and tempted to turn back or send her an *emergencia* message, but what would I say in the message? That I received her message? That I'll call her as soon as I can? And I need to keep my powder dry as the possibility of reaching the SBN ship forces me forward. I've come too far to turn back now.

"How long until we arrive?" I ask, reorienting myself toward the journey forward. I make a hand gesture trying to express what I am saying.

"*Quatro horas*," he says. "Four."

"*Gracias*."

"What there?" he asks.

"Boat," I say, tracing the outlines of our boat with my finger. "*Barco*."

Flores eyes me suspiciously, I'm sure he's wondering what kind of boat we are meeting so far into the open sea.

I have no idea how to say aircraft carrier in Spanish but sense it's probably best to not try.

"How GPS?" I say.

He takes the small device out of his pocket. It is oddly rectangular, like an old iPhone. I haven't seen a relic like this in years. The arrow on the screen points and our rickety fishing boat is heading in the same direction. The distance counter rolls down slowly. My agitation builds with every wave we crest.

Flores walks toward me with a small cardboard box. "*Tiene hambre?* You eat?" He shakes the box to counter my hesitation.

I reach out tentatively. Pulling open the flap of Flores's box, I realize what he meant when he told me a few hours ago we were supplied for the trip. The plastic-wrapped chicharron fried pork skins seem entirely unappealing, so I go for the Crokatto peanut bars. The bar almost fights back as I gnaw at it, trying to bite off a chunk. "*Gracias.*" I slur the words through the peanut clusters still congealed around my teeth.

Every twenty minutes or so, I step into the navigation room to have a look at Flores's device. Forty-two nautical miles, thirty-seven, thirty-two, twenty-nine. The number slowly ticks down as we thrust forward. At three, I can feel my heartbeat accelerating. At one, the beating becomes pounding.

At zero, my heart sinks.

Flores cuts the engine. Our small boat bobs up and down, alone atop the vast ocean.

It's a fucking ship, you idiot, I say to myself. *A ship moves. Maybe it was once here. Now it's somewhere else. Just because Gillespie said the SBN vessel tried not to move doesn't mean it can't. And now you're here in the middle of the fucking ocean and Toni is alone and you are a moron.*

I calm my internal critic a moment to think.

"*Capitan*, are you sure this works?" I say, pointing to the Chinese-made GPS device. "It works? *Funciona?*"

"*Si, funciona*," he says, looking around us wondering, I'm sure, what about this patch of ocean was worth four thousand dollars to me. "We go *casa?*"

I force my mind to focus. The SBN ship may be long gone but I am already here. Could Gillespie have given me the wrong coordinates? Could Flores's antiquated machine be off? Could the boat be listing somewhere nearby? I have no idea, but I've come this far and I'm not giving up the search without a fight.

"No *casa*. We make circle?" I say, pointing my finger in a loop around the boat.

Flores eyes me suspiciously. Wider circle patterns around a central spot are exactly what we would make if we were searching for drugs dropped from an airplane.

I start to sense why Flores has been so reticent.

"No time," he says. "Go *casa. Mal tiempo* coming."

The skies are a fierce blue but as I gaze up into the sky, I notice the ashen clouds collecting in the distance.

"We need to go circle," I say, again with my hand gesture.

"*Non*," Flores says in a voice far more forceful than I've heard from him before.

I'd found him amiable enough over the course of the day, but I only now fully realize I'm in the middle of the ocean with a lot of cash in my bag and a man I hardly know. "One hour circle," I offer. "I pay two thousand dollars more."

He shakes his head in a way I interpret more as suggesting I'm an idiot than rejecting my offer outright. "*Una hora*, four thousand dollar more."

I stare at him defiantly for only a moment, then hand him the cash.

Flores tracks our course haphazardly on his GPS machine and our dwindling time meticulously on his watch. Forty-five minutes. Nothing. Thirty minutes. Nothing. Twenty minutes . . .

Anxiety begins to overtake me as the clock ticks down. A cloud of self-doubt, of deep anger at myself, begins to form. I'm out in the middle of the open sea, sequestered and alone. It's not just that I'm here, it's that I've left everyone else in my world in order to be here. It's that I've become my own little island, bobbing up and down in the ocean of my own isolation. I feel a surge of self-loathing bubbling up from deep within. Its presence becomes almost physiological, a strange buzzing flowing through my head. I place my face in my hands. *What the fuck am I doing? What the fuck am I doing here?*

And then I notice it.

The buzzing hasn't stopped.

I look down at my hands, then hold them over my ears. The buzzing, and the sounds of the blowing wind, calms. I remove my hands and the buzzing ramps up again.

The buzzing isn't in my head.

"Do you hear that, the noise?" I shout frantically at Flores.

He stares at me, nonplussed.

I twist my head frantically in all directions trying to track the sound amid the shifting ocean air. Where, where, where? I look up. Nothing.

And then I spot it.

It could easily be missed. The small, twirling blades are almost too well camouflaged to be seen, probably digitally cloaked to match the sky. But the refraction of the sun's rays bouncing off the water creates a slight contrast.

"What's that?" I yell to Flores, pointing up.

He looks up but doesn't see it. "No see. *Que?*"

"Look. There," I say again, pointing to what now appears to be a miniature helicopter floating above us, its deep blue camouflaging it against the sky.

"*Vehículo aéreo no tripulado,*" he says.

My Spanish sucks but the English word is far simpler. Drone.

My angst vanishes as my mind swings into gear. A drone like that can't be on its own in the high seas, at least not at such a low altitude. It can't be a coincidence that both it and we are here in the same place.

"*Capitan,*" I say firmly. "I need you to radio your base. Radio. *Emergencia.*"

He stares at me blankly."

"*Emergencia!*" I repeat more forcefully.

He nods, then leads me back into the control room.

I write down the number for the base to call and spell out the name. "S-I-E-R-R-A H-A-L-L-E-Y. Tell her to make the call. Make call. *Llamada.* You understand?"

"*Si,*" Flores says, then radios in the request.

"We keep circling," I say excitedly.

"*Non, Señor,*" he says abruptly, pointing to his watch, "*diez minutos.*"

"*Non,* diez minutos," I say. "Two thousand dollars more."

"*Non.*"

His bark pushes me back, making me suddenly fear we may be on the verge of physical confrontation.

"*Mal tiempo* coming. We go *casa*, must go *casa*," he orders.

"*Capitan*, no," I plead. "*Capitan—*"

"*La creta que baina!*" A look of wonder crosses Flores's face as his eyes widen and shift focus from my face to a space over my shoulder.

I turn slowly and behold the light blue hull of the massive carrier floating city-like in the distance.

46

"Cut your engine immediately or you vill be fired upon."

The accented English booms from the helicopter drone, now hovering about twenty feet above us and no longer playing for stealth.

"I repeat, if you do not cut your engine immediately you vill be fired upon. Cut your engine *now*."

I flash Flores a hand gesture of my finger across my throat. He flips the switch.

"Take out the pistol in the floorboard in the captain's room," the voice from the drone continues. "Show me you have it, then throw it in the ocean."

I nervously make a gun gesture for Flores then point at the floor. The drone must have some kind of thermal imaging technology. Flores lifts a wooden floorboard apprehensively and takes out the gun. I take it from him gently, holding it from the tip, walk out to the front of the boat, wave it in the air, then toss it in the ocean.

"Now both of you come to the front of the boat and lie down on your stomachs vith your arms and legs spread apart."

I look over at Flores apologetically. His angry eyes make clear who he blames for getting him into this situation. His hands are shaking.

I try to keep eye contact with him as I lie down, signaling for him to do the same.

"A boarding party is heading out to you. Do not move. I repeat, *do not move*."

I hear the rev of the engine growing louder as the boat approaches, then the vibration as the boat locks on to ours. Our wooden floor-boards shake with the heavy footsteps of the boarding men. I count six pairs of black boots.

"Put your hands behind your backs," one of the men shouts in what seems a slightly Middle Eastern accent.

"My friend doesn't speak much English," I say into the floor.

"*Espanol?*" the man asks.

"*Si,*" Flores responds nervously.

"*Pon tus manos detrás de la espalda, rapido,*" he barks.

I feel the jerk of Flores's quick movements as he complies, then my u.D being stripped from my wrist and the pressure of the plastic cuff replacing it. I hear the zip as they lock down Flores's arms.

Two men grab my arms and flip me up, then push me down with my back to the boat wall. Flores doesn't resist as they do the same to him.

The six men are all dressed in black cargo pants with black boots and light blue Dri-fit polo shirts. All have close-cropped dark hair and angular, muscular bodies and appear to be in their thirties or forties. Their focused glares suggest an iron discipline and a comfort with force. I breathe deeply in a vain effort to remain calm.

"The GPS tracker is in the stern target's front right pocket," the voice from the helicopter drone says.

I look at Flores to warn him but one of the commandos is already reaching into Flores's pocket. He yanks out the GPS, places it into a small electric box they've brought aboard, then dumps the smoking mess of what's left of it into the ocean.

Flores is shaking. I sense he knows far better than I what can happen in the no man's land of the high seas.

Another commando enters the wheelhouse and comes back with the radio he's pulled from its mooring and stuffs it into the box.

"I'm going to ask you this once," the ominous voice from the drone says. "Who are you and vy are you here?"

"My name," I begin to say, my voice cracking. "My name is—"

"Stop," the voice commands. "Stand by."

I gape at the six men. The silence lingers. Their fierce faces betray nothing, as if they are prepared to do whatever needs to be done. Only the shaking Flores and I are expressive.

"Dikran Azadian?" the voice from the drone says.

"Yes?" I say, slowly and guardedly.

"You and your colleague will now be escorted to the ship. We will speak further upon your arrival."

The commandos nod to a message being fed through their earpieces. They pull Flores and me up and pass us over the side of their boat and into their Zodiac.

As the boat pulls away, I notice Flores beginning to calm.

Until the small explosion smashes through the sound of the waves.

We turn to see the burning *Perseverencia* sinking into the deep blue sea.

47

"Ship" does not feel like the right word for the colossal structure dominating the space in front of us. It's more like a land mass with a runway on top. A tall control tower with a large white ball at its head reaches from the top of the deck to the sky. A flap opens out from the back of the carrier as we approach. Our Zodiac maneuvers into the hold.

The massive landing area at the back of the ship is almost a marina in itself. Zodiacs and other small craft are suspended in the air on large conveyors. A bright spotlight beaming from above illuminates a path for our craft on the water toward a designated docking point. Reaching that place, I feel the mechanical arms lifting us from below, placing the Zodiac at equal level with the dock.

"Stand," one of the commandos orders.

Two others lift me and then Flores to our feet as a third cuts the cuffs from each of our legs. Two commandos then climb onto the dock before we are instructed to follow.

The blue jeans, T-shirt, and leather sandals of the man stepping out to meet us on the dock do nothing to make him look casual. His deeply tanned face is weathered and creased under the dome of his bald head; his graying eyebrows jut over penetrating blue eyes. His body is wiry and short like a wrestler's.

"Velcome to the SBNS *Singularity*," he says, neither his words nor tone betraying a hint of warmth.

"Quite a welcome," I say pointedly, recognizing the voice from the drone. "That ship was the captain's livelihood."

The man stares at me as if my words do not merit a response. "I'm sure you will understand, Mr. Azadian, that security here is always paramount."

He takes my arm and moves to place a small blue biometric bracelet around my wrist. His grip deepens as I instinctively pull back.

"*Everyone* on the ship has their vitals monitored at all times. It's how we maintain our health standards. We also have suppository sensors if the wrist monitor is not possible."

I relax my arm and the bracelet locks on.

Flores is still clearly shaken up by the loss of his boat and acquiesces more easily.

"Now exhale into this."

A commando lifts a small Menssanalysis device to my face. I hold my breath, not wanting to so easily provide access to my health indicators.

"The easy way or the hard way," the man says.

I lock my eyes on his, then look down and breathe. Flores follows suit.

"We have agreed to bring you and your colleague on board, to ensure your safety," the man continues. "The plane will arrive for you tomorrow morning. You will be our guests for approximately eighteen hours, and we will treat you as such. You will remain in your rooms, where you will find what you need to be moderately comfortable."

"I need to make a call," I say, "and I need to meet with the SBN Council of Elders."

He shakes his head slightly with incredulity. "Follow me."

We walk behind him through a small metal door and into a large hall lined floor to ceiling with a vast array of small drones: airplane, helicopter, and submersible. Commandos and other crew scurry purposefully about, a few augmented by exoskeletons helping them carry heavy equipment. We pass through a seemingly endless maze of long hallways and metal doors, unlocked and resealed by the commandos as we move through the ship. The walls are lined with gaudy wallpaper.

Our host notices my attention. "You are aboard a former Kiev class carrier of the Soviet navy."

"This is interesting, believe me," I say, "but I need—"

The man holds up his hand to stop me, then continues with his tour as if determined to fulfill his obligation

"The technology of the ship has been completely revamped, but the taste is actually Chinese. They bought it from the Russians in 1996 and converted it into the Tianjin Aircraft Carrier Hotel. We acquired it from them."

"My call? The elders?"

The man looks at me but doesn't answer. With a hand gesture, he tells two of his men to take Flores to his room. Flores's eyes dart at me nervously, then angrily, as the three peel off.

As we approach what appears to be my room, my panic intensifies. If he deposits me here and I'm whooshed away tomorrow morning, where will I be? He moves his open palm toward the bioscanner beside the door.

"Wait," I say sharply.

His hand keeps lifting.

"I'm not moving until you respond to my requests."

He ignores me and places his palm on the scanner. The door opens but I do not walk through.

My level of desperation is rising fast but I steady myself to take my best shot. "I know you want me off of this ship," I say. "That is clear. But you know from Shelton who I am. I'm a reporter. You can contact my editor if you like. Her name is Martina Hernandez. I can give you her contact information. I have a lot of pieces of this story. The missing scientists, the murder of Noam Heller, Heller's research, Adam Shelton's and Heller's links with Scientists Beyond Nations. We have most of the files splashed up in a conference room. If you just kick me off the ship we're going with the story tomorrow. We don't have every piece of it, but what do you think it will mean for you if we report that Heller had links with SBN, that you've kidnapped the scientists from hospices, and that you may possess the secret of total cellular reversion? Do you think the world will leave you alone? Do you think you'll be safe even in the middle of the ocean, even in your fifty-year-old aircraft carrier?"

His eyes lock angrily on mine.

"And how do you think I found you?" I press on. "Do you think I'm some kind of nautical genius? I just called a friend who used to work for American intelligence. He doesn't even work there anymore. If I can find you, you can guarantee that lots of people are going to find you if you force my paper to print the story we have, if we tell the world the fountain of youth is located on this fucking ship."

I stop a moment to let my now bulging veins calm.

"So now I'm asking you," I say, slowly and intensely. "Are you going to introduce me to the Council of Elders or are you going to grab your umbrella to prepare for the shit storm heading your way if you don't?"

48

If I were coming home drunk from a night of gambling in a Chinese casino, I'm sure this room would be perfect. The round white bed, the silver drapes, the space-age chaise longue, the zebra skin spread across the beige carpet, could all be used as a photo dictionary definition of the word "garish."

But languishing in this locked room for over an hour under the glare of the poorly hidden surveillance cameras, watching the rain pelt against my porthole window and waiting to see if my desperate words have had any effect on the imposing man in jeans, feeling my clock ticking down toward my departure, I feel imprisoned. I pace back and forth nervously.

"Mr. Azadian, I'm opening the door." The man's voice sounds from an intercom embedded in the ceiling.

I stand in the middle of the room, facing the door as it opens. The host stares at me as if sizing me up. I still don't know his name.

"Come with me."

"My call?"

"Come with me," he repeats, this time more forcefully.

I don't move.

"Please." The small word seems to pain him.

I follow him silently through multiple metal doors down a long corridor. We enter another large hall, this one with twenty or so whirling 3D printers and about ten robotic hologrometers along one of its walls. When we reach an elevator bank covered with gold mirrors, he presses a button and the doors open to reveal a red velvet and crystal-adorned interior.

"Nice," I say as I enter.

"*Xie xie*," he mutters, hardly moving a facial muscle.

The elevator goes up two levels and opens to a corridor lined with long couches upholstered in gold. He walks me to the end of the corridor, then knocks on a large door framed by silver flowers.

"It used to be the Soviet navy officer's mess. The Chinese turned it into a disco," he says, responding to the ironic smirk on my face.

The door opens electronically. He leads me in. The room is mostly dim. A plume of light highlights the six elderly people, four men and two women, standing in a loose semi-circle in the middle of what appears to be a dance floor.

I take in a deep breath, realizing where I am, as a silver-haired woman looking to be in her seventies or eighties walks toward me. Her face has a glow of wisdom, her hazel eyes radiating kindness.

"Welcome, Mr. Azadian," she says warmly.

I'm unable to speak.

"Thank you, Captain Golan," she says to the man, smiling at him until he gets the message.

"Madam," he says deferentially with a slight bow. The door closes behind him as he exits.

"We're very impressed you found us," the woman continues.

Something about her draws me in, but I still hesitate.

"Oh, I'm sorry to be so impolite," she says as if reading my hesitation. "I think you know what we are."

I nod stupidly, aware I have yet to utter a single word.

"But please allow me to tell you *who* we are."

She leads me toward the center of the room.

"My name is Lynette Margolies. The council operates as a collective, but I guess you could say I'm the secretary."

"If secretary is synonymous with queen," an elderly gaunt gentleman in a tweed jacket says in the King's English with a devilish grin.

"Oh quiet, you," she shoots back. "I guess we can start our introductions with this inveterate troublemaker."

The man frowns unconvincingly.

"Bartholomew Penrose was an Oxford don for fifty years and one of the great geniuses of mathematical physics."

"Was?" Penrose queries, feigning hurt.

"He's no longer twenty—"

Penrose's theatrical cough silences Margolies momentarily.

"But," she continues, "we get the sense once in a while he still has a few tricks up his sleeve." She points to the diminutive slouched man to her right. "Shinobu Yakamoto here was the first to develop a process for inducing any type of cell to become a stem cell, which blew open the doors of personalized and regenerative medicine."

"Doors, of course, are meant to be opened," he says slowly in a Japanese accent.

"They are indeed, Shinobu-san." Margolies points to the tall woman with cropped silver hair standing next to Yakamoto. Her posture is surprisingly erect for a woman of her age. "This is our real superstar, Frederica Singer, recipient of two Nobel prizes for her work on the biochemistry of proteins."

"Yes," Singer says, "in 1874 and 1896."

"Bite your tongue, young lady. You are a spring chicken," Margolies responds, turning back to me. "Don't believe a word of it."

I can't help but smile. I'm starting to feel like either I've stepped into the middle of a comedy routine or there is genuine warmth between the members of the council.

But an urgent thought penetrates my wonder. "I'm really honored to meet you all, but is there any way I can make a call? It's *really* important. You seem to be getting messages from Adam Shelton somehow."

"We are very sorry, Mr. Azadian," Margolies says solemnly. "Our protocols for connecting with the rest of the world do not allow that, and we are all bound absolutely to following them."

"But—"

She takes my hand in hers, then covers it warmly with her left hand. "I really hope you can understand. You will be able to communicate with the outside world during your flight tomorrow. That's not very long from now." She looks deep into my eyes and squeezes my hand gently. "Please. We don't have much time."

My face softens.

"Thank you," she says sympathetically, leading me toward another council member. "Francis Achebe here might be the greatest African scientist ever. He developed a computer model that simulated the network connections of bee colonies, which had huge implications for network architecture and data analysis."

"And it got me stung quite a few times, I might add," the elderly African man says in his buttery accent.

"And rounding out our merry little band is the indefatigable Clinton Richards, another Oxford don. We seem to be drowning in them. He is, of course, the great expert in genetics and evolution and the man who single-handedly declared war on Jehovah."

"He stah-ted it," Richards says dryly, flicking a tuft of long silver hair away from his eyes. "And, if I may," he adds, bowing slightly to the woman, "our queen—or did you say secretary, madam—in addition to her charming personality, is the mother of endosymbiotic theory, the simple yet radical idea that all species evolve in interaction with each other."

"Or at least it proves that your pain impacts my *derriere*," Margolies retorts.

The six elders face me quietly.

I stand nonplussed.

"You may speak if you like," Margolies says warmly.

"I have to admit I'm just a bit overwhelmed," I stutter. "I have a thousand questions, but . . . it's just, just so nice to meet all of you. I hadn't imagined . . ."

"We understand," Margolies says. "What we're doing is quite revolutionary. Scientists have often had troubled relations with their governments. Wernher von Braun wanted to send rockets to space and ended up being a tool of the Nazis. Heisenberg, too. Even Einstein, who escaped to America and helped win the war, had second thoughts about how his theories were used to develop the bomb. J. Robert played along but got crushed anyway."

"And so . . ." I stammer.

"And so," Richards responds, "with the dawn of this spectacular age of superconvergence, of breakthroughs folding into each other and causing the pace of technological change to increase exponentially, a number of us old timers got to thinking that science needed to advance but that governments could not be fully trusted to do the right thing."

"Scientists Beyond Nations?"

"The name is a bit gimmicky, we admit," Frederica Singer says, "but it makes the point. Beyond nations but not beyond accountability. That's what our council is about. We don't believe in stopping the progress of science. Quite the opposite, actually. We only believe in filtering some of its most potentially dangerous applications, or, should I say, protecting them from being monopolized and used for nefarious purposes by governments or others with ulterior motives."

"Is that even possible?"

"We think so." Singer leans in to make her point. "We're not against governments and others having access to this science. Not at all. We just try to influence how, how much, and when it is made available. We try to hold ourselves to a higher standard of global accountability. Will our approach work over time? Our hypothesis will need to stand up under observation and challenge."

"And experimentation?" I ask, my mind shifting to thoughts of Heller.

"We know that is why you are here, Mr. Azadian," Margolies says, "and, to be quite honest, we are a bit desperate to learn more of what you know."

Recognizing I may have something of value to this illustrious team gives me a small burst of confidence. "I believe you already may have learned quite a bit from Adam Shelton."

"Yes, of course." Margolies nods. "But we need to hear it from you and we have many more questions."

"I have a lot of questions, too."

"And we will answer them," Achebe tells me, his tone authoritative and convincing as he leads me toward a circle of chairs just beside the dance floor. "Please let us all sit down and begin our conversation. May we offer you some tea? This will likely be a long night."

<u>49</u>

A small voice in my head advises caution, but something about this warm, wise, and brilliant group overcomes my reservations. In a strange way, Heller has brought us together by dividing up access to his files. I'm in desperate need of information they have and sense deeply that the only way I'll get it is by trusting them.

I walk them through every detail of what I've learned over the past eight days since I first showed up at the Kansas City hospice. They fire questions at me as I speak, asking for more specific details about my conversations with Heller, the configuration of his lab, what happened when Heller was alone with Toni in the dark room. It's an exhausting interrogation, but as my story brings me to the SBN ship, it is time for the tables to turn.

"Thank you for your candor," Margolies says. "We appreciate it greatly."

I nod. "Are *you* ready?'

"Of course we are," Penrose says. "We would not have let you get this far if we were not. But before we go on, we must establish one basic ground rule."

I bristle. We've been at this for over three hours, I've laid my cards on the table, and *now* we need to establish ground rules?

Penrose seems to read my expression. "You have put your faith in us, and we will do the same with you, but, to quote the Bible and Spider-Man, 'with great knowledge comes great responsibility.'"

"It's 'great power,' Bartholomew," Singer interjects.

"Of course, dear," he says quietly under his breath. "I've taken the liberty of improvisation."

"What he's trying to say, or would be trying to say if he ever got around to it," Margolies jumps in, rolling her eyes, "is that you cannot publish anything that would compromise the safety and security of our mission here."

"That's a pretty broad request."

"We're at least smart enough to know," she continues, "that our only meaningful leverage with you is our mutual trust. Everything else is mere formality. We made a collective decision to trust you after you arrived on this ship. You have already demonstrated your trust in us. All we are saying is we must simply operationalize the trust we have in each other. Do you understand?"

"May I ask why you decided to trust me?"

"You are obviously a smart and resourceful person with respectable, if sometimes risky, judgment."

"And?" I ask, not fully convinced I've received the full answer.

"And because we are so concerned about the death of Noam Heller. Noam was a gifted scientist and a great man," Penrose says. "Forces beyond our control are at play. To counter them, we simply must know more, and trust is a two-way street."

"I only met Heller briefly," I say, "but from what I experienced, I would tend to agree he was a great man." I pause to let my words settle. "But I'm here because I believe there's a connection between Heller's research, the disappearance of Hart, Wolfson, and the others, Heller's death, and the two explosions."

"Of course there is," Margolies says softly, "but if we had all the answers, you would not be here right now. Please ask us your questions, Mr. Azadian. Before you begin, however, let me state categorically on behalf of all of us that SBN had nothing to do with Heller's death or the destruction of Heller's lab or Ms. Hewitt's home. On that we give you our word."

Margolies only confirms what I feel in my gut to be true, but her words launch an avalanche of worry in my brain. If SBN was not involved, who is? And what are they doing now? The urgent questions pile up. I feel the conflicting urges to stay here and have them answered and to rush home as quickly as possible. But the plane will not arrive for four more hours. For now, I have only one choice.

"Heller's lab notes described the process of total cellular reversion," I say. "My friend, Professor Franklin Chou—of the University of Missouri–Kansas City, did the cellular analysis of Heller's dog and the results indicated the process worked. My first question is whether total cellular reversion works, does it work on humans, and, as I presume to be the case, are Hart and Wolfson and the others on board this ship?"

The six elders look at each other and nod slightly before Yakamoto speaks. "Yes, yes, and yes. Next question?"

I breathe in deeply. "Dr. Heller provided the two encryption keys to gain access to his database. I gave one to Adam Shelton a few days ago. May I assume that he gave it to you and that you have accessed Heller's database?"

"Yes," Margolies replies, "of course."

"And that you changed the encryption signature once you were in?"

"Yes," she repeats. "Well, we ourselves didn't do that, but SBN did."

"And that you have access to the final file in which the formula for Heller's catalytic compound formula is described?"

Silence blankets the room.

"No," Professor Penrose says after the heavy pause. "That catalytic compound is the key to the reversion process. We have the limited amount of the substance itself provided to us by Noam, but its folded proteins make it impossible to reverse engineer. Without the formula for how to create the compound, reversions will be impossible after the meager doses we have run out. We had hoped you might provide us with additional information about where the formula might be found."

"Unfortunately, I've told you all I know."

"So what basis do you have for your theory that Heller transferred that information to Ms. Hewitt in their moments together in the lab?" Singer asks.

"I don't think it's just a theory anymore. Toni left me a message saying she's starting to remember fragments of her experience in Heller's jellyfish room. She thinks he may have told her about a place."

"What kind of place?" Singer asks.

"I don't know. That's why I'm so desperate to call her. Maybe a remote server where an encrypted digital file is hidden. It could be a lot of things."

Achebe chuckles. "Mr. Azadian, I studied bees, very simple organisms, to demonstrate how many simple actions can collectively create a complex system. We should at least consider the possibility that Heller's formula is not stored electronically. For all we know he could have told her to look under a certain tree beside the river."

"How much of the catalytic compound did Heller provide in the vial he gave you?"

"Not a great deal," Richards replies, shaking his head slightly.

"Which means?"

"Enough for two more reversions at most, with a small sample put aside for further analysis."

"Who are you reverting?"

The elders look at each other cautiously before Margolies speaks.

"Five of the scientists went through the procedure at Heller's lab in Kansas City, including Professor Hart and Dr. Wolfson. Once we understood the process and had the vials Noam shared with us, three others were given the treatment here."

"And why?" I ask, suspecting I may already know the answer.

"The child is the father of the man, Mr. Azadian," she continues. "We believe in the promise of our mission but can't guarantee we will always have the brainpower to remain at the forefront of scientific discovery. Our plan was and is to bring great scientists to our cause and our ship and to have the elders reverted to earlier versions of themselves, mentoring a generation of assistants and then in turn becoming assistants to their former assistants. Of course they lose the memories of their older selves in the reversion process, but it's far better to engage their newly young minds than take their old wisdom to the grave."

Singer picks up where Margolies leaves off. "It's a way of harnessing spectacular brainpower to boomerang scientific discovery *ad infinitum*. We're making progress in telekinesis, neural network emulation, and connectomics, so someday we'll be good enough at downloading minds that the mental reversion could become obsolete. Now, we're only at the beginning of that process."

"And Heller's work was the key to everything?" I say as if chancing on the realization I've just been spoon-fed.

"Of course. That's why we funded it so generously once we learned of his progress," Richards says.

"But I though the big health company was funding him?"

Richards brushes the sinking tuft of hair back toward his forehead. "They were funding his cancer research. What he needed to prove his theory of total cellular reversion went far beyond what they were capable of providing or what he would trust them to do. It required some of the greatest minds and most sophisticated computer modeling systems ever applied. Heller kept his cards close to his vest, so to speak, but he could never have progressed as he did without a great deal of assistance. In the later stages, his work also required human subjects that are rather difficult to acquire."

My mind shifts back to the Kansas City hospice. "And you are trying to tell me that a bunch of, forgive me, elderly scientists on a ship in the middle of the ocean arranged for people to be kidnapped from hospices across the United States, maybe around the world, hacking into security systems to bypass video feeds and erasing personal files?"

"As I'm sure we are making quite clear, Mr. Azadian," Dr. Singer says testily, her back even straighter than before, "you should never underestimate the power of the determined elderly."

"And the two hundred and seventy-four scientists on this vessel are not just old codgers like us," Richards adds. "We have brilliant scientists of all ages toiling away in the nooks and crannies. The pipeline of innovations is breathtaking."

"But presumably all of you would be reverted if you had the formula or enough of the catalytic compound?"

"That would go without saying," Margolies says, "at least over time."

"But until then," Achebe adds, "the greatest contribution we can make is in the application of what wisdom we have sometimes painfully accrued over the many years of our lives. None of us may be as sharp as we once were, but we've all become better people as our brains have continuously slowed. Aging can be cruel, but we should never forget its magnificence."

I push on. "My contact in the US intelligence community told me of rumors that SBN is funded by and is a front organization for the Israeli Scientific Service, of Israeli intelligence. There seem to be a lot of commandos with Middle Eastern accents on this ship."

The elders look nervously at each other before Margolies speaks.

"We do have Israelis on this ship. We also have one hundred and five Filipinos and eighty-three Mongolians on its crew."

I eye her suspiciously.

"We can neither confirm nor deny that assertion, Mr. Azadian, but some have called us partially funded, possibly connected—not a front organization. But even if that were true, one might theoretically assume there could be a mutuality of interest, a desire on our part to expand the frontiers and applications of revolutionary science and, perhaps, a desire of theirs to gain access to new technologies that could provide a key to national survival. Survival is our species' most basic instinct, a laudable one. From that perspective, it might sound like a fair deal. One might imagine that Noam Heller understood that and came to the same conclusion."

I realize she is saying as much as she possibly can and decide not to push. "So they were the ones who kidnapped Hart, Wolfson, and the others?" I grant myself an exception.

"Kidnapped is a loaded word," Richards says. "Those men were rescued from the cruel fangs of nature."

"And their families?"

"Their families would have mourned them either way. By the laws of uncountered nature, their families had experienced all there was of those men, perhaps minus a few dying words as their hearts flatlined."

The words are harsh, perhaps almost as harsh as nature. "And Shelton, his background in Israel?"

"One could imagine that Shelton, SBN, and the Israelis are each playing an essential and complementary role making all this possible. Shelton might be connected to the same intelligence agency, but it would not be for us to divulge," Margolies says. "Just like our deadly serious Captain Golan here. He tries to hide it with the jeans and T-shirt, but he might as well have his professional identity written on his forehead."

The data floods my brain. I imagine throwing each bit of information up on the wall in our *Star* conference room as I struggle to pull the pieces together. "I need two things from you," I say firmly, "and I will not take no for an answer."

The elders stare at me through the silence.

"I will protect you as much as possible and appropriately," I say, "but I demand your firm commitment that you, and I mean all of you and Israeli intelligence and Shelton and anyone else you can muster, will do everything in your power to help me find out who killed Heller and triggered the explosions . . . and help me protect Antonia Hewitt."

Margolies responds without hesitation. "It is in our interest to find out who killed Heller, may have stolen the vial, and threatened Ms. Hewitt," she says. "We give you our word we will do all we can. Second?"

My mind shifts back to Katherine Hart staring longingly at the photo in her living room. "I am leaving this ship in three and a half hours. Before I go, I insist that I meet with Hart and Wolfson."

50

The tour is at best half-assed and at worst grudging. But Lynette Margolies's instructions that I should be "shown around" on my way to the coffee salon were clear and Captain Golan is, at least technically, complying.

We pass through a long hall where additional small helicopters and fixed wing drone aircraft rest on conveyors. Robotic Delivery Carts roll quietly along.

"When the ship was being used by the Soviet navy," Golan offers, "it was always surrounded by a battle group. We don't have that, so we try to make do with our stealth technology and low electromagnetic profile on the one hand and with circling drones and free electron lasers on the other. Not perfect, but not bad."

"And what do you do for energy?" I ask. "I can't imagine you pulling into gas stations."

"The entire ship has been configured for sustainability and self-reliance. The flight deck runway is made of solar panels. We have a magnetic fusion reactor in the aft and ferromagnetic buoys trailing the ship feeding energy from ocean waves into our magnetostriction generator."

"And food?"

Golan's face animates. "There's a greenhouse on the flight deck, but most of our gardening is done in one of the interior airplane storage facilities that we converted into a vertical indoor farm. Each plant gets the right wavelength of light from our hydroponic light-emitting diode system and the exact nutrients it needs based on constant sensing. Water is desalinated through the reactor and recycled continuously. We culture our meat and dairy in vitro. Conservation is our obsession, the key to our survival."

The ship is huge, with hundreds of different rooms and halls. He walks me quickly through the extensive bio lab, the robotics factory, the particle physics workshop, as well as the ship clinic, where he shows me the 3D bioprinters pumping out personalized bioceuticals matching the genomic indicators of each patient and customizing tissues for implantation. It's the middle of the night, but the machines are humming and scientists working away.

It starts to feel claustrophobic. "What about connecting to the outside world? Science doesn't exist in a vacuum," I say.

"We are connected to the grid," Golan says, "just insulated from it as well. Our scientists have access to all of the research papers from anywhere in the world. Secure conversations with scientists not on the ship are more complicated, but we're able to accomplish a great deal with holoportation."

"And people just work here, all day and all night, almost entirely cut off . . . forever?"

"Some people have bigger goals than just entertainment," Golan says derisively.

"Like living their lives?"

The look on Golan's face makes clear once again that he doesn't appreciate my snarkiness. "We have coffee salons, lecture series, our own internal university, and virtual reality pods where people can spend hours exploring other worlds," he says, giving me the impression he sees entering virtual reality as a mark of weakness. "We even have our own transcranial direct-current stimulation room and a karaoke bar," he adds with a hint of a smile, "apparently a must on any vessel carrying so many Filipinos."

He leads me through a small metal door into the coffee salon. The room's velvet chairs and dark wooden paneling give it the feel of an old Viennese café.

I sit nervously and wait. I know intellectually what is coming, but I sense that no amount of thinking can prepare me for what I am about to experience. Sebastian was one thing, but I never met his wife. The fact of him didn't fundamentally transform human mortality. I brace myself to enter, perhaps once and for all, a world where the basic axiom of human existence is forever turned on its head. It's one thing in principle, quite another over coffee.

The door swings open and the two men stride in. I recognize them immediately. They are roughly my age. Hart is tall and gangly, his movements almost awkward. His wavy brown hair and thick glasses rest over an intelligent smile. Wolfson is short and round with frizzy reddish hair, bushy eyebrows, shiny green eyes, and an impish grin.

I stand, unable to move any further. I reach out to touch them as if feeling the skin on their hands will somehow confirm this unbelievable miracle is real. Wolfson leans toward me, but Hart lifts his hand to meet mine. I grab it softly and rub it around, then gently squeeze his forearm. I stare back and forth between the two of them.

"Well, hello to you," Hart says wryly.

His strong voice knocks me from my spell. "I'm so sorry," I say quietly, "it's just I was in your home in Overland Park a week ago."

"What house—" He cuts himself off mid-sentence. "I'm sorry. Sometimes it's easy to forget."

I don't let go of his hand, holding it softly as my words slip past the gates of my consciousness. "I sat in your living room with your wife Katherine. She told me about your daughters, Dalia and Ofira."

Tears well in Hart's eyes. "My babies . . ."

"Are married with babies. Five grandchildren, I think she said. She showed me a record you gave her for your fifth anniversary."

His head droops before a distant smile crosses his face. "'Crazy Little Thing Called Love,'" he whispers wistfully. "I remember it like it was yesterday. For me, it almost was. Would you mind telling me every detail of your interaction?"

He holds onto my words as if each is a rope dangling from another life, a past that will never be his future.

"And I spoke with your grandson in St. Louis," I add, looking at Wolfson. "He seems like a good kid."

Wolfson nods soberly. "They've told us about our histories," he says after a heavy pause. "We just don't remember them."

The two men seem to recuperate in the silence from the emotional shock of my words.

"Can we offer you more coffee?" Wolfson adds. "We even have *sachertorte* if you like that sort of thing."

It is still unclear if I am their potential liberator or they are my hosts. I look them each in the eye, then nod slightly. "A plane is coming for me in two and a half hours," I say.

"We know," Hart says.

"And I have so much I need to discuss with you before I go."

"It's four thirty in the morning," Hart says. "Sometimes an entire lifetime must be condensed into a few hours."

"They briefed you?" I say.

"They had an entire dossier on each of us," Wolfson says. "As many digital photos as they could grab from our networks, the research files and papers we'd amassed over our careers, videos from vacations . . ."

"Ofira's bat mitzvah party," Hart says with a surprising smile.

"The recipe for my wife's tiramisu," Wolfson adds, plugging into Hart's rally.

"We can't tell you how much time we've spent trying to decipher the memory fragments they downloaded from our brains during the reversion process."

My mind races back to the helmet I'd observed in Heller's lab just after we found his body floating in the jellyfish tank. "Can you tell me more about that?"

"That's yet another thing that's blown us away," Hart says, "Forty years ago, no one had ever heard of neuroinformatics, connectomics, or brain-computer interfaces. No one could have imagined what a functional MRI machine could do or even pronounced the word electrocorticography. We've just started learning and it still feels like magic. They told us it was only in an experimental phase, but apparently there's a way to download memories as they are being erased during the reversion process."

"Does it work?" I ask incredulously.

"Bits and pieces," Wolfson says with a shrug. "It's almost like a fuzzy slide show with a lot of the slides missing. We've been in constant training these past weeks, filling in the gaps with electronic education modules and all kinds of reading about the past forty years."

"But was going through the reversion your choice?"

"How could we have made a choice like that?" Wolfson asks, as if my question is absurd. "We were both practically vegetables."

"Or at least they told us we were vegetables. We had videos and photos and medical records for that, too," Hart says.

"And when you woke up you were forty years younger?"

"Something like that," Hart admits, "just suddenly a bit discombobulated and in a strange new place."

"And truly with no memories of ever being fifty or sixty or seventy?"

"None," Hart says. "I had a strange scar on my stomach I didn't remember. I was missing a few teeth. Frankly, if they hadn't done such a good job of convincing us, I'm sure we'd have both thought this entire thing was a hoax."

"You have to understand," Wolfson adds, "our minds were still both in the middle of the 1980s. You're probably too young to remember, but the computer era was just starting. Ronald Reagan was president.

"We were both pretty hesitant at first, but they showed us the diode screens, the digital walls, the Augmented Retinal Display lenses, the fMRI magnetic electrocorticography helmets, the miracle of miracles you call the Internet. It was clear pretty quickly that either we'd been abducted by futuristic space aliens who happened to speak our language or what they were telling us might actually be true."

"But did you actually make a decision?" I repeat.

"It's impossible to answer that question," Hart says. "Once

we accepted their version of what had happened, we could have demanded to be returned to our families, to our children who were now our own age, to our wives who were now older than the age of our mothers, at least the age we thought our mothers were. What would we have done? Of course we miss our wives, the families as we knew them. There's hardly a moment that goes by when I don't think of Katherine." Hart's eyes begin to glaze. "She's in my dreams every night . . ."

"And where would we have gone?" Wolfson jumps in to relieve Hart. "They told us we had been chosen and they were right. As far as we know, eight people in the history of our species have ever been reverted to an earlier age on a cellular level. Ephraim, Michaela, Solomon, the two of us who went through the process with Noam, and David, Sasha, and Vlad who did it on the ship. And to have been brought back to live another life dedicated to the pursuit of scientific knowledge with a lab to die for, well"—he reconsiders—"not really, and unlimited funding?"

"Bill is right," Hart interjects. "Maybe we could have gone back. Maybe we could have made a run for it, even though they were careful to not give us the chance. But nature is cruel and it just may be that tricking nature requires a certain level of ingenuity, maybe sometimes even a commensurate cruelty of its own."

"And Katherine?" I say, perhaps cruelly.

"I can't know the woman she is now, what she must be like, but I know who she was, and I know how much she loved knowledge. And if she is mourning me having disappeared, I imagine she would also be mourning me if I were truly gone. I can't even imagine what she's going through. I've been given a great gift, but I also began mourning Katherine the moment I accepted what had happened. I've seen the photos and the video of the past decades, I've seen the blurred images from the fMRI and the ECoG, but in my head she is still thirty-two and doing back flips in the pool, still beaming at me when I surprised her on her birthday at her lab at Kansas University Medical Center; she's still painting cat whiskers on the girls' faces."

"It's ironic," Wolfson says, "they've gone to such lengths to recreate memories of our past lives but also to cover their tracks by destroying the records of our existence available to the outside world.

"And what about Heller?"

"Noam was a great man, a great scientist, a genius," Wolfson says wistfully. "He sat with each of us all night after our transfusions. It was an incredible shock, of course, but he eased and welcomed us into our new reality."

"Your eternal sonata," I add. *A tribute to your wife, the music never stops.* Heller had lost Yael but his eternal sonata was not only the music, it was Sebastian as the continuation of Yael's parting gift, it was Hart and Wolfson and the others carrying their thirsts for knowledge in perpetuity, it was overcoming death itself while recognizing the wonder and the danger of what he had accomplished.

"Do you know that Heller is dead?" I ask.

Pain blankets both of their faces.

"We do," Hart says softly.

"It's funny," Wolfson says, "Noam was chronologically younger than us but he's also our father in some ways."

"And we are technically the same age as the people you just met with from the Council of Elders, but now we are their research assistants," Hart adds. "If we crack the code of Heller's formula for the catalytic compound, some day they will be ours."

"How did you get out of Heller's lab?"

"New identity papers, a private plane," Wolfson says, then describes the longer journey.

"Courtesy of Israeli intelligence?"

"Not all intelligence is stupid, Mr. Azadian," Hart says, responding to my tone. "What's happening here could very well be called enlightened."

"Even if it's benefiting one country?"

"One country that's trying to save itself from destruction. It can't be lost on you or any of us that the eight chosen ones, the immortals for now, are all Jews. Both of us were born in the mid-forties. For

Jews and maybe for all people who have faced extinction, survival isn't something to be taken for granted. Sometimes it even needs to be fought for," Hart says.

"I'm an Armenian American," I say. "Believe me, I know that from my own history."

"And if a country is going to fight," Wolfson adds, "how wonderful it tries to do so by advancing human knowledge. This same level of effort dedicated to nuclear or chemical weapons and biological warfare agents could have also been a strategy for Israel. In the relative scheme of things, helping a bunch of idealistic scientists float around the open ocean doing research and trying to figure out how best to use it would not be such a terrible thing."

"Even for the scientists *beyond* nations?"

"I guess there are gradations of that word," Hart replies. "If the world were simpler, our jobs would be a lot easier and life would be far less painful."

"And far less magical," Wolfson adds, a twinkle in his eye.

After two hours of conversation, Golan strides back into the room. My body instinctively stiffens as I see him.

"The plane will be here in thirty minutes. We need to be on the flight deck in twenty," he says politely, as though he can read the emotional signature of the room. "I'll need to take you up in ten." He turns back toward the door and steps out obsequiously.

The mention of the clock retriggers mine. Two burning questions sear themselves back into my brain with a burning intensity.

"Can both of you please tell me," I say softly, "what you think I should tell your families?"

Hart and Wolfson look at each other. I get the feeling traveling through mortality together has given them some kind of existential connection.

"We thank you for all you have done, Mr. Azadian," Hart says, "but those lives, those wonderful lives that we've studied but feel like we've never known, are better left untouched. We are here with the memories of the lives we know and I hope our families are cherishing the memories of the lives we lived but don't remember. Perhaps," he says with a profound sadness, "it is better to leave things as they are."

The second set of questions overcomes even the intense profundity of this moment.

I am here, on this ship, in this ocean, facing the miracle of our species' transcendence.

I have learned so much but my every fiber knows I have answered nothing.

I have come so far but the questions that propelled me here remain terrifyingly unanswered.

Who killed Noam Heller?

Who destroyed Heller Labs?

Who blew up Toni's house?

Who may be still trying to kill Toni even now as I sit with this stupid fucking coffee cup in my hand in the middle of fucking nowhere?

51

The six elders greet me warmly as I enter the glass-enclosed command room overlooking the flight deck.

Lynette Margolies reads the nervousness on my face. "I hope you understand by now how much trust we're placing in you with the sensitive information we have shared."

"I do."

"And we hope you accept we had nothing to do with the murder of Noam Heller or the two explosions. Why would we harm the one person whose knowledge contains the key to our future? Noam should have been one of us instead of facing such a tragic end."

I've been mulling that question all night and have arrived at the same conclusion.

She takes my hand and cradles it in both of hers. "The world is a dangerous place, Mr. Azadian. We know that. That is why we are here in the first place. There are many people, many organizations, many intelligence services, even, who are profoundly opposed to what little they know about us. I imagine if they knew everything, we might simultaneously have greater leverage and face greater dangers. Do you understand?"

"Yes," I say. I appreciate her words but am beyond eager to get moving.

"We don't know who killed Noam and threatened your lady-friend, but whoever or whatever organization did those things is as much a threat to us as it is to you. Are you following me?"

I nod. "And I am also mindful of the promises you've made to me."

"Good." She turns toward Captain Golan and gives him a signal to speak.

"When the plane arrives in four minutes, you and Captain Flores will be onboarded at the far end of the runway," Golan says. "The plane will only stop for a matter of minutes, so you will need to move quickly."

Margolies gives Golan a hand signal to speed things up.

"You have asked about communications systems on the plane," Golan continues. "The plane has an Iridium Telephonic Communication System. The ITCS will not be activated for security reasons for the first thirty minutes of your flight."

"And Flores?" I ask.

"The plane will stop momentarily at Mr. Shelton's compound in Cuba. Captain Flores will get off the plane at that time and arrangements will be made for his return to Arroyo Barril."

"How will he support himself now that—"

"You are a good man to ask that question." Francis Achebe says, taking a small step forward. "Arrangements will be made for the provision of a new boat, a much better boat. This has already been communicated to Captain Flores."

"Here is your universal.Device," Golan adds, reaching down to wrap it around my right wrist, then unlocking and removing the biosensor bracelet from my left. "I have transferred a biometric application to your u.D that will first learn and then respond to your cardiac signature only. If and when you want to contact us you must open this application while the u.D is on your wrist with your biometric settings on. At that time, an access number will flash momentarily on your screen. Each time you do this, the number will be different. No number will ever be used twice. Call that number and leave a message. It will be delivered to us immediately. And by the way, your potassium levels are low. You should be eating more spinach."

I look at Golan, not sure how to respond. The transformation of my experience on the ship from entry to exit is too profound.

"*Et voila*," he adds, looking out the window wall at Shelton's Airbus fast approaching. "*Yallah*."

I turn to face the six elders, feeling a strange cocktail of emotions.

Shinobu Yakamoto is first to break the awkwardness. He steps forward.

"*Domo arigato*, Mr. Azadian," he says before bowing.

I match his bow. "You should write a song about that," I murmur, unable to help myself.

"I assure you," Frederica Singer says with a slight grin, "he has not the faintest idea what you're talking about, but on behalf of all of us we want to thank you and stress again how essential it is that we maintain our bond of mutual respect and support, that you will respect our absolute need for discretion."

The rest of the elders circle closely around me, shaking my hand, patting me on the back, or, in the case of Margolies and Achebe, hugging me warmly.

It doesn't take much for Golan to pull me away. As connected as I feel to the elders, I know where I need to be.

We meet Flores and the two commandos with him on the runway. Flores is wearing new khaki pants and an oxford shirt and carrying a *cerveza*. His wide smile confirms to me they've already told him about his boat. We shake hands.

As we approach the taxiing plane, I observe the massive greenhouse lining the runway and the running track and vitacourse extending the full length of the ship. Crew members in T-shirts and shorts run up and down. In the madness of this extreme isolation, it seems a strange new form of community is budding, a Noah's Ark for the exponential future.

The plane comes to a stop and its door opens. Paige Newmark, as perfectly put together and formal as ever, steps down to meet us.

"*Maher, maher*," Golan barks, "let's go." He practically pushes us up the stairs.

Flores's mouth drops as he takes in the luxuriousness of the interior. "*He visto mejores*," he says with a smile.

"You'll need to strap yourselves in tightly," Paige Newmark says as the door closes. "I don't know if you've experienced a carrier take-off before, but the G-force from the electromagnetic launch can be quite powerful."

The ground crew turns the plane and locks us on to the magnetic catapult. I look out my window to see the elders watching solemnly from their perch. Then I glance down at my u.D and set the timer to thirty minutes.

The magnetic lunge slings us into the air and we are gone.

Twenty-nine, twenty-eight, twenty-seven, twenty-six.

Each minute feels like an hour.

Seventeen, sixteen, fifteen.

Maybe everything is fine, or at least as it was when I left Kansas City two days ago. It's just that I don't know. It's just that I need to hear Toni's voice telling me it is, telling me what she has remembered.

Five, four, three . . .

My u.D flashes zero. I put in the earpiece and tap the instruction on my wrist.

System not activated.

"I was told the phone would be functioning thirty minutes after takeoff," I plead to Ms. Newmark.

She looks down at her u.D. "Let me speak with the captain."

She steps into the cockpit and returns a couple of long minutes later. "It is now working. You may place your calls."

My heart races as I tap in. It's six thirty in the morning in Kansas City. I picture Toni lying in my bed or preparing her morning coffee.

Ring, ring.

Come on, baby, pick up.

Ring, ring.

"This is Toni," the voicemail says. "I'm so sorry to have missed you . . ."

Could she still be asleep? I kill the call and try again.

My body tenses with each ring.

"This is Toni," her voice again says sweetly. "I'm so sorry to have . . ."

Fuck.

I tap my u.D to call up her mother's number.

"Mrs. Hewitt, Elizabeth," I say, trying to maintain an element of calm in my voice, "it's Rich."

"Good morning, Rich," she says groggily. "Is everything okay?"

"I'm sure it is," I say unconvincingly. "I'm flying back to Kansas City this morning. I just tried Toni on her phone and she didn't answer. I wanted to see if you knew anything."

"She was going back to work this morning. The shifts got rearranged when she took her days off and they hadn't expected her to come back so soon. She told us yesterday she was on the early shift for the rest of the week, starting at five in the morning."

"Thanks so much for letting me know," I say, feeling a bit relieved. "Sorry to have bothered you. Please go back to sleep."

"Call any time, Rich," she says before the connection cuts.

My body begins to relax as I place the next call.

"NICU," the duty nurse answers.

"Good morning," I say. "This is Rich Azadian, Antonia Hewitt's boyfriend."

"I know who you are, Rich," she says warmly.

"I'm calling to talk with Toni if she's available, please."

"I'm sorry, she's not here yet."

I feel the knot yanking my stomach. "Wasn't her shift supposed to start an hour and forty minutes ago?"

"It was, but we know she's been through a lot these past days and she's not exactly used to the early mornings. We're more than happy to cover for her all morning if she's still asleep."

My pounding heart shakes my entire body. Could she be still asleep? I call her two more times. Still no answer. When we land momentarily in Shelton's private airport in Cuba to drop Flores off, I take the captain's hand quickly and tell him goodbye, but my mind is frantically elsewhere as the plane takes off again. *Where could she be?*

A calming thought enters my mind. Haruki. I tap an icon on my u.D I've never before used.

"Yes, Dikran-san?" he says. "How may I be of service?"

His cheery voice soothes me. "I need you to tell me if Toni is still in the house."

"No, Dikran-san."

I feel my heart falling. "What time did she leave?"

"She left at 4:47 a.m. central daylight time, Dikran-san."

"What was she wearing, Haruki?" I ask, the fear rising within me.

"A white uniform traditionally worn by those in the nursing profession. May I—"

I tap off Haruki and urgently scroll for Maurice.

"Back from the beyond?" he says after tapping in.

"I can't get hold of Toni."

"All right," he says calmly. "I understand my men are still with her."

"She's not answering her phone. She left the house at a quarter to five this morning in her nurse's uniform. She was supposed to be on the 5 a.m. shift at Truman but didn't show up. I need to know if she's with your protection team."

"I imagine she is but stand by, Rich," Maurice says. "I'm putting you on hold."

I try to control my nerves as the line goes silent.

Maurice returns a few moments later. His voice is entirely changed. "They escorted her to the hospital at 4:59 a.m. She told them she didn't need security in the hospital so they waited outside. They're still there."

Every nerve in my body activates in panic. "What the fuck, Maurice?"

"I've ordered my men into the hospital to search for her. I've got three more cars on their way. We're in touch with hospital security. I'm heading over there now. It's premature to jump to conclusions."

"Premature?" I shout, beside myself. "Those guys were supposed to be protecting her."

"I know, Rich," Maurice says. "I get it. She's most likely still in the hospital. I'm getting in my car now. I'll be there in ten minutes. Call me in fifteen."

I can hardly breathe as the line drops.

"Is everything okay?" Ms. Newmark asks.

My face is too paralyzed to answer.

After thirteen minutes I can't take it any longer.

I feel the weight of Maurice's silence as the line connects. A part of me fears breaking it.

"The surveillance cameras show her being approached by a man and a woman as she passes through the lobby," he says quietly. "Both of them are wearing hats obscuring their faces from the cameras. The feeds show them walking her to a room, then emerging ten minutes later."

It takes every ounce of energy I have to fight the convulsions of fear surging through my body.

"I'm sorry, Rich," Maurice says gravely, "but the cameras show the two people dressed in scrubs and masks coming out of the same room wheeling out a body under a sheet. They took her to an ambulance we've so far been unable to track. I've got my top people on this, Rich. When do you land?"

52

Maurice is waiting for me on the runway as Shelton's plane taxis to a stop.

His impassive face is a complete response to the question I don't need to ask as I race down the steps. "This is our number one priority right now," he says softly.

I feel the blood surging through my veins; my hands are shaking. "Have you tracked the ambulance?"

"We're still looking. All of our personnel have been notified. I've issued a national missing persons alert."

I stare wildly at Maurice. This may be the best he can do, but it seems pitifully inadequate. It's hard to believe Maurice's approach will work given the sophistication of whoever we are dealing with. It's painfully, depressingly, urgently clear to me that my team will need to figure out the big picture ourselves to have any chance of finding Toni. "I need to get to the *Star* right now."

"I'll drive you there. We can talk on the way."

Maurice speeds me through traffic, the siren screeching from the roof of the car as the self-driving vehicles pull over automatically. But no matter how fast we go it still feels to me like we're crawling.

Arriving at the *Star*, I run up the stairs and into our digital conference room. Martina and Sierra are there waiting. I give them a staccato summary of what I've learned and about Toni, pausing for only a moment to tell of my promise to the SBN elders. With Toni missing, I've too much to lose to be cagey.

Martina steps up. "We need to know the details of all this. Halley, focus on the money."

"We need more help," I interject. "Where is Joseph?"

"He's out on the Brain-Pulse story," Martina says. "Another rave last night. I—"

"We need him here *now*."

Martina looks at me preparing for battle, then relents. "Call him."

Joseph answers after the third ring.

"Joseph, I need you in the conference room right away."

I feel the silence on the other end of the line.

"Joseph?"

Still no reply.

"Toni is missing. She's been kidnapped."

"I'll be there in fifteen minutes, boss."

Joseph rushes in anxiously twelve minutes later and trains his ancient eyes on mine as I'm detailing more of what I learned and mapping the options for where Toni could be. As always, his unspoken emotions are expressed through his quiet presence.

"Abraham," Martina barks, "you need to dig into the SBN organization and Israeli intelligence. Azadian, continue."

"On it," Joseph replies, tapping his u.D as he takes his position in front of one of the data walls.

I rush through the relevant details from the ship, filtering out only the most sensitive. My head is about to explode, but I calm myself. If I lose it now, I sense, I'll never find her.

A stunned silence permeates the room as I come to the end of my report.

Then the data starts splashing up on the walls.

"There's a story here," Martina says, her voice more reflective than I've ever heard it before. "Let's fucking find it."

We spend over two hours in frantic dialogue, fighting to narrow down the options. If SBN and the Israelis didn't kill Heller, who did? A rival intelligence service? A big health company? I step out every few moments to check in with Maurice or call Toni's frantic parents to give them an update. Part of me feels I should be out searching for Toni, but I know the path to finding Toni is figuring out the bigger picture and that's only going to happen here. The digital walls fill fast with words, images, and stacked files, but even after all we've learned, the amassing jigsaw pieces still don't come together as much as I desperately need them to.

"That's interesting," Sierra murmurs into her screen, breaking a momentary silence.

"Well?" Martina says, seeming annoyed she has to ask.

"It's a press advisory from Santique Health. They'll be making a major announcement today at four."

"What does that mean?" I ask, desperate for any additional information.

"Usually companies do this sort of thing for a product launch, something they think will get a lot of media attention and bump up their share price. They do it at the end of the day so media sources won't have time to do much background and have to go with what the company says for the morning news cycle. The news can build all night to drive a big surge in share prices the next morning."

"Any indication of what they'll be announcing?" I ask.

"No," Sierra says. "It's the usual 'hide the ball.'"

"Can you find out?" Martina asks.

"Maybe," Sierra says tentatively. "Probably."

"What are you doing standing around, then?" Martina barks.

Sierra looks momentarily shaken, then regains her composure and marches out.

"What about Shelton?" Joseph asks softly.

"How do you mean?" I ask.

"Can we be so sure that Shelton, SBN, and the Israelis are all on the same team? Could they have different interests that might make them collaborate in some ways and compete in others?"

Joseph's words are so thoughtful and reasoned they push my mind into rewind. "It's definitely a possibility," I say, sitting down a moment and trying to force myself to calm, but all I can think about is Toni.

Martina perks up. "Play that out."

We open a new space on the wall where I splash out the four categories into columns. Under each of the names I add a section labeled *individual interests* then add a full row underneath labeled *common interests*. New questions jump out as we begin dictating to fill the coordinates. The process is too slow, but I'm desperate for anything. I squeeze the sides of my chair to hold myself down.

Our questions stack up on the wall, taunting us with their importance and unanswerability and making me even more crazed than I already am.

"A revolutionary stem cell treatment for cancer." Sierra's breathless words reverberate through our brains. She stands fiercely just inside the door, her hands at her hips.

It takes only a fraction of a second for the words to sink in.

"Joseph," I order, "unpack the Santique hub."

He waves his hands over the section of the wall where all of our data about Santique has been stored. The files and images minimize the other hubs as they spread across the wall.

"So Santique learns of Heller's cancer research, they recruit him as a contractor and fund his work," I begin, hypothesizing aloud. "The research is promising on worms and mice but the data from the human trials less so. Then why would they be announcing the results of those trials now? Why wouldn't they start a new trial to reach a better outcome?"

"Maybe they had multiple trials going," Sierra fires back. "Maybe some other pressure is pushing them forward. Maybe Heller didn't know all they were up to. Didn't Heller mention something about that in the letter he embedded in the dog's DNA?"

"I think—"

Joseph's actions are a fraction of a second faster than my thought. We race through the letter he's splashed on the wall until we find it.

"*Although Santique was not, by my design, aware of my total organ-*

ism cellular reversion research, they were well aware of the progress I made in cellular reversion as a potential treatment for cancer and had begun additional research in their corporate labs based on my preliminary findings. Independent of me, Santique made the decision to go forward with experimental human trials in early 2025."

"So there could be a whole other strain of Santique's work that grows out of Heller's research but is also independent of it," Sierra muses.

"And either the timing is extremely coincidental or somehow the two strains remain connected," I add. We're getting more information but still don't have clarity. Not enough to feed my desperate drive to figure out how and where I can find Toni. "Could the timing be linked to Toni's . . . ?"

"We've got to explore all of the options," Martina declares. "Maybe they lied about the research. Maybe they got rid of the evidence that things weren't going well."

Her words rattle me. "The cancer treatment didn't work on Hart and Wolfson. Heller knew that," I add.

"How do we know?" Sierra challenges. "Heller didn't think the cancer treatments worked on humans but maybe he didn't know everything. Hart and Wolfson certainly got a lot better. And even if Santique didn't know about the age reversion, all three are out of the picture in one way or another."

Joseph reads the strange look on my face. "Where would Toni fit in this?"

"The kidnapping this morning, the timing of the Santique press announcement today," I say softly. "The coincidences are too great. There's got to be a connection. And if there is a connection, there's got to be a link somewhere in the company's network." My shaking finger taps my u.D, and Jerry Weisberg's sweaty face appears in a box on the wall.

"Jerry," I say, "I need you to drop everything. I need you—"

"I'm finalizing the firewall around Heller's files. You don't want—"

"It doesn't matter. Toni is missing, kidnapped. I need you to do something. Now."

He stares back, awaiting additional information.

"She was taken from the hospital this morning. The police are trying to find her. I don't give them much of a chance. We're starting to think there's a connection between her disappearance this morning and an announcement coming later today from Santique about a revolutionary new cancer treatment."

"What kind of connection?" Jerry asks nervously.

"We don't exactly know." I feel my face falling. I clench my jaw muscles, tightening to keep it up. "There are too many coincidences piling up. We don't have any better options."

"What do you need?"

"Full access to the Santique system."

Jerry blanches. "Multinational firms like that, with so much intellectual property and deep political connections, have some of the best security systems in the world, protected by quantum photon encryption. It could take months to get in if it's even possible at all."

"Jerry," I say, my whole body trembling, "you've got to do better. Someone's got Toni. They could've easily killed her this morning and left her body somewhere in the hospital. I have to think she's alive and there's a chance, there's got to be a chance, there's information somewhere in their system that can help us find her."

"I want to help you, Rich," Jerry says with absolute earnestness. "I'd do anything." His voice softens. "I just don't have the processing power it would take to crack this kind of system. Physics is the limitation."

"Franklin Chou plugged in to the UMKC system to do the genetic analysis of the dog. Could doing that help?"

Jerry shakes his head. "You don't understand what I'm saying. Multiply that by a thousand, a million. A company like Santique already has a system far more powerful than the university's. There may be only ten or twelve exascale supercomputers in the world with the processing power it would take to even have a chance of getting in."

I am too desperate to stop asking questions. "Okay then," I

challenge, as if the very existence of such supercomputers is a cause for hope. "Where are they?"

"Probably four or five of them are in China and controlled by their government in one way or another. Three are part of the US government—with the Department of Defense, the CIA, and the Data Analytics Agency—and completely unavailable. The rest are probably with the few national intelligence agencies with the sophistication, resources, and will to operate at that level."

I freeze.

"What?" Jerry asks, noticing my sudden change of expression, my eyes widening, my mouth opening.

I am too focused to respond. My mind locks in. The single thought takes hold of my being.

I slap my u.D with an intensity that stings, tap my biometric icon, then swipe frantically until I find it. In an instant the box appears on the conference room wall. The ten-digit number flashes for five seconds before disappearing.

53

"What the hell was that?" Martina says.

I dictate the numbers to my u.D.

The line rings twice before it connects.

Beep.

I hesitate a moment before realizing this single beep is all there is. "This is Rich Azadian," I say as quickly as I can, not knowing how much time I have. "My girlfriend Antonia Hewitt was kidnapped from Truman Medical Center in Kansas City this morning. I fear for her life and desperately need your help. You pledged on the ship you'd help me protect her. If that meant anything, I need you now. There may be a connection between her disappearance and a press announcement about a new cancer treatment to be released today at 4 p.m. central time by the Santique Health Corporation. We need to hack into the Santique system but can only do it with your immediate help. Please!" I turn to face Jerry on the screen. "My friend Jerry Weisberg is a computer expert." I point at Jerry. "Jerry, say exactly what you need."

Jerry hesitates, confused.

I raise my voice. "Jerry, dammit, if you could have any assistance in the world what would it be?"

"Um, um," he stutters, "a quantum supercomputer and a team of twenty of the best hackers in the world?" His expression asks if I've lost my mind.

I repeat Jerry's words into my earpiece.

"How would they connect with you?" I yell at Jerry.

"Um, um, through the bash management system. They need to have my IP address to give me admin credentials," he yells back.

"What is it?"

I repeat it as he reads it to me.

"I'm old school, Jerry," I say. "Give me your u.D access code."

Jerry stutters it out. "I'll need to confirm the link with a retinal scan."

I pass on the information.

"We need some indication you've received this message. We need you *now*," I shout into my earpiece.

I don't fully realize how much I'm shaking until I tap off the connection.

"And now come the ten plagues?" Martina asks cynically.

"Better ideas?" I snap.

She swivels to face me.

"Let's take another look at what we have on the wall," Sierra interjects.

My depression mounts by the second. We slide the data around the wall for tens of minutes that feel to me like tens of hours. We sift through the Santique section, each of us trying to move the content around in a way that completes the tale. Sierra tracks down her contacts to try to learn more about the cancer announcement. I send a message asking Franklin Chou to rush over to help. Each moment I imagine Toni, lost, afraid, alone. I feel a pulsing energy and a petrifying numbness battling for control of my body, as if a part of me is dying even as I struggle for Toni's life. Our pitiful efforts in this pitiful room for this pitiful paper all seem wholly, violently, dangerously inadequate.

Then the gentle vibration on my right wrist radiates through me like lightning.

My left hand swings to tap it.

A Hebrew message flashes momentarily across our wall:

זעוי בורב העושתו

"What the fuck is that?" Martina asks.

The English version flashes a moment later: "In the multitude of counselors there is safety."

"What the *fuck* is that supposed to mean?" she repeats.

"It's Proverbs 11:14," Joseph says quietly, as if his long silence and Catholic upbringing have been a preparation for this moment.

"Which means?" Martina demands.

Joseph ignores her assault. He leans back in his chair and looks up at the ceiling before focusing his eyes on me. "That we're stronger when we work together."

"It also looks like it's part of the motto of Israeli intelligence, the Mossad," Sierra calls out, reading from her search query on the other side of the room.

"Wait a second," Jerry yells, "my system is connecting." He begins waving his hands, excitedly conducting the symphony of invisible screens around him. "The Privileged Access Management package is downloading onto my system . . . I'm credentialing in to the Santique system . . . I'm being granted root access . . . Holy shit . . ." His eyes are scanning wildly side to side, his pitch escalating to a frenzy. "They are disabling the logbots around me . . . I've never seen anything like this. We've breached the system. I need a place to download the data . . . Plugging in to the VPN. Transfer happening now. Two hundred and forty seconds . . . 220 . . . 170 . . ."

We all stand amazed, watching Jerry work.

"One-ten . . . Seventy seconds . . . Forty . . . Ten . . . Three seconds, two, one. Got it!"

"Great, Jerry," I shout. "How can we get access?"

"I'm setting up a data link to the university server now. Should have the access code on your u.D in a few. You should have it . . . now."

My left hand flies toward the vibration on my right wrist. "Open file," I bark at my u.D.

The tidal wave of files floods our walls.

"We need to narrow this down," I say.

"Search terms?" Jerry asks.

All of us begin splashing them up. *Noam Heller. Total cellular reversion. Antonia Hewitt.* Turritopsis nutricula melanaster. *Benjamin Hart. William Wolfson. Adam Shelton.*

Joseph pools the terms and sets the search. Piles of files, represented by what look like individual sheets of paper, start growing up from the bottom of our electronic wall, pushing each of our search terms toward the ceiling by the files containing each reference.

"How many?" I ask.

"Six thousand two hundred forty-seven have at least one of our search terms," Joseph says.

"Fuck," I say, "that's a lot."

"We divide it up," Martina orders. "Fifteen hundred each."

"On it," Joseph says, waving his hands in the air to splash fifteen hundred files on each of the room's four walls.

Each pile feels dangerously tall, too vast a trove to sort through as quickly as we need. "We don't have time—"

"So shut the fuck up and start looking," Martina utters over her shoulder.

I've got fifteen hundred files on my wall and don't even know what I'm looking for. My body is shaking.

"Just keep searching, Jorge," Martina adds, this time more gently.

Swiping frantically through the files, I'm jarred by Martina's name for me. I realize I'm Borges's Librarian of Babylon trying to catalog the entirety of human knowledge without any kind of guide, searching endlessly for the catalog of catalogs he is destined to never find. I feel an intense pain in my gut. Six thousand files with potential clues contained within them. But Toni is gone, missing, and I know to the depths of my being I have far less than forever to find her.

We flip wildly through the files as time passes. Most of them deal with Heller's research and the setup of the human trials. Chou arrives breathlessly and sits beside us to help.

Seconds become minutes, minutes become hours. I'm racing through the files but the time bomb is ticking away in my heart. Toni, Toni, Toni. Her name repeated in each tick. I force myself to focus.

At four, Sierra links in to the media event.

I turn away from my wall display to watch the svelte and tanned Swiss appear on the screen in his shiny blue suit and silver tie. Short brown hair graying slightly at his temples, he looks like someone who owns a yacht.

"Hello and good evening," the man says smoothly. "My name is Arnaud Beauvais, chairman and chief executive officer of Santique Health."

I turn back to keep working through my documents, still listening to the voice wafting over my shoulder.

"For all of our species' history," he continues, "we have been victimized by a terrible killer who has lived among us. This killer has taken our mothers, fathers, friends, even our children. We have fought back. We have fought back valiantly and yet generation after generation we have failed in our struggle. The killer, of course, is cancer, *all* forms of cancer. Ladies and gentlemen, *madames et monsieurs, nushimen he xianshengmen,* as of today this killer has been stopped. The cure is the proprietary process for the total cellular reversion of cancer cells we have been developing for many years and which I have the honor to announce tonight."

"Do you have any idea what this means?" Sierra says excitedly over Beauvais's voice as his remarks continue. "After this announcement, they will be one of the highest valued stocks in the world by the end of the week."

"Even if it doesn't work?" Chou asks skeptically.

"For the short-term, it doesn't matter. Maybe it does work. Or who knows how they may have manipulated the regulatory process? When the stock shoots up, they'll be able to go on a buying spree scooping up other companies. Even if the cancer miracle doesn't pan out, the research pipelines of the companies they acquire will be theirs and the Santique shareholders who know the truth will be long gone by the time anyone figures that out," she says.

"Keep going through the files," Martina admonishes. "Has anyone seen reports on Hart and Wolfson's treatment?"

Our collective "no" reverberates through the room as Beauvais takes a few softball questions from the virtual forum.

"When will this treatment be available?"

"Is this treatment only for cancer or can it cure other diseases?"

"Will it be available in all markets?"

Beauvais answers each question with an Olympian benevolence. "According to our plans, the treatment will be available in major markets beginning in late 2026 and expand quickly across the globe in close consultation with world governments and institutions. So far, we have focused on cancer, but there is no reason to believe the same approach might not also apply to many other diseases . . ."

"Rich, can you come over here?" Joseph says softly, like a student asking his teacher to review his work.

Something about his tone catches my attention. I rush over.

"Look at this," Joseph says. "A bunch of the files are classified under the name Michel Noland."

"The one who published the article with Heller three years ago, the only article Heller published as a Santique researcher."

"Yes," Joseph says. "Look here. Noland was in charge of overseeing Heller's work. Then Noland takes over the cancer research program himself."

"We knew that. And?"

"Noland oversaw the work at Santique extending Heller's research, even when Heller was no longer involved," Joseph continues. "Then he authorizes the human trials."

"So if Heller said he was being pressured by Santique to begin human trials, we can assume that pressure might have been coming from Noland," I say.

"That's what I'm thinking, but look here," Joseph says, pointing. "All of the files have subcategories under the subheading of TCCRT, which the files identify as meaning Total Cancer Cellular Reversion Therapy.

"And look at these files." Joseph pulls up another batch. "Same name, Michel Noland, subcategory here is called TCRT. That could probably either mean Total Cancer Reversion Therapy or Total Cellular Reversion Therapy."

Now we're all crowding behind Joseph.

"But when I try to open these files, they're empty. So are the Noland files on Heller. It looks like they've been washed, with only the file names remaining elsewhere in the system architecture."

"What does that suggest?" Martina asks.

"That someone is cleaning the files dealing with exactly what we are looking for, maybe storing them in a manner even more secure then encrypted digital files," Joseph says.

"Like?" I ask, trying to push Joseph forward.

"I don't know. Maybe encrypting them in another place or another way."

"Michel Noland," Sierra reads from her screen, "forty-seven years old. MD, PhD. Graduate of the Pierre and Marie Curie University in Paris. Cancer specialist. Chief scientific officer at Santique until he comes to Kansas City four years ago to supervise the building of the new Santique Research Center. Seems like quite a company star. His title is listed as advisor for special projects. Here's a photo from their personnel file."

The image splashing on our wall could be of a model in a cologne ad. His short, dark hair and thinly cropped beard frame sardonic brown eyes.

"And look at this," Joseph adds. "When I search for Noland in the full data set, again most of the files are also scrubbed, both the references to him in other files and his own document folder."

"Are we sure he even still works there?" Martina asks.

Joseph waves his hands in the air a few moments more until he finds what he's looking for. "Yes, we are," he says proudly, "the company has to list its non-US nationals annually for its visa filings. It's the same information I have to provide."

Now Joseph is rapid-fire swatting his hand to pass through the documents flying across the wall.

Until his hand stops abruptly in mid-air.

We stare, transfixed, at the file name floating on the electronic wall.

Root Directory File: *Michel Noland*; Sub-Directory File: *Antonia Hewitt.*

Martina's command breaks the stunned silence. "What the fuck are you waiting for?"

I hesitate a fraction of a second, too shocked to move.

"Sierra and Joseph, you stay here and keep digging," Martina orders. "Tell us immediately anything interesting you find. Azadian, let's go."

I shake myself to action. "Franklin, you come with us to Santique," I order Chou, thinking we may need him to understand whatever we might find. I call Maurice on my u.D as we run down to the parking lot and pile into the Lincoln. "It looks like there's a link with Santique," I shout breathlessly. "They've got a file on Toni. There's someone there who might be a key to the whole thing."

"Looks like? Might?" Maurice responds suspiciously.

I explode. "Do you have anything? Do you know where Toni is? Have you tracked the ambulance? They've got a fucking file on Toni. I need you there now."

"All right," Maurice declares. "I'll be there."

"This is the only lead we have," I plead. "Please, for the love of God, send the fucking cavalry."

54

Callahan screeches the Lincoln to a halt in the Santique Research Center's front parking lot. I jump out and run to the door, feeling the cold, blowing rain piercing my skin. I tap my fingers on the control panel beside the door with increasing force.

"Fuck," I shriek, banging it.

I know from last week that even during business hours there won't be a live person inside the lobby to hear me, let alone in the dark of night. I bang on the glass.

"Is there another door?" Chou yells.

"You go left, I'll go right," I shout. "Martina, you drive the circumference of the building with Callahan."

I start running. Chou streaks in the opposite direction. We meet on the other side of the massive building a few minutes later. The thick frosted glass of the employee entrance is locked. I bang desperately on the door and control panel. No response.

"There's a loading dock just around the corner," Chou gasps through heavy breath. "I tried pulling on the metal grate. It's fully shuttered."

"Dammit," I curse. "Where the hell are you, Maurice?"

Martina and Callahan pull in behind us in the Lincoln. "It looks like the only other entry points are this one and the loading dock," Callahan confirms.

I tap the control panel outside the entry, again to no avail. I feel desperately out of place as the wet cold reaches my bones. The quiet whirl of sirens rises to a roar. Maurice's car streaks around the corner, lights blazing, and pulls to a stop behind us.

"The doors are locked," I yell as he jumps out of his car. "We've got to get in."

"You are sure about this?" Maurice asks.

"Maurice, we've got to get in. The key to all of this has to be here. I was right that we needed to break into Heller's lab and I'm betting I'm right now," I say frantically. "It's all I have. Please."

Maurice looks at me, weighing the options. I know him well enough to believe my desperation about Toni is on the scale. "Okay, my friend," he says cautiously.

His radio squawks. "Deputy Chief Henderson, we have the chief of security for the Santique research facility on the line."

"Roger that," Maurice says. "Put him through."

"This is Jacques—"

"I don't care what your name is," Maurice barks. "This is Deputy Chief Henderson. I've got men stationed at each door of your facility. Either one or more of these doors opens in the next two minutes or we break them down. Am I clear?"

"May I ask under what authority you are seeking to enter our premises?" the security chief asks coolly.

"Reasonable suspicion," Maurice says, looking over at me. "One minute and forty-five seconds."

"Hold on just one moment," the man says. "Reasonable suspicion of what?"

"Reasonable suspicion of exigent circumstances. One minute and thirty seconds."

"You can't just break into our facility. You need—"

Maurice cuts him off. "I have reasonable suspicion, sir."

"I am sure this must be some kind of misunderstanding we can easily clear up," the man says. "I'm at home now but can get in my car immediately. Would it be okay if I meet you just where you are in, say, fifteen minutes?"

"That would be wonderful. Thank you for offering," Maurice says matter-of-factly.

My head juts forward.

Maurice lifts the handset to his mouth. "But if one of these doors is not open in fifty-three seconds you'll be able to drive straight into your building when you get here."

"Now just hold on one second, sir," the increasingly nervous voice says. "You have no authority to enter our premises."

"Forty-one seconds."

"Please stand down. I'm on my way. We have strict security protocols."

"Thirty-two seconds."

"Sir, you don't understand what you're doing. We have strong connections with the governor. We have lawyers—"

Martina looks enraged by the reference to the governor but Maurice remains calm.

"We are forcibly entering your premises in twenty seconds."

"Sir—"

"Ten seconds, five, out." Maurice lowers the radio and looks over at me. "I hope you're right about all this."

Chou steps forward. "I think the metal door on the loading dock might be easiest to get through."

"Where is it?"

"Just around the corner there." Chou points.

"Get in," Maurice orders.

We jump in the car and Maurice speeds over, calling two patrol cars to meet him at the loading dock. The officers rush out and connect long thick chains between the metal gate and the hitches on the backs of their cars.

Maurice launches the count. "One, two, three, pull."

The three cars pull away from the gate like dogs straining at the end of a taut leash. Their engines rev, the tires screech, a smell of burning rubber permeates the air. The loading dock gate does not move.

"Stop," Maurice yells into his radio. The engines quiet. "Pull back two feet. Let's try this again. One, two, three, go."

Our wheels connect with the pavement as we lurch forward for a fraction of a second, then bang our heads into the back of our seats.

"Stop," Maurice shouts again. "Blow it."

In minutes, another patrol car arrives. Two men in black uniforms get out and walk over to Maurice. He gives them the orders before all the cars pull back.

"On your call, sir," one of the men says over the radio after the explosives are set.

"Do it."

The explosion is not huge but leaves the gate a shattered mess.

"Let's go," Maurice says.

Martina, Chou, and I follow him through the smoldering hole.

"What the hell . . ." the stunned security guard says, rushing over to us in the hall. "I was told you have not been authorized for entry."

"You were told wrong," Maurice snaps. "We're looking for . . ." He turns to me.

"An employee of yours named Michel Noland," I say.

"Is he here?" Maurice asks aggressively.

"I'm not authorized to provide any information about our—"

Maurice gets in front of the guard and stops him in his tracks. The guard's bulging neck muscles make him an imposing match for Maurice's tall, muscular frame. "You are going to tell us right now whether he's here."

The guard shrivels. "I don't know—"

"Take us to his office," Maurice commands.

"It's in the restricted—"

"I don't give a damn where it is," Maurice orders, "take us there right now. Do I make myself clear?"

"Yes, sir," the man shrinks obsequiously, "but it's in—"

"Take us there *now*."

The guard puts his head down and leads. We follow him to an

elevator bank and then up to the eighth floor. The hall only extends about fifty feet before it's blocked by a thick metal door.

"I was trying to explain to you," the nervous guard says, "this is our high-security zone. The only way in is with retinal verification and a personal security code."

"Are you authorized?" Maurice asks.

"I-I . . ." the man stutters.

"Don't say a word," a tense voice yells from behind.

We turn to see a tall, burly man rushing toward us.

"Don't say a word," he repeats. "They have no authority to be here. Our lawyers are on the way."

"I was trying to explain to them—" the guard says.

"Oh, shut up," the man barks.

Maurice only smiles. "And you are?"

"Jacques Malraux, chief of security."

"Very nice to meet you, sir," Maurice says politely.

I'm not surprised by Maurice's formality and have a sense of what's coming next.

Malraux looks at Maurice, confused.

"I'm just going to need to borrow something for a moment," Maurice says.

"You've got to be—"

Malraux's words are cut short by the firm clasp of Maurice's hand around the back of his shoulder-length hair. Maurice forcefully yanks Malraux's face in front of the scanner.

The words RETINAL SCAN AFFIRMATIVE flash across the monitor.

"You idiots," Malraux says. "You also need a personal identification number."

Maurice lets go of Malraux's hair. "Darn it," he says, walking a few steps back. "I guess I didn't think of that." He pauses a moment before he speaks. "All right guys, blow it."

I get a certain perverse pleasure observing the transformation of Malraux's face.

"Wait just one second," Malraux yells. "You can't just storm into our building and blow out our walls. This is the United States of America."

Maurice doesn't even look in his direction. "Set the charges," he orders his two men in black.

The men pull the small explosives from their belts and rip the covers off their adhesives.

"Wait, wait, wait," Malraux says. "*Merde*. There is going to be hell to pay for this." He begins tapping a code into the control panel. The door glides open.

"Now take us to the office of Michel Noland." Maurice's tone makes clear he will brook no dissent.

Malraux grudgingly leads the way. We arrive at a large corner office blocked off by a security wall similar to the one we just breached. I feel my pulse surging.

Maurice glares at Malraux.

"Even I don't have access to this office," Malraux says.

"Show me."

Malraux places his face in front of the scanner.

Retinal Scan Negative.

"All right, boys," Maurice says nonchalantly.

We step back as they strategically place the explosives.

"Wait, stop," Malraux shrieks. "You can't do this. You can't just barge into our building and start blowing up things. You can't—"

"On my mark. Five, four, three . . . I'd suggest you step back."

Malraux stares at Maurice, his eyes bulging until the countdown registers in his mind. As he jumps back away from the metal door, I catch the nervous smile on Martina's face.

"Good . . . Two, one, execute."

Boosh. The room fills with dust. The doors stand, but barely.

"Crowbar," Maurice orders.

In sixty seconds we are in. The large office is all windows on two sides facing the building's exterior. It is sparsely decorated with a minimalist, almost Zen feel.

"Look at this," Chou says after opening what looks like a closet door. "I haven't seen anything like this in years."

I enter the room just as he puts words to what he is seeing.

"Paper files," he says incredulously.

The walls are lined with old-fashioned, color-coded folders like a twentieth-century doctor's office. It's far more information than we can absorb quickly, especially without the assistance of technology, but we begin desperately leafing through the files. The categories are all there. *Noam Heller. Heller research. Total Cancer Cellular Reversion Treatment. Trial protocols. Benjamin Hart. William Wolfson. Total Cellular Reversion Treatment. Heller SBN. Heller formula. Heller vial inventory. November 7 security breach. Antonia Hewitt.*

My hands shake as I open the thick file with Toni's name on it. I scan the handwritten notes referencing her role in the November 7 security breach by Dr. Heller, summarizing our conversations in Heller's lab, and noting that Toni spent thirteen minutes with Dr. Heller in the jellyfish aquarium room when no surveillance information was available. The reports track her every move from the time we visited Heller's lab, at her house before the explosion and at mine after, and includes photographs of her house, of Sebastian inside it, of my house, of the hospital. A document transcribes all of the messages from the past week going to and from her u.D. Another details the extraction of her 2021 blood sample from the National Biostorage Facility, immediate preparation for her procedure in the "treatment module." I flip frantically through the documents, feeling the blood drain from my head.

My eyes are bulging but my mind locks into gear. "They're starting her today on some kind of procedure," I shout urgently to Chou. "It says she's in the treatment module. Where the fuck is that?"

"Where is it?" Maurice yells at Malraux.

"I am not able to communicate absent the presence of counsel."

Maurice walks toward Malraux and Chou and I flip through the files desperately. My heart pounds. *Toni, Toni, Toni. Fuck, fuck, fuck.*

"Here," Chou yells.

I rush over.

"It's in the Parkville Underground," he says. "The limestone caves up north. 8800 Northwest River Park Drive, lot forty-one. It's the caves the university used to own."

"Grab the file. We've got to go," I say turning toward the door.

Maurice orders his men to set up a command post at Santique and then calls into his handset, "I want all available cars going to 8800 Northwest River Park Drive in Parkville."

I'm desperate to leave but quickly pull Martina into the file room. "The rest of the story is here, Martina," I plead. "Stay here as long as you can."

55

We're at nearly a hundred and ten miles per hour weaving through traffic up US 71 North to Highway 169. Maurice keeps tabs on the fifteen police cars heading in the same direction.

I frantically read the file on Toni over and over, searching for even the smallest shreds of additional information. What type of procedure? Why? How long does it take? All I can think of is Toni lying inert, being wheeled from the hospital. Toni alone and afraid in a dark limestone cave deep below the surface.

Come on, Maurice, I think. *Drive. Drive!*

From 169, we make a screeching turn on Highway 9. I can hear the throng of sirens converging behind us. Maurice races toward the entrance of the cave, honking his horn for the guard to lift the rail. The rail stays put and Maurice crashes through. The road funnel loops deeper and deeper down into the cool, white limestone. The screech of the tires and the reverberating roar of the sirens amplify exponentially in the enclosed space. After five complete spirals down, we corkscrew onto a level road and speed past the glass-enclosed numbered lots.

One, three, five, seven. The odd numbered lots to our left flow sequentially. The frosted glass entryway of each is embedded into the surrounding limestone, each opening to a series of smaller interior caves from the central atrium.

Faster, Maurice. Hold on, baby.

Twenty-seven, twenty-nine, thirty-one.

I jump out of the car and bang on the frosted glass door of lot forty-one. Maurice follows immediately behind, rapping the door with the back of his flashlight.

"Stand back," Maurice orders. He hacks his crowbar into the area around the clasp, then lifts his leg and smashes the same area with his heel. The glass cracks but holds. He lifts the crowbar again. With five whacks the door is breached.

I dart in front of him as the officers fill in behind. The polished limestone of the domed central atrium is covered by a thin film of clear polyurethane. Spartan modernist furniture gives the atrium a Japanese feel that reminds me of Noland's office. Eight small doors line the circumference of the room, with plastic sheets creating a sterile zone separating each door from the air of the central space.

I charge through the plastic of the first door, yelling, "Toni, Toni!" It's an operating room like the one I saw in Heller's lab, but it's empty. I jump out.

"Toni," I yell again, rushing in to the second.

Nothing.

"Baby," I shout as I rip through the third.

A man and woman in surgical masks and white lab coats look up at me and raise their hands, signaling me to stand back.

My eyes feel like they're bulging from my head. I hardly see the two people. Every ounce of me is focused on Toni lying inert on the operating table. Red tubes pass from each of her arms, sending her blood into a machine, where it seems to spin through a clear cylinder. Her mouth is covered with an oxygen mask and her head surrounded by an electrocorticography helmet with hundreds of cords passing from patches stuck to her scalp and into a large processor. Digital displays monitor her bodily functions.

I leap toward her. "Baby, can you hear me?"

She doesn't move.

"What the fuck are you doing to her?" I shout, pushing the two people aggressively.

"Stop." Franklin Chou's strong word echoes through the room. "Stop, Rich," he begs.

Maurice and three officers file in behind him with their pistols drawn. "Put your hands in the air where I can see them," Maurice shouts at the two people.

They lift their hands. "You don't understand," the man says in a French accent through his surgical mask.

"Where I can see them," Maurice orders.

An officer comes behind each and jams their hands behind their backs before placing them in plastic cuffs, then pulls off their surgical masks and pushes them down on the ground.

As the masks come off, I recognize the cropped beard and the mocking, intelligent eyes from the research files. And I feel an instinctual urge to tear Michel Noland to pieces.

"I'm telling you," Noland says calmly, "don't touch anything. You don't understand what you are doing. This is a very delicate procedure."

"He's right," Chou declares from behind me. "Total Cellular Reversion Treatment?"

Noland's contemptuous eyes confirm.

"When did the process begin?" Chou asks, his voice retaining its calm.

Noland doesn't answer.

"When?" Maurice shouts.

"I am not at liberty to answer your questions absent the presence of counsel."

I lunge toward Noland, but Maurice gets there first. He lifts Noland up by his shirt and presses him into the limestone wall. "When did it begin?"

"This afternoon," Noland grunts.

Maurice eases his grip, and Noland sinks to the ground.

I place my hand on Toni's forehead. *Baby, baby, baby.* She is completely nonresponsive. Panic overtakes me. "What does that mean?" I fire at Chou.

"I don't know," he says contritely. "All of my knowledge about this is theoretical. We've only just begun our experiments on the roundworms and mice."

"Can we stop it?" I shriek.

"It looks like they've already begun the cellular reversion process. If Heller's notes are correct, the transfusion and genomic alteration should take approximately six days. We don't know anything about stopping in the middle."

"Which is exactly what I was trying to tell you," Noland pronounces from the floor.

"You have the right to remain silent," Maurice says, shaking his head in disgust.

Chou is already immersed in the science. "If they're using genetic materials from her 2021 blood sample, she now has a mix of cells with different age signatures inside of her. It's got to be incredibly confusing for her body. Heller's process requires complete sedation during the transfusion because the struggle between the old and new cells can be extremely traumatic—"

"Can we stop it?" I repeat.

"I don't know," Chou says nervously. "Shutting it down now could be extremely dangerous for her."

"What about all of the blood in her body? She can't have been here for more than twelve hours."

"If I'm right," Chou says, "then all of her current genetic material has already been compromised."

"Morons," Noland says under his breath, "of course it has."

I take an aggressive step toward Noland, my predatory instinct fully activated.

Chou places his arm across my chest as he speaks. "We would need more recent genetic materials, if a reversal is even possible."

"And the additional catalytic compound you don't have," Noland mutters.

My heart sinks as I turn toward Toni. I have tried to protect her and failed. She lies motionless, being morphed into an earlier version of herself with the last four years of her life—the three years we've known each other, her dreams and hopes and pains—vanishing through the transfusion tubes. I think of Katherine Hart mourning a man who has lost forty years of their life together. Time, cruel and unforgiving, is also, I suddenly realize, the ultimate carrier of the true meaning of our lives.

My mind whirls frantically. More genetic material. My body freezes as my brain locks on to the idea. I stand up straight and turn toward Chou. "I've got it."

"Got what?"

"Last Saturday Toni had her eggs extracted and a skin graft taken. They've just been deposited with Kansas City Cryobank."

"But you'd need someone who actually knows what the hell they're doing to do the procedure, if it's even possible at all," Noland declares, recognizing his opportunity.

I turn my head slowly and bend down to face his. Then I grab his shoulders and ram him violently against the wall. "And it sure as fuck is not going to be you."

But the urge to take care of Toni overpowers my drive to harm Noland. I let go of his shoulders and stand. My mind locks in. "Where do we need to take her?"

"Hospital's the best bet," Chou says. "We don't even know what we don't know. We're going to need a lot of help."

"Of course you are," Noland murmurs from against the wall. "So this may be a good time for us to negotiate."

I take an instinctive step toward him, then stop myself, the idea suddenly becoming clear in my head. I turn toward Maurice. "Can you please get this asshole out of here?"

Maurice signals his men who grab Noland and his colleague and begin dragging them out. "You are making a terrible mistake," Noland yells, "I am willing to neg—"

Chou eyes me nervously as the closing door cuts off Noland's voice. "Plan B?"

"We can do better," I say, slapping my u.D and swiping frantically for the icon. I find it and tap. Nothing. "Shit."

"The limestone is blocking the signal," Chou says. "Looks like there's no repeater."

"I've got to get above ground."

Maurice jumps in. "I'll drive you. We need to call the ambulance."

I'm pulled in two directions. I need to get above ground but can't bear to leave Toni.

"I'll keep an eye on her," Chou implores, recognizing my agony. "We shouldn't wait. We need to get her to the hospital. Go!"

Maurice pulls me away and into his car. We screech down the drive and then up the loops and out the ground level exit. I can't tap my u.D fast enough. "Come on," I mutter.

The ten-digit number flashes for five seconds on my u.D's monitor before disappearing.

I'm shaking as I dictate the numbers into my wrist.

Beep.

"This is Rich Azadian," I yell. "I'm in Kansas City. My girlfriend is stuck halfway through a reversion process. I need your help right now. I need you to get me the catalytic compound and your best scientists from the ship to reverse the transfusion. I know this is a lot to ask but I'm taking you at your word. I'm begging for your help." I pause to collect my thoughts then drop my tone a notch. "You asked me to pledge mutual respect and support and I did. Now I need you to do your part."

I tap off the call as Maurice orders the ambulance on his radio.

"Confirmed. Ambulance will arrive in seven minutes," the dispatcher says.

Maurice hits the gas and U-turns the car back toward the cave entrance.

"Wait," I yell, opening the door. "You go. I need to wait for the response."

Maurice slams on the brakes, then looks at me and nods.

As he drives away, I feel the dark of the windy plains, a cold aloneness, seeping into me. I cradle my u.D and right wrist in my left hand as if I can rub it into action. The silent u.D mocks me with indifference. The seconds tick away. "Come on," I murmur, hoping against hope that the Council of Elders is deep in discussion right now. I have no way of knowing. I hear the siren growing louder, then watch the ambulance jet through the broken gate into the cave. The u.D doesn't peep.

Self-doubt begins to overtake me. How stupid to send Noland away. Was he Toni's only hope? Did my selfish anger put her in even greater danger than she's already in? I step in front of the ambulance rolling back out of the entrance with my hands up, then rush around and jump in the back. Chou and an EMT are kneeling over Toni in the cramped space jammed full with the machines from the operating room inside the caves.

"We've kept her hooked up to everything," Chou says as I maneuver toward Toni. "Hopefully we can figure this out at Truman."

I blanch. "Didn't you say you had a plan B?" Chou asks, the nervousness registering on his face.

My silence hangs painfully, overcoming even the clamor of the sirens around us.

"I-I . . ." I stammer, feeling the full weight of my doubt descend upon me.

And then my u.D vibrates. The message flashes across its small screen:

Received. Considered. Confirmed.

56

The room is silent but for the quiet whir of the transfusion machine and the steady beep of the biorhythm monitor. The Hewitts stand nervously beside the bed. My efforts to explain what's going on to them has only made them more nervous. Chou is busy prepping for the procedure. All I can do is stare at Toni. She lies peacefully, but I have no idea what damage may be visiting her on a cellular level.

It's been twelve hours since we arrived at the hospital. Those twelve hours have been forever, only punctuated by the series of short data blasts on my u.D.

Cargo arriving Wheeler Airport 9 p.m. CST; arrange pickup. Maintain strict operational security. No media coverage whatsoever. Minimal contact with external medical personnel.

I had Joseph pick them up.

The two women march in purposefully, already in scrubs. Each pulls a rolling case. They both appear to be in their forties and in impeccable physical condition. The taller one has medium-length blonde hair pulled into a bun and razor-like features. The shorter one has a darker complexion and deep, penetrating brown eyes. Every aspect of their demeanor indicates they are here to do a job and nothing else. I stand to greet them but Joseph signals me back.

The women acknowledge me, Chou, and the Hewitts, then set down their cases and begin unpacking their supplies, placing a metal box like the ones used to carry transplant organs on a table beside the bed.

"Is that what I think—"

The taller woman's stare cuts off my sentence.

"Please step outside while we prepare," she says in a sharp accent I recognize as Hebrew. Her request to me and the Hewitts is really more of an order. "I will join you in a moment to explain the risks."

The three of us hesitate before following the instructions. Something about the way she refers to "the risks" is deeply unsettling to me. The Hewitts sit in the waiting room of the hospital suite while I pace nervously. None of us speak.

About fifteen minutes later, the taller doctor steps out. "We believe the safest option that will cause her the least amount of systemic trauma is to push forward the transfusion using her most recent genetic materials—those taken when her eggs were extracted thirteen days ago. But this procedure has never been carried out before. We have no way of reliably predicting the outcome."

I gasp.

"Another possibility," she continues, "is that the first cellular reversion will complete regardless of our actions and she could be physically younger with no knowledge of the past four years. This could happen if her cells have passed a point of no return in the reversion process. It is also very possible that something else could happen which we cannot predict."

Every muscle in my body tenses. "You can't say anything more certain than that?"

"The human brain consists of hundreds of billions of neurons with almost a hundred trillion synapses connecting them. This is extremely complicated work. Now if you will please excuse me."

Elizabeth Hewitt steps forward as the taller doctor is turning back. She places her hand on the doctor's arm in a way that reminds me of Toni and looks warmly into the doctor's eyes. "Thank you for being here," she says.

The doctor's iciness shows a first hint of thaw. "We will do our best."

The wait is excruciating while the procedure rolls on in the next room. We watch on the monitor as the doctors carefully calibrate the transfusion machine and biorhythm monitor and exchange a few words with Chou in English. I don't understand all that is happening there but keep my eyes locked on the screen until I feel the vibration of Sierra's message on my wrist.

Arriving.

Per my instructions, she walks in alone, her posture as erect as her aged bones can support. A large scarf is wrapped around her head. I'd known when I contacted Sierra that I only had a small window to fulfill my promise; the unmarked SBN plane parked at Wheeler Airport the only ticket to make it possible.

Katherine Hart takes off the scarf and looks deeply into my eyes.

"I gave you my word I would find your husband and let you be with him again," I say.

"I had a feeling about you," she says tenderly, taking my hand.

I smile as much as the fear still surging through me allows. "What I'm about to offer may not be exactly what you had in mind. Can I start at the beginning?"

Two hours later, she has journeyed through a lifetime that has somehow, somewhere, been lost. Her facial expressions have traveled the full spectrum, back and forth, between the poles of horror and joy, understanding and consternation, love and loss, life and death. "He was, he is, the love of my life, and I will always miss him," she says softly, "but I'd much rather have him where he is right now, doing what he loves, than dead or dying or lost." Her words float in the profound silence. "I only hope he's not alone."

My mind wanders to Wolfson and Margolies and Singer and the others, to Toni in the operating room just beside me. What does it mean to be alone? What type of connection does it take to break that spell? "That's why I've invited you here. Can I ask you an impossible question?"

"Ben used to say no questions are impossible; it's just the answers are sometimes harder to find."

I lay out the idea.

"Oh my, that *is* an impossible question."

"I promised I would bring you together. I'm offering you the chance to be together for decades more, maybe forever. There's only enough catalytic compound left for one more reversion and I believe it should be used on you, to bring you and Ben together, but only if that's what you want. I'm so sorry to rush you, but you've got about four hours to make your decision and you would have to give me your sacred word this would only be between us."

"What would I tell the children, the grandchildren, the . . ."

"You'd have to figure that out."

"And if I decide to do it?"

"I'll need you to let me know within three hours and be at Wheeler Airport in four."

Katherine Hart looks deep into my eyes as if, through me, imagining another world, another life, a future. Then she stands and rushes out the door.

Three and a half nervous hours later, the tall doctor invites us in. It's been a nearly six-hour procedure and everything looks exactly as it did in the beginning. Toni is still lying inert on her back, eyes closed, not moving, the blood surging in and out of the transfusion machine tubes. Watching her, I feel as if the life is being sucked out of me as well. The shorter doctor gives us specific instructions for what we need to do to care for her over the next five days until the parabiotic transfusion process is complete.

"If you need us," she says, "Mr. Azadian knows how to reach us."

I don't want to leave Toni's side, but I dart out to ambush the doctors as they prepare to leave.

"Impossible," the exasperated taller one replies to my request. "Dr. Heller's second vial looks like it's lost, we've just used a dose to restore your friend, and this is how we should use what might be the last existing dose of the catalytic compound?"

I shrug.

"Anyway, a decision like that is not for us to make."

"I understand," I say, tapping my u.D. The ten-digit number flashes for five seconds on my u.D's monitor before disappearing.

I place the call.

Beep.

I know I'm pushing my luck, but it wasn't me who made this mess in the first place. "Benjamin Hart never volunteered for this. You took him. Maybe his and Katherine's last moment in the hospice would have been forever for them. They never had it. Now you've got to help make this right. People cannot be pawns, whatever the stakes, and a classically trained neurobiologist wouldn't be a terrible addition to the SBN team. I don't mean to be a pain," I add, "but if this doesn't happen I would consider it a significant blow to the deep relationship of trust between us and would need to reconsider my commitments accordingly."

I understand I may be playing the same game as SBN, deciding who lives forever based on my own sense of what is good. But life is a balance and sometimes actions require reactions to keep it.

In ten minutes, the acceptance of my "request" flashes across the screen for the three of us to see.

"This is a mistake," the taller doctor says.

I stare at her for a moment longer than comfortable. "It's a crazy little thing called love."

The two women shake their heads.

"*Meshuggah*," the shorter one grumbles.

57

The next four days are a continuous flow of meetings and updates, with Maurice, Martina, Sierra, Joseph, and Toni's parents joining me in my constant vigil over Toni. We even infiltrate lovable Dreyfus in a rolling suitcase, hoping his presence might bring positive energy to the room.

But Toni still lies motionless and unconscious. The only signs of life are her slow breath and the whirl of her blood passing through the tubes. Not knowing all that's happened to her cells, her history, her health, fills me with constant dread.

"The FBI and NIH are now all over this," Maurice tells me during one of his visits, "and KCPD is on it full tilt. Noland and six of his colleagues are in custody, all of them cooperating fully to try to save themselves from the death penalty for the murder of my two men. It looks like Noland was the one masterminding the cancer program and then manipulating the data from the early trials after it started coming back less promisingly than expected."

"So why fake it?"

"Once he discovered Heller had figured out how to reverse people's ages, Noland knew that breakthrough was potentially far bigger than a cure for cancer could ever be. His idea was to use the cancer announcement to drive up Santique's stock price and then leverage the higher valuation to begin a massive roll up of all the technologies they'd need to bring age reversion to market. They knew Heller was hiding things from them, but they'd already built surveillance systems into Heller's lab that tracked everything, even over the constant music Heller played trying to drown out their systems."

"Except for inside the jellyfish room," I say.

"Heller figured out they were getting his information, but he engineered that one room to be safe, divided up his files, and put the coded message in the dog's DNA as a backup. He must have felt the noose was closing on him when he invited you and Toni into the lab."

"He told us we'd come at a serendipitous moment. But why did they kill Heller?"

"Noland knew that Heller's invention could make Santique the most powerful company in the world. At first, Noland wanted to do a deal with Heller guaranteeing Santique a monopoly on Heller's work, but Heller told them to go to hell, that he'd only give the data to people he could trust. Noland's thugs suspected that the formula for producing the catalytic compound, without which the reversion process could not work, had potentially been passed when you and Toni visited. They checked in on Heller after the two of you left to get him to talk and things got ugly. They snuck out the back door with the vial of Heller's reversion formula when you started banging on Heller's front door, but not before throwing his body into the jellyfish tank to try to cover their tracks. If we hadn't broken in that day, we never would have found Heller's body. Then they started tracking you and Toni, getting a lot of information from hacking your u.Ds."

"I thought those things were supposed to be Silent Circle encrypted, unhackable."

"Apparently not," Maurice says. "That's how they realized their tracks weren't covered, why they destroyed Heller's lab and went after the dog at Toni's house."

"Went after? They blew up the damn house. How did they—" My mind answers my question. "They heard my call to Franklin Chou about Sebastian?"

"Yes. And they thought they were protected after Heller's lab was destroyed and the dog was incinerated, until they intercepted the message Toni left on your u.D saying she was remembering what Heller told her about how to find the catalytic compound formula. They were desperate to get control of the formula before anyone else did."

The pieces start to fit together in my head. The electrocorticography helmet in Heller's operating room, Hart and Wolfson's memories being recorded when they were being reverted to earlier ages. "But they knew she wouldn't tell them, so they reverted Toni to try to capture her memories."

"That's what it looks like," Maurice says. "That formula was the key to everything. They had a small dose of the catalytic compound they'd stolen from Heller's lab, good enough for maybe one reversion. The compound itself could not be reverse engineered, so they desperately needed the formula to make it possible to bring the reversion process to an industrial scale. They knew that if Toni told you and the catalytic compound formula got to SBN and others, the monopoly would be broken. Their only option was to revert Toni before she could tell anyone and try to download what Heller told her in the jellyfish room. With so much at stake, they decided to move up the announcement of their cancer program as a precaution."

I feel a chill in my spine. "And if that's why they were reverting her, it's hard to believe they would have just sent her back home four years younger once they were done."

Maurice purses his lips. "That's why we're charging them with the attempted murder of Toni in addition to the murders of Heller and my men and everything else."

I put my hands over my face. Maybe we did save Toni from a worse fate, but her new reality remains deeply uncertain.

"Downloadable memory, the damn scientific age," Maurice mumbles, trying to ease the tension. "I'm probably going to need my son to explain it all to me."

I look up and smile fleetingly. Downloadable memory. Neural computing. Artificial intelligence. Life. Death. Immortality. Maurice is finally looking at the big picture, but that picture may be too big these days for any of us to accurately see. His son's philosophy books are as good a place to start as any. "What will happen to Noland?"

"Life, for sure," Maurice says. "I'd be happier with execution. But his complete cooperation now will probably spare him. Of course, your article is confusing things."

"My article?"

"Don't play stupid with me, Dikran. Just because your name isn't on the byline doesn't mean you're not behind it."

I shrug.

"Joseph Abraham and Sierra Halley are getting a lot of attention around town. Hell, around the world. The mania about defeating cancer and the possibility of someday defeating mortality is starting to swirl across the globe like a virus. The immortality tidal wave looks like it's only beginning."

"It's strange," I say, the errant thought darting through my brain, "people waste so much time in their actual lives but still can't resist the drive to live forever."

Maurice shakes his head. "Of course, Senator King is organizing hearings, trying to blame President Lewis and Jack Alvarez for letting this happen under their watch, asking why they let the big health companies get so politically powerful. The parties are rushing to give back the political contributions they've received from Santique. People are amazed that anyone in the media has finally taken on the health companies and are calling Abraham and Halley the next Dikran Azadians."

I appreciate Maurice's efforts to lighten things up and try to play along. "I'm not that confident in Dikran 1.0, Maurice."

"But I've read all the stories multiple times and I still get the feeling it's not all there, that you're influencing things behind the scenes, protecting people by withholding critical pieces of information."

"Well, I didn't write those stories, but that's a very interesting theory."

Maurice lifts an eyebrow before patting me on the shoulder and leaving the room.

I return to the procedure room and resume my vigil. Closing my eyes a moment, I picture the SBN ship floating on, imagine Katherine Hart lying motionless in one of its operating rooms with the tubes of blood going in and out of her arms, the history of the last forty years of her life vanishing and a new future opening. I open my eyes and see my story, the story of my life, of my future, of a tomorrow I no longer dread but am willing to embrace as a treasure trove of shifting, exciting, graying possibilities, resting in the body lying before me in this painfully silent room.

58

The movement is so slight it hardly even registers. But I'm watching Toni's face like a hawk, and nothing is going to get by me.

"I think her eye just twitched," I say excitedly to Elizabeth and Owen. I put my mouth close to her ear. "Baby, can you hear me?"

She doesn't move. The computer has been slowly decreasing her level of anesthetic for the past two hours.

"It's me, Rich. I'm here with your parents."

Nothing.

"I just spoke with Nayiri. She and Maya and my mom . . . they all send their love."

I stare at her desperately. "I really think I saw something, a flutter."

Elizabeth Hewitt places a gentle hand on my shoulder. "Maybe it will take a little time."

My nervousness doesn't allow for such patience. "Baby," I whisper again, "I just—"

Toni's eyelids flutter, then open gently halfway. I feel the surge of blood pumping through my heart as her eyelids battle the array of drugs and bodily forces pulling them closed. Her powers of wakefulness struggle to gain the upper hand.

Her eyes pull partly open.

They are not the sharp green eyes I know so well but foggy and glassy, unfocused.

"Baby, it's me," I say, trying to stay calm. "I'm here with you in the hospital. Your parents are here with me."

Her pupils shift toward me without locking. A strange look of confusion crosses her face. My anxiety begins to swell.

Who ultimately knows what a human is made of? Maybe it's just carbon and a spark of electricity. Toni's cells have been hacked and re-hacked, even her memories perhaps erased along with the neurons in her brain. A lost toenail can grow back, but what happens to a lost memory?

I take her hand. "Just relax, sweetheart, breathe. You've been through a lot."

Her eyes betray no awareness. Her pupils drift fleetingly around the room, not seeming to recognize anything or anyone.

Images of our history together flash through my mind. Meeting at the Jazzoo Gala, our first date to Union Station, our trip to watch the prairie grasses burn in Cottonwood Falls, racing out of Rapture Ranch in Waco, fighting for our lives in the trashy hotel room in Oklahoma, pushing to get in front of each other during our video calls with Nayiri, eating chocolate mint ice cream out of the container while resting lazily on her couch. Maybe our histories exist in some objective realm because they actually happened, but what can they mean beyond their being recorded in another person? What remains of a life if the memory of it is erased?

"Toni," I say desperately, "can you hear me?"

Silence permeates the room.

My mind darts to the Israeli doctor's warning of an unknown outcome.

Her unfocused pupils drift lazily toward her eyelids.

I fight the panic overtaking me, the horror of history, memory, love, life, identity being sucked into the black hole of loss. With every moment, the possibility increases that a piece of her, our life together, has been lost.

Then, in an instant, her eyes widen. Her retinas lock on mine.

"Rich?" she says hoarsely.

I feel every ounce of my being rising, something old yet new being reborn. "Baby," I say through my tears.

There will be time, I now know, to tell Toni the full story of what's happened. There will be time to tell her how the world has spun, the oceans have rolled, how I boarded a giant ship to track down the secrets of immortality and protect the one thing I now fully realize I value most in the world—all since she dropped by the OB/GYN ward two weeks ago. There will be time to tell her that as far as we know the vials of Heller's catalytic compound are used up or lost, that whatever Heller might have told her in a dark room at a time she may never remember might end up being the key to transcending the mortality of our species. There will even be time to tell her I am ready for a life together.

But that time is not now.

For now, the only immortality I seek is the transcendence of this one feeling.

Toni looks up at me with a strange, beatific smile. It's a smile I've only seen once before. I stare back at her, bursting with wonder, then interrupt the thought.

Hope springs eternal, I think, gazing deeply into Toni's awakening eyes, but love is forever.

Acknowledgements

Writing can be a solo pursuit, but it takes a proverbial village to transform words and ideas into a book. I am grateful to the many special people who provided helpful comments on all or part of earlier drafts of *Eternal Sonata*. Thank you to Cori Bargmann, Mallika Bhargava, Jim Lovgren, Deborah Devedjian, Houman Hemmati, Zachary Kaufman, Kurt Metzl, Marilyn Metzl, Caren Meyers, Lindsey Meyers, Judy Sternlight, Bill Swersey, and Vinai Trichur. An extra special thank you to my dear and brilliant friend Rakhi Varma, who read the manuscript twice and provided invaluable suggestions for improvement. The final version is significantly better because of her. (I keep telling Rakhi she should become a professional editor, but she is shy. Let this be her first advertisement.) Thank you to my tireless agent, Jill Marsal, my excellent and extremely conscientious editors at Arcade, Cal Barksdale and Chelsey Emmelhainz, and to the Skyhorse publicity team, including Lauren Jackson and Bri Scharfenberg. I dedicate this book to my family (including my grandfather George, who always called himself a "recycled teenager"), to my friend and mentor Richard Clarke, to Rita and Irwin Blitt, and to the loving memory of Tyler Preston.

About the Author

Jamie Metzl is a Senior Fellow of the Atlantic Council, novelist, blogger, syndicated columnist, media commentator, and expert in international affairs and biotechnology policy. He previously served as Executive Vice President of the Asia Society, Deputy Staff Director of the US Senate Foreign Relations Committee, Senior Coordinator for International Public Information at the US State Department, Director for Multilateral Affairs on the National Security Council, and as a Human Rights Officer for the United Nations in Cambodia. He is a former partner and current Advisory Board member of a global investment firm, was chief strategy officer for a biotechnology company, and in 2004 ran unsuccessfully for the US House of Representatives from Missouri's Fifth Congressional District in Kansas City. He has served as an election monitor in Afghanistan and the Philippines, advised the government of North Korea on the establishment of Special Economic Zones, and is the Honorary Ambassador to North America of the Korean Ministry of Trade, Industry, and Energy.

Jamie appears regularly in national and international media, and his syndicated columns and other writing on Asian affairs, genetics, virtual reality, and other topics are featured regularly in publications around the world. He has testified before Congress outlining emergency preparedness recommendations after 9/11 and the national security implications of the biotechnology and genomics revolutions. In addition to *Eternal Sonata*, Jamie is the author of a history of the

Cambodian genocide and the novels *The Depths of the Sea* and *Genesis Code*.

A founder and co-chair of the national security organization Partnership for a Secure America, Jamie is a board member of the International Center for Transitional Justice and the American University in Mongolia, a member of the advisory boards of the Brandeis International Center for Ethics, Justice, and Public Life and of 92Y's Center for Innovation and Social Impact, and a former board member of Park University and of the Jewish refugee agency HIAS. A member of the Council on Foreign Relations and a former White House Fellow and Aspen Institute Crown Fellow, Jamie holds a PhD in Asian history from Oxford, a JD from Harvard Law School, and is a magna cum laude, Phi Beta Kappa graduate of Brown University. He has completed thirteen Ironman triathlons, thirty marathons, and eleven ultramarathons.

Jamie speaks frequently to corporate, nonprofit, and academic audiences.

www.jamiemetzl.com